Conspiracy

Lunnaria Trilogy II

by Luiza Dobrzynska

PAPERBACK ISBN: ISBN: 978-1-7353456-6-6
EPUB ISBN: 978-1-3930935-8-9

***

WRITTEN BY LUIZA DOBRZYNSKA
PUBLISHED BY ROYAL HAWAIIAN PRESS
COVER ART BY TYRONE ROSHANTHA
TRANSLATED BY RAFAL STACHOWSKY
PUBLISHING ASSISTANCE: DOROTA RESZKE

***

FOR MORE WORKS BY THIS AUTHOR, PLEASE VISIT:
WWW.ROYALHAWAIIANPRESS.COM

***

VERSION NUMBER 1.00

I float freely in space, free of body weight. All around me swirl galaxies, nebulas, peculiar creations of the cosmos. I see places where new stars are born, voracious black holes with endless dark space that lies beyond the event horizon. I feel good, I'm calm, I feel no emotions. I died. My free consciousness can freely traverse the vastness of the universe, connecting in a cycle of birth and death with everything that ever existed. Time has no meaning, space doesn't matter. I am surrounded by great, wonderful peace, unwavering confidence that everything is exactly as it should be, and the matters of the tiny Earth do not matter at all in front of the wonders that I am looking at now. That I will look at forever.

And suddenly something grabs me, pulls me down with such incomprehensible force that I begin to lose my breath and consciousness.

I

"You had some damn luck, the bullet bounced off the titanium implant and ripped your muscles, but it didn't damage any major organs or large vessels," said Scott Cavanaugh, settling himself on an uncomfortable hospital stool next to my bed. "How are you? Did they tire you too much?"

"I'm fine," I murmured. "They gave me some painkillers and there's a buzzing in my head."

Of course, it's buzzing, I thought. *I was shot on duty, that's quite something. The doctors had to do a dozen stitches, I was kept in a regenerative coma for a week, and I received artificial blood. Apparently, it's better than the real one, because there is no danger of shock or infectious diseases, but it also has disadvantages. I now have a foul taste in my mouth. In addition, I felt like I was on a swing with the medicines I received.*

"Boss, do you know, who was the shooter?"

Cavanaugh shrugged.

"The vehicle was quickly identified, but that didn't help us much. It was stolen from a rental shop, no significant traces except the residue of liquid nitrogen fumes and high levels of carbon dioxide, which helped us identify the weapon. You were shot with a frisial rifle. It's an illegal weapon, beloved by criminals."

"I thought firearms were only available to authorized services."

"Don't kid yourself. Just because something is forbidden doesn't mean the criminal underground won't get access to it."

I felt dizzy, I was confused, but I still had to ask one more question.

"This rifle... what's so special about it?"

Scotty has improved on the stool.

"It's a BB gun, at least in a sense. Uses cartridges with compressed liquid nitrogen. The projectile is made of dry ice, so nothing we can examine. In many ways, it's the perfect weapon."

I closed my eyes. At this point I should be shaking with fear, but I have gone through too many things, and a danger to my life no longer frightened me. Life is not a movie, the sent murderer doesn't always succeed. Oh, and the question remains: who was he aiming at? At me, or...?

"Monty... how is he?"

"Sue took care of him. He is sitting at home and doesn't leave. We are not sure who the target was. I can see by your expression that it's what you're thinking about too."

What a relief. Before the inspector visited me, I had no idea if the attackers were only able to hit me, and the anxiety about the android was killing me. The doctors and nurses obviously knew nothing about him, and I couldn't call anyone in my state.

"What now?"

"Good question. I mean, I guess we know who's behind this, but we have no evidence, just circumstantial evidence."

He looked at me with care and attention.

"We must continue this investigation. Will you be afraid?"

I thought about it and then shook my head.

"Probably not. You know, Scotty, I feel less and less fear. I think it's adaptation."

He smiled with obvious satisfaction.

"You could call it that. All right, get back to health, I'm going back to work. And so that you don't feel too lonely, someone is here to see you."

"Sue?"

"No, she won't visit you until tonight. She's working on some data for me. Someone else is waiting until I let them come in."

He stood up and opened the door.

"Chris!"

A moment later he was hugging me, just like when we were kids, when I was returning from a school trip, and he was running to greet me, always cheerful and smiling. Only now he had to bend down because I still couldn't get up on my own.

"How did you get here, brother?"

"I got a referral for a holiday internship at a shuttle maintenance facility. I am supposed to learn how to work in the conditions of zero-g. The professors believe I have some great prospects and promised me a referral to the Marathon space station next year. After just two months of studying, I was enrolled into an entire cycle of university! You know what that means? Not just one year, but all four years, provided we assume that my average doesn't drop! And I will try my best to ensure that it doesn't. I'll pass all the exams and become a space engineer. You see yourself now that dreams sometimes come true."

It would be hard to deny that. Chris was beaming with happiness, and I looked at him with the affection of an older sister. He was thinner than before, he also shortened his hair a bit, but overall he didn't change at all. He was still the same boy for me whom I looked after and who treated me like a surrogate mother. In his understanding, I deserved this title more than Cynthia Lara, just and wise, but always dry. I don't think she loved any of us, although she liked us – the way one would like the children of neighbors or friends. In retrospect, I saw that this cool attitude towards raising orphans was helping her not to favor any of the pupils and to avoid overly emotional reactions when we did something bad. As a result, we had a stable, peaceful and safe home, conducive to harmonious development.

We all respected Cynthia and were obedient kids. We had to admit, however, that we loved Sean much more, who kissed us goodnight, carried us piggyback and willingly made small, pleasant surprises.

"How did you find me?" I asked.

"Oh, that was less difficult than you think. I watched a news report from the guest house Blue Moment and then, at one point, who do I see? My dear older sister, in a police uniform. At first I thought she was just some woman who looked similar, especially since the surname was different, but I decided to go to the police station and ask."

"Ohoho, how are your first impressions?"

"Fantastic, I 'd say. Your boss ordered me to be locked up and ironed for several hours before he became convinced that I had no bad intentions. He ID'ed me from everything back to the maternity room, called the factory and the college, he acted as if you were the English queen and he was your bodyguard."

He looked at me closely.

"What is this about? How did you, so gentle and friendly, end up working at the police? You've always hated violence, you preferred to give way rather than fight for yours. The police are the last place where I would expect to find you. And your sign... you were regrouped. This explains the different name."

He touched the class symbol on my forehead with his fingers. I fell on the pillows with sudden discouragement. I couldn't tell Chris nearly anything, so how was I to explain it all? The truth was out of the question, and on the other hand he was too perceptive to let it go at anything but that. It was always difficult to trick him.

"I'm caught up in a nasty scenario," I murmured finally. "I had to finally join the witness protection program and that's how I got here."

He nodded.

"You can't talk about it, I understand. So, this thing is really serious. I'm sorry, my dear sister."

I patted him on the back of his hand. He showed me that charming, boyish smile that I missed so much. Chris was probably the only person I really cared about in my previous life – maybe because he was so adorable and fawning as a child. Three years younger, just enough for him to think of me as the 'older one', he chose me for his 'little mommy', as Cynthia Lara used to say with an indulgent smile. Why did I take this role? I don't even know myself, maybe the reason was what I just mentioned – that he was such a sweet little kid. He never complained or whined, he liked to give kisses, he had a face like a painting and beautiful curls.

It was nice to show up to places with a little brother like that, even if we were only 'social family', not a real one. Growing up, Chris kept his former beauty, a bit girlish and gentle, thanks to regular physical exercises he had a shapely figure, so I could only imagine how many girls' eyes were looking in his direction.

"Are you enjoying the university?"

"Very! But, better tell me how you are doing. I heard you are leading a really colorful life now. And also... that you have an android that you treat like a human."

Serious.

"Have you been told about Monty?"

He nodded.

"Well, I wasn't surprised, you know?"

"Why?"

"You prefer the company of technical products rather than people, I know that well. You've always been this way. Do you remember Lalinda?"

How could I forget? When I was ten years old, I fell off the climbing wall for children, and in such an unlucky way that I broke my arm at the elbow. It became necessary to reconstruct the joints, fortunately without artificial components, and with the help of cartilage taken from the ribs. The whole procedure was cumbersome and the rehabilitation was painful. To make it up to me, Sean Lara bought an interactive doll at a warehouse sale. It was almost new and had a fairly large range of words registered. She walked, sat down, gave her hand, tilted her head, blinked, moved her lips to speak. Using the remote control with the keyboard and display, you could program the sentences she said and code them into memory.

I could sit in the nursery for hours and talk to her as if she was my best friend. I got so attached to Lalinda that when she finally broke down for good, I forced my social parents to go out of town and organize the doll's funeral. I never even wanted to have another one, even the most similar toy. Either way, I was already too big for dolls. I was fifteen...

"Do you think that's bad?" I asked.

Chris shook his head.

"Everyone has some preferences. You are fascinated by robots and computers. I am surprised that you succumbed to a vocational counselor and didn't go to an electronic technical college. I'm sure that you'd feel just like a fish in water."

I shrugged my shoulders. He was probably right, but only recently – under Scott's influence – did I learn to be more assertive. Cynthia Lara didn't consider electronics to be a good direction for a young girl, and I – as usual – obediently followed her suggestions. Contrary to appearances, the adviser had little to say, while my social mother – a lot.

She's always been overbearing and strict, although all in all she's a good woman. From our entire group, Mia was the only one who could stand up against her and go her own way. Maybe it was because she was the youngest and the most pampered by everyone? Or maybe she just had the strongest character.

"Do you know how Mia is doing?" I asked.

My brother grinned.

"She got herself a great job," he answered enthusiastically. "She is an assistant to a market researcher and travels with him around the world. She always wanted that and believed that she would achieve it."

"Market researcher? That's a job?"

"Yes, sister. It's someone who looks into economic needs of people living in a given region and prepares sales forecasts for producers and store chains. Actually, a person like that is always traveling, and Mia has the nature of a wanderer. She enjoys this kind of life."

"That's good. She deserves to live however she wants..."

I'm one of the few people who would ever say that. Mia had the nature of a 'rebel without a cause', a hot-tempered tongue and a rough personality. Dark-haired, constantly glowing black eyes, with her behavior she resembled living silver and it was impossible to feel bored with her. The children at school called her 'Basilisk' and avoided her as much as they could, because she was quick to turn to violence. At the age of twelve, she cut her beautiful hair down to the skin with manicure scissors and insisted that from now on she would only wear men's pants and shirts. There was no point arguing with her, and when someone tried to persuade her to submit to the will of our parents, she responded with screams and throwing herself to the floor.

Visits to psychologists and educators didn't help, because during such meetings Mia was polite and sweet to the point of admiration, she only 'winded up' back at home. It took quite a long time before Cynthia and Sean learned how to deal with her. Our adoptive siblings loved the youngest 'little sister', perhaps paradoxically partly because she was such an unbearable little devil.

We spent a long time talking about the old days, until finally the nurse came and chased Chris out of the room. As he left, he promised to visit me at the police headquarters as soon as he was free.

Two days later, I was discharged to go back home with a recommendation of at least two weeks of rest, and Sue came for me in a police rover, with two stormtroopers as guards. She looked very proud of such an escort, and it certainly amused her. She had already patched the gaps in her wardrobe. She was wearing a synthetic satin blouse, wide pants, and shoes studded with jets that had to cost a fortune. She also went to the hairdresser. She was in a great mood, who would have thought that just recently she was forced to leave her apartment in a hurry and move into the premises guarded by the police system.

"You have no idea what was happening when you were taken to the hospital," she chattered when I got inside. "Scotty ordered a roundup, shut down the entire sector, and was so enraged that everyone was practically running away from him. And Monty, like a skipping record, kept saying: Everything's gonna be all right, until it finally started to get on my nerves."

"Did they arrest anyone? Scotty didn't want to say anything."

"They did, and with a whole parade! The deputy prosecutor, this smooth asshole Johnson, turned out to be the mole he was looking for. He was the one who gave information to Romain Corporation. He is now in custody and awaiting extradition."

"He was the one who told them to shoot me, right?"

Sue shrugged.

"He's not admitting to it. He isn't saying anything at all. A difficult case. Prosecutor Cable had his house searched and all his accounts frozen. He has far too much on them and isn't able to explain where some of the income came from, so far that's all I know."

I felt a great urge to spit, but I refrained from this inelegant reflex. We were in a rover, and I was brought up too well. I felt disgust, as if I had eaten something rotten. I have always been convinced that judges and prosecutors are perfectly clean people who can be believed without reservation, but instead I'm met with such a surprise. Either way, after we discovered Johnson's almost twin similarity to the wanted Mr. Brel, we could expect further unpleasant revelations.

While lying in the hospital, I didn't think about anything related to work, probably because I was given strong painkillers and anti-inflammatory drugs. I felt great after them. Not only did the pain go away, but my thoughts didn't revolve around unpleasant things, it's as if these things didn't exist at all. Now the reality was coming back to me, I had to again get on the treadmill that is police work. Although I did get two more weeks off, I felt like it would be better if I didn't use them.

Monty was waiting in the hallway – I would bet that he's been there like a statue since Sue left, but I don't even know if that was anything unusual for him. The feeling of passing time is so abstract that I have not been able to determine yet if Monty could feel it. We couldn't agree on the issue. In the other corner of the corridor, Sid was lying and playing lazily with a feather ball. He sprang up at my sight and mewed loudly, as if with a grudge.

"I'm sorry, little guy," I said, crouching next to him. "I was in the hospital but I'm back now."

I stroked his bent back, his smooth head, and he rubbed his face against my knees.

"Does this being understand your words?" asked Monty.

"As if!" Sue snorted in amusement.

I got up and went to the android.

"Are you all right, Monty?"

"Yes. I didn't receive any damage. You stood between me and those who shot at us."

I remembered it as if through a fog. Was it really that I wanted to shield Monty from the attackers? I reacted instinctively, in a split second, terrified of the prospect of losing an artificial friend. If all this happened in one of the futuristic novels, where robots accompany people as helpers, then he would have been the first to get shot, since that's the role he played in the story. They were to die instead of the people they helped, that's what the introduced program commanded.

Human life was most important in these books, and yet the robot or android was not an independent, equal human being there. If one were to think about it, even now, when the writers' fantasies are beginning to turn into reality, only me and Henry Karpinsky recognized the new generation of androids as 'beings', not things. Even Sue didn't believe in Monty's self-awareness, that he could think independently, on his own. His behavior was due to some very complicated program, which she didn't know and could not 'figure out'. She liked him, of course – the way you like a mechanical toy, but she laughed at my attachment and how precious Monty was to me.

And was I precious to him? Everything pointed to the fact that I was, although I didn't know whether such a concept as 'the value of something' is understandable to an android. The sphere of abstract concepts is something that is difficult to navigate when you're dealing with artificial intelligence.

We attribute various feelings to higher animals, because to some extent we can prove that they possess them," Henry Karpinsky wrote to me. *"They can be happy or sad, restless or bored, show love, indifference or aversion. However, we don't know anything about the sphere of feelings of reptiles and amphibians, let alone insects. We have no reference points, and we gain little by observation. For example, ants or bees show social behavior, but they do it to the same extent as small robots programmed for specific activities. All it takes is cutting them off from the swarm and they become helpless.*

The same applies to wasps. They feed the young, but do they love them? Not likely, because they don't even recognize their own larva if it goes outside the nest and eat it. The program, or rather instinct, tells them to feed the creature in the nest. Otherwise, it becomes the same food as the other insects it hunts. Even in the case of birds, we don't know whether a higher feeling is possible at their development level, except in cases such as parrots or ravens. Thinking about things in human terms, bird parents love children, devote a lot of care, strength and attention to them, but why don't they react when one chick pushes the other out of the nest? These are things we cannot understand, we can only speculate about what these creatures feel deep inside their tiny nerve centers. If what I wrote seems long, please forgive me. There are some things I wanted to clarify for you.

When it comes to artificial intelligence, we have the possibility of verbal communication, but there is also a serious danger of projection, transferring human patterns into a being that is not human. An android is able to use words that it learns from us, but behind which will be no real meaning. We know for sure what other people feel because we are people ourselves. We guess the feelings of higher animals because they are evolutionarily close to people. But how do we know what an artificial creature feels? The reactions of the androids that I studied pointed to the action of emotions, and according to theory they shouldn't exist.

The main disadvantage of typical microprocessors was their coercion and limitation in the possibilities of communication between individual memory blocks. That's why I decided to use unconventional building blocks for their brains. I connected a typical mnemonic mesh with a chemogel, of which recipe only I know. Its bindings are able to form any bridges between the android's memory banks. This increased the brain's efficiency by a factor of a hundred and also multiplied its unpredictability. Perhaps this is what caused my creations to rise above the ordinary electron brain and what formed the appearance of emotions in the androids. Please consider this when you teach him how he should behave.

I kept this letter, along with others. We corresponded with the engineer since his departure to Central Island, and citizen Hakat pretended he knew nothing about it. I described Monty's progress to Karpinsky, he commented on my observations and thanks to these letters I had the impression that we knew each other better and better. Unnoticed, more personal content crept into the technical details. We both had a deep affection for what his hands and mind created, and perhaps we were the only people who granted him the right to self-determination. Everyone else would consider it insane.

"Did you miss me, Monty?" I asked.

Android bowed his head slightly.

"What does it mean 'miss me'"?

I thought about it.

"Did it cause you any discomfort that I wasn't home? Any instability?"

He was silent for a few minutes, then suddenly nodded.

"I felt like I was constantly receiving the command to stare at the door, but no one gave me such a command. It came from somewhere inside..."

He put a hand to his temple. A human would likely point to their heart instead, but Monty didn't understand such associations. He would treat expressions such as 'think with the heart' as illogical and I don't think he could understand what they meant. The world of poetic metaphors was inaccessible to him and he had to come to terms with it.

"Lie down," Sue interrupted our conversation. "You still need to rest. Do you remember what the doctor said?"

"I feel fine."

"So what? You are a convalescent, my dear, and you won't convince me that the stitches are not affecting you."

She was right. Despite the painkiller that I got in the hospital, I still felt unpleasant stinging around the left clavicle and I felt like I was hit there with a heavy rock. It felt strange, I used to think that a gunshot wound would feel entirely different. Sue had a point, though, I should rest and above all work on my hand. It wasn't entirely paralyzed, but it was heavy and I had problems moving it – temporarily, as the doctor claimed.

"All right, I'm going to bed, you win," I grunted in made up resentment.

Sue patted my back.

"Lie down, I'll bring you some meat broth. They make them for takeaway at the La Paloma restaurant. My mom always said it was a reliable remedy for every illness."

She stopped in the doorway.

"Whenever I was sick, she would buy the meat broth and heat it back home on a stove. I still remember the smell that filled the house. When I think about her, I can almost smell it. I miss her so much."

I listened while changing into pajamas.

"I nearly don't remember my biological mother," I confessed after a moment. "I mean, I have one memory of her zipping up my sweater. I was maybe two years old and she was bending over me... she had a fashionable hairstyle and a cheerful gaze. That's all I have left."

"Did she die after that?"

"She died as a result of a gas leak at a laboratory. They worked there, both mother and father. After their death, I was given over to Sean Lara and his wife. At that time I was their fourth social child."

"Were they good to you?" she looked at me questioningly.

"Oh, yes, especially Sean. I quickly got used to them and my new siblings, children adapt quickly. However, whenever one of us was sick Cynthia gave powders and syrups instead of a broth. You know, she is a supporter of a cold-hearted type of raising, she didn't spoil us, but she didn't hurt us in any way either. She could be described as 'just and consistent, but also forgiving'."

"I bet she punished you, and then he comforted you. All right, I'll go for the broth, and you lie down and turn on the TV. Today is the coverage of the Miss Universum in Bogota, live broadcast."

I had to admit, it's not even a comparison between lying in your own bed and staying in a hospital. Even if the facility's staff is 100% involved in the work, the hospital always feels like a prison, and home is always home. It's your own, friendly environment, a bed, and I was next to Monty at that, who was ready for any request. The sheets smelling like my favorite washing liquid, the cat purring on the quilt. The television murmuring quietly.

As I lay there, stroking Sid, curled up in a fluffy ball, I realized that for the first time I have somewhere where I feel 'at home'. Living with my social parents I felt more or less like on holidays with my aunt. As an adult, I moved several times, but the rented premises were emotionally indifferent to me. I became lost in thoughts.

It only happened once I started living in Sue's messy apartment, built in a moonlike style – that is, sparingly, without sliding walls or the possibility of changing the color of the interior, filled with furniture attached to the floor and walls with special clamps – that it became like a real home. The police headquarters to which we were moved after the burglary was so similar to it that I barely felt a difference. It had the same style, and when our furniture was placed inside, it gained the same friendly atmosphere. I liked its warmly. The architecture on Lunnar was necessarily old-fashioned, simple and solid, and that's something that suits me. Thick walls, small armored glass windows and tightly closed doors give a sense of security, which is probably what I lacked before.

Yes, now that I think about it, that must be what I needed to feel comfortable.

Or maybe I was drawing the wrong conclusions? Maybe the feelings of security came more from Monty and the cheerful, friendly girl I got to live with? Although Sue seemed to be a typical virtualist, she unveiled her second side to me without resistance. Perhaps earlier, before I came to the Moon, she really worked all the time, with breaks only for food and sleep, and that was what really affected my predecessor's nerves. However, I met her from a different angle. From the first day, we were united by an agreement of our souls, as if we had known each other for centuries.

With me, Sue, one could say, regained her youth. When she stepped away from the computer, she became lively, I would even say that she was a rather wild girl, longing for company and fun. This did didn't fit the typical view of virtualists, not at all! And yet my friend was one of the best in her profession and, according to logic, she should be the biggest weirdo. Meanwhile, for a virtualist, she seemed extremely normal, although I admit that in order to understand that, you had to get to know her well first.

"Do you need anything that I can bring you?" Monty asked, leaning over me with his angular face with sharp features.

Derailed from the track of lazy thoughts, I looked at him. I already knew that the external appearance of the android was modeled on the dead friend of engineer Karpinsky, but even he admitted that the physical resemblance is not everything. I had no doubt that Monty wasn't really anyone's copy, but a completely separate being – although it was hard to deny that the creator's goal was different. He was meant to be a copy, but instead became an original, unique, self-thinking individuality. A human being? Perhaps, though slightly different. Either way, he had feelings, some of which were towards me. For lack of better terms, they could be called attachment and he showed them in different ways – sometimes in ways very touching.

"I don't need anything right now," I said. "Just stay with me. That's enough. I like when you are close."

"That means I'm doing my task."

"Your task?" I was surprised. "Who gave it to you?"

"Mr. Karpinsky. He said that a person should feel comfortable in my company and that it should be my priority."

"Don't you subconsciously feel that it limits you?"

He tilted his head to his left shoulder, as always when something surprised him.

"Subconsciously? What does that mean? I don't think we have such a thing."

I forgot about that. In one of the letters, the engineer wrote to me about the basic differences in the operation of the artificial mind and one resulting from natural evolution.

"Together with a set of genes, everyone inherits from their ancestors some of their experiences in the form of subconscious memories. This is why we react automatically to certain threats, even before the brain can digest the received information. The artificial mind is deprived of that."

Something else struck me in Monty's statement. He spoke not specifically about himself, but about all androids, as if there were many more in the world, and yet he was the first prototype. Did he have any sense of... tribal belonging? Racial belonging? How could that be determined?

"Do you feel like you're a part of the android community?" I asked, fixing myself on the bed. Monty shook his head steadily for a moment, then answered:

"I don't know for sure. I've never seen others like me, but Dr. Oenas referred to me in conversation with engineer Karpinski as 'number 27'. It could mean that there are at least twenty-six Montys. Am I reasoning in accordance with logic?"

"Of course. And you say very interesting things, although I do not agree that there is any 'other Montys'. You are unique."

In Laboratory F, where a team of illegally working scientists was arrested, we didn't find any finished artificial beings. There were several projects started, one almost completed, and two or three half assembled, but none of them were operational. Among the secured parts and apparatus there was also nothing that could be considered as an out of use or scrapped android.

Monty's words indicated that Henry Karpinsky was silent about something important and must have had a reason for that. I felt sorry about the fact that I will have to find out why he did that. I didn't want to act against the sympathetic engineer, but I was a policewoman. I felt it more clearly than ever before.

"Have you never heard of people like you being sent somewhere? Maybe to the mines?" I asked after a while.

He shook his head.

"I know nothing about that. I once asked the engineer why he wouldn't build more like me, but he said that it was not my business and that I should not ask about certain things."

"What things?"

"About anatomical details of my body. He said that if I knew too much, I could replicate myself, and this must not be allowed."

He was silent a few minutes, then asked:

"Leeta, why can't I build an android myself, and a human being must do it instead? What is the substantive difference?"

"Well, there must be something," I began uncertainly, but at the same moment I heard the door open.

Sue peered into the room.

"I have some tasty soup!" she called cheerfully. "I'll heat it up in a minute."

She soon came back with a steaming mug. I've never had any meat soup before. I didn't like the real meat that I've tried, but the decoction turned out to be very tasty. I drank with pleasure and felt a nice warmth spreading all over my body.

"Oh geez, I feel so hot now..."

"You should," Sue said cheerfully. "My mother always said that it's best to sweat out the disease and I imagine it usually works, although the family doctor said it was a stupid superstition from the Middle Ages.

I smiled.

"Sean Lara used to say that doctors aren't always right. He didn't like them. I don't know exactly why."

"He must have had a reason. Doctors can be weird. My grandfather was one. Mom had been in conflict with him since I was a child, and probably began to study old books on herbal medicine and other folk medicine practices out of anger. She told me about it a lot."

She sat down at the edge of the bed. Her round face with large eyes became serious, as always when she remembered her mother. Despite my will, I envied her this sadness because it showed she had some beautiful memories that I was deprived of. Even though I didn't really remember my biological parents and went through my childhood quite comfortably, I sometimes felt I've lacked somebody I could refer to as 'mom'. Cynthia Lara wouldn't allow us to call her that.

"Why didn't she want to become a doctor, like her father?" I asked. "Did she have a lower classification?"

Things like that happen all the time. Although there is an axiom in current-day medicine which states that a child of two Class A partners will have the same grade, in practice it varies. The synaptic density measuring instrument is relentless and the result must be accepted without questions, even if they weren't favorable for the parents. I knew those who for years fought for additional tests for their offspring in order to give them higher classification. This was not always successful, even after giving the kid phosphorus preparations and torturing them with an intensified learning program.

Sue shook her head.

"That wasn't the point. My mother had rebellious nature, she didn't listen to anyone, she didn't allow anyone to dictate her career path. She became an actress, even though the whole family responded in outrage. Actually, uncle was the only one who supported her."

"You mean Citizen Hakat?"

"Yes, yes... Citizen Hakat for you, for me just my uncle. I've known him since my earliest memories. He carried me piggyback, took me to the amusement park and the cinema, and it's hard to think of him as the very important Chief of Arms."

She didn't have to explain herself. During Hakat's visit to Lunnar, I had the opportunity to observe their mutual relations and clearly saw that Sue was fond of her uncle and he adores her in return. I thought then that he probably directed her to work on the Moon as it was somewhere she was safe. Otherwise he would've had to always keep her close and she would be his Achilles heel. I was just wondering how he convinced everyone that he didn't care about family relationships and his niece – because surely many knew that he had one. He must have done it cleverly, because during training on Central Island I only heard once that my supervisor had relatives.

Tanith Kelso, one of the government cabinet secretaries, mentioned it when I asked her whether she thinks that Hakat cares about me.

"You're insane!" she exclaimed. "He doesn't even care about his own family!"

"Does he have any relatives?"

"Oh, yes. As far as I know, he had a sister who died many years ago, and several other relatives besides her. He doesn't keep in touch with any of them. And once, when a cousin of his was arrested in a bar fight, I heard myself, when asked to intervene, that they could even hang him for all he cares. Give it up if you think you mean anything to   him."

Hakat was playing a complicated game and I didn't think he would show his true self to anybody. Perhaps the one most true was the one I had the opportunity to see while visiting Sue, but I wouldn't give my head for that. Although I was curious how much Mabel, his current official companion, knew about him. I haven't been able to talk to her in private lately, which is a pity. There's so much I wanted to know.

The methods of treating the sick that Sue's mother believed in may have been unconventional, but I liked them. My friend fed me the hot broth, massaged my hand and cheered me up with carefree chatter, especially in the evenings when I fell into melancholy for incomprehensible reasons.

Inspector Cavanaugh finally reached out to me on my fifth day of staying at home. I expected him to do it earlier, but he gave me a few days to rest before he called with a short order to appear at the police station.

"But you are still on leave!" Sue exclaimed in shock when I repeated his words.

"Just help me dress up. I had a feeling that my boss won't let me be sick in peace, not right now. I can only imagine what's currently happening over there. The arrest of the deputy prosecutor must have caused a real storm."

I buttoned up, feeling the adrenaline rush in my veins. I missed my job. I wasn't born to laze around in bed. I never liked it, even when I was a child, and working in the police changed me into somebody really passionate about my new profession. I didn't realize this until they put me in the hospital after the attack.

It wasn't until I was lying down and looking mindlessly at the television that I realized that I'd rather work any kind of job. Even sitting at a desk and viewing thousands of documents would've been better. Idleness depressed me, took away all the joy of life and made me feel empty. I couldn't imagine how the people who used to be condemned to unemployment must have suffered. Today it's hard to believe that such a sick system could exist, but it has existed for centuries. I learned about it at school and at the university's library.

Living so close to the workplace has its advantages. I didn't need to call in a cab, all I had to do was cross the internal courtyard to the service entrance – the police quarters were located in the back of the main headquarters, in a solid building, secured in every possible way.

Check-in was just about to end at the police station's office. Inspector Cavanaugh stopped reading the assignments and snorted angrily:

"You've finally decided to show up!"

"I'm still on leave," I grunted.

He threw up his arms.

"You can get sick later. For now, there's no time for that. Don't make such an expression, I'm not sending you to suppress riots. You'll mainly work from the office. I need the help of anyone capable of thinking, and there aren't many of those in this damn place."

"I'm still learning."

"And I know what I know! Take a seat behind the desk and wait, we'll talk in a moment."

He glanced at me with his eye implants and went back to sorting today's tasks. I took my seat and waited for him to finish. Not long ago, I still shared this desk with Silvana Evans, murdered by a man named Brel. We haven't known each other long enough to have formed a real bond that should exist between partners at work, but I liked her and now began to miss her company. Even though Silvana had a C1 class, I felt like she had IQ above 105 points, which was the upper limit for class C. She was far too clever, ambitious and logical for this sub-class.

I looked over at Scott, who was explaining something in a low voice to the patrol group. I tried to imagine what his thoughts were like when I was placed in the hospital. I was hoping that he cared for me at least a little bit, and hence – I wondered if he was worried. He didn't say anything about it when he paid me a visit, but that didn't surprise me. He wasn't an ordinary, average man. His professional career was dominated by fighting criminals of the heaviest caliber and nothing else than work mattered to him. I suspected that he had been married once, and he took off the wedding ring quite recently, because the ring finger on his left hand showed a strip of pale skin, but I haven't had the chance to ask him about that yet.

On the other hand, he did hint on the fact that he avoids women, and they avoid him. He believed that the disfiguring scars and eye implants deter the representatives of the opposite sex – he wasn't wrong, because this type of dentures, so large that they didn't fit the eye sockets and had to cover the forehead and cheekbones, were out of use long ago. The advancement of biotechnology has made disabilities invisible, and such old, massive implants could indeed seem repugnant. Modern humanity is accustomed to bodies which, if they weren't healthy and beautiful, at least gave that impression. You quickly get used to that, as it turns out, and the sight of mutilation becomes difficult to look at.

He was right in a lot of ways. However, you simply needed to get to know him a little better, and the mechanical implants no longer matter, just like the old scars. It would have been easy to remove them confidently, but Scott didn't care for beauty and wasn't going to lose allotment points to the cosmetic regeneration clinic. In general, he spent surprisingly little on himself. Subordinates suspected that he was simply stingy, though I preferred to refrain from being judgmental. I still didn't know enough.

At first, his appearance frightened me, I was afraid of him, but I quickly got used to it and learned to look at this man in a different way. Even those nightmarish scars stopped affecting me, they were, after all, a part of Scott, to whom I was getting closer. Ever since we ran into each other at the dating center, I felt like we've become significantly closer.

It had nothing to do with what we were doing. People meeting in the dating centers had no obligations to each other and that was the main advantage of those places. If anybody tried to claim that the person they met at the dating center owed them anything, they would be laughed off. Even so, I felt a peculiar relationship with Scott, only I wondered whether he felt the same way about me. It would be best to ask him, but I didn't have enough courage.

The inspector finally finished talking to the patrol and walked over to my desk. He pulled up a vacant chair and sat down.

"First of all, welcome back," he said. "I know that you're on leave, now's not the time. The police follow a different set of rules and we respect these types of papers only in really justified situations."

"I'm not quite back in shape yet."

"I know. Still, I had to get you out of bed. Things got a little complicated."

"How complicated?" I tried to keep my voice from shaking, but I failed.

Scott pursed his lips for a moment.

"A little more than I would've liked," he admitted. "We have to go to Earth to participate in the deputy prosecutor's trial. It'll take some two or three days, we're no longer living in the times of processes that drag on for months like gum. Our testimony is crucial. Monty must also accompany us."

"Why?!"

"Don't shout, I'm not deaf," he scolded me. "Monty is a witness, the most important one at that, his admission will, however, require a change in applicable criminal law. The prosecutor general decided to submit the appropriate application at the next meeting of the government... that is, it happened two days ago. And since last night I've received confirmation of the subpoenaing, then I'm guessing they passed it."

He paused, took a piece of chamois from his pocket, and began to wipe the visor of the left implant. It was not the first time that I thought that he had to be persuaded somehow to replace the outdated, coarse prosthesis with a better model, one that would not require cleaning and would be a bit... more discreet. Right now, however, there were more important things.

"How is this going to take place?" I asked helplessly. "How will we convince the judges that he's not some self-winding machine, but a self-thinking being?"

Scott shrugged and hid the chamois.

"Karpinsky will convince them. How he does that is his problem."

He was clearly hesitating whether to say anything else, so I waited patiently without saying anything.

"Chris Nikanov is coming with us."

"What?" I got up from my seat.

"Sit down, idiot. It can't be helped, the boy dug himself in this hole. Before he came to the police station, he joyfully bragged to his colleagues at the factory that he found his sister."

"Oh, mother..."

"Exactly. After all, you're here as part of the witness protection program, not a living soul was supposed to know... at least not one from outside your agency. And then comes the overjoyed blonde boy and everything falls apart."

My heart ached painfully. What's going to happen now? It all depended on Hakat, and he didn't succumb to sentiments, except when he took me into his care. What will be his decision about Chris? Poor kid, he fought for the right to study at university for so many years, and now he could lose everything because of a stupid mistake. I felt guilty, even though I had nothing to do with it.

"Can we somehow... affect it?" I moaned.

The inspector shook his head firmly.

"How? Too many people about it. I'm sorry but your brother can't go back to the university."

"Scotty, please! This will kill him!"

"As if. It's not that easy to die of unfulfilled aspirations. Anyway, everything depends on your smooth boss."

He said these words with such disgust that I was surprised. To this day I didn't know that Scott knew Hakat, although it made scene. The Chief of Arms sent me to him for a reason, when I needed to hide myself from the people I helped unmask. He must have had a good opinion of Inspector Cavanaugh, though – strangely enough – it didn't seem to be mutual.

"You don't like Citizen Hakat?" I asked.

"He's a bastard, like all politicians," he replied shortly. "He uses people and treats them like objects. He eliminates the unnecessary. You don't know him at all."

"Maybe, but he did help me."

"Because he had a reason to. Don't trust him, Leeta."

I felt that he was right somewhere deep inside, and I saw myself as a fly trapped in a spider's web. Whatever game Citizen Hakat playing,

I was an unimportant pawn, like Scotty or Mabel, and even Sue. She was the daughter of the Chief of Arms' sister, but something told me that if the need arose, he would sacrifice her as easily as me or anyone else."

"How's the investigation going?" I asked, wanting to divert the conversation to other topics.

Scotty took the remote control and switched the caffetino maker on.

"We're stuck again," he said. "That Brel guy, or whatever he's called, simply dissolved in thin air. The undercovers sweep the underground, patrols have this guy's portfolio and we still have nothing."

"Wait, what portfolio?"

"Ah, you don't know about this procedure yet. The picture has been processed by graphic designers so that you can see how the wanted man would look with a beard, without a beard, with a different hair color and with a shaved head. It usually helps. For now, however, no one has encountered him."

"Maybe he left Lunnar?"

"We are considering this possibility, but it's hard to confirm that right now. When we get back from Earth, we'll have to get serious about working out all the threads. Maybe..."

"What?" I encouraged him as the silence began to lengthen.

"Maybe someone on Earth will finally hear me out and we can get some additional recruits. I dream of a real investigation team, and right now I only have you, Kunch, plus Kell and Miss Herefort. Of course, I'm not counting the stormtroopers from the intervention brigade and the patrol people, they're all class C and it's hard to demand detective skills from them."

"And the secret agents that you mentioned?"

He waved his hand in discouragement.

"They're not even officers, they're volunteers from the civilian population. They are very useful, yes, but as eyes and ears, nothing more. I need an investigation team, dear. I can't do much without one."

He stood up and poured caffetino into the earthenware cups. *A little pointless,* I thought, *that I miss the porcelain, and glass from earth.* The utensils used on the Moon had to be made of durable material because of the frequent meteor strikes against the shield protecting the city's dome. The vibrations caused by the impact spread to the dome's structure, and the residents felt in the form of ground tremors. Most of the time they were harmless, but couldn't be called imperceptible. These slight shocks actually caused glass dishes to collide with each other in the cupboards, and sometimes fell and broke into pieces. The thick faience was more resistant and worked much better.

"Where are Sue and Kelley?" I asked.

Scotty brought me some sweetener. I had to admit that, ever since I tried real sugar, I wasn't very fond of the artificial substitute – unlike meat. In Lunnar, however, real sugar was not available, unless someone brought it from Earth on their own for personal use, and even if it was on sale, I wouldn't be able to afford it. The artificial sweetener didn't taste great, but there was no choice.

"Miss Herefort and Kell are in the laboratory," said the inspector. "They're working on some material evidence. They make a great team."

He took a small sip and changed the subject.

"All right. I need to familiarize you with some details and maybe we'll come up with something together."

When I informed Monty about my planned trip to Earth, I had the impression that he was both surprised and happy.

"Does this mean that I will be able to talk to engineer Karpinski?" he asked.

"I think so. He'll be something like a guarantor in court."

"Guarantor?"

"Yes, his job will be to convince the judges that your words can be trusted. You must understand that you will be the first... representative of artificial intelligence to be called as a witness in court. Lawyers will not know how to treat your testimony."

Monty looked at me, tilting his head slightly. His face wasn't able to express feelings, it could copy them at best, but I saw with amazement that he was trying to arrange the artificial mimic muscles as if he was about to make an astonished expression.

"But I always speak the truth."

"I know, and so does your creator it, but others may think that you could simply repeat what I tell you to say."

He nodded gravely.

"I'd do it if you gave such an order, though I wouldn't see any sense in it."

"I know, Monty," I barely controlled my reflex to embrace him and hold my head to his broad chest. "But the point is, I don't command you to do anything. You are not my slave, but my friend."

He was silent for a long moment.

"Only humans can be friends," he said finally.

"That's not true," I denied. "Animals can also be friends, Sid for example, so why not androids?"

"I don't know. That's what I was told."

I took his hand. It was calm as usual, stable, cool to the touch and smooth.

"You were told wrong. You are a friend to me."

"Friend," he repeated in an unnaturally deep voice, releasing the spoken word slower, like a slowed down player.

I would give a lot to know what he was thinking in this moment.

Perhaps we will never fully understand the reasoning of androids," Karpinsky wrote to me. *"The problem is that the human brain has been conditioned to think with words, while they think with images. That's an enormous difference. They also don't experience phases necessary for the development a human being's personality, such as a phase of rebellion against authorities or a phase of hormone storms, because they appear in this world immediately as an 'adult' and don't have the equivalent of a human endocrine system. They absorb knowledge about the world via a computer, and absorb what they see there several dozen times faster than a human. Their personality is uniform, while human is made up of many, often seemingly mutually exclusive elements. This difference between natural and artificial intelligence was predicted by the writer Stanislaus Lem from many centuries ago, but this doesn't carry the negative side effects he predicted.*

Sure, I couldn't fully understand Monty, but what significance did that have? None to me. In the absence of a better word, I found his reaction to be emotional. Ultimately, why wouldn't I? After all, it's hard to find a name for voltage changes that occur in the artificial brain and affect the mental balance of the android. I thought it would be worth asking him about it now, but it was at that time that the videophone buzzer sounded.

Sue's embarrassed face appeared on the screen.

"Honey, come back to the police station, right now," she said. "We've got an arrest of a big-shot, he's saying some interesting things."

"I'll be right there."

I turned off the device, took Sid off my lap and stood up. Monty was looking at me expectantly, so I explained:

"I have to go back to work. We'll talk again when I come back. For now, pack three sets of my underwear, two pairs of pants and five blouses into a travel bag."

"Which clothes should I take?"

"Doesn't matter. The first ones you find. I'm not going to a fashion show. Put one set of your own clothes, too. Preferably some more formal ones."

While I was in the hospital, Sue took on the responsibility of providing the android with new clothes. Among other things, she purchased an elegant suit according to what has been currently fashionable for men – pants with narrow legs fastened at the ankles with decorative clasps, a shirt with a high collar and wristbands reaching nearly to the elbow, along with a short jacket without clasps. She really went all out. Such a set, even ready-made, cost a fortune, and this one was purchased in an exclusive store at that, where the clothes were matched to the figure of the customer.

When I asked Sue where she got the points for something so dearly expensive, she replied carelessly that she got a briefing from the Horus Corporation. The company's bosses terminated her contract after learning that she would now work for the police. It surprised me, I admit. Horus was honest, at least as far as I knew, and the code of virtualists forbade any deceit against clients, though on the other hand, it didn't declare loyalty towards othem, on the contrary. In order to provide the police with data obtained while working for Horus, Sue would only have to inform the company heads first. And if Horus were as honest as it was thought, the bosses would not be afraid that a virtualist in the services of the main police force would find anything in them.

"Don't be naive. Nobody likes the police," Sue answered my doubts.

She was right. Society, even in modern times, simply hates uniformed services. It is a remnant of the times when a policeman or a soldier could shoot the perpetrator captured at the crime scene without any consequences, which in truth wasn't that rare. The times immediately after the ecological disaster were very difficult and horrifying things happened. The army and the police had to maintain order among the population which was demoralized thanks to hunger and the lack of a feeling of security. The restoration of any kind of order took not years but decades and cost the lives of many citizens.

All this has long since passed, but to this day, the special powers of both services arouse deep resentment at best.

Scott, accompanied by our pathologist and Sue, waited in the office. A young man in a suit sat in the chair interrogation chair, thin as a rake, swarthy and dark-haired, clearly resigned and overwhelmed by what had happened to him.

"Who is this?" I asked.

"Alexander Kensell. One of the CEOs of the Sidney Glory Company, mining and processing of helium three. Patrol number five caught him at the casino Las Lunnas with a certain Bertie Shakespeare, when they both tried to cheat at the locale's disadvantage via fake dice and a roulette manipulation device."

I furrowed my eyebrows, again something banged in my head. I wasn't quite healthy yet, and truth be told, I should be in bed right now, not participating in the investigation. However, the inspector was right. There were not enough of us that we could afford to be sick at will.

"Bertie Shakespeare? I've heard that name somewhere."

"You sure did," Scotty agreed. "Silvana Evans was investigating her. Until now, we thought she was a petty criminal, another derailed woman trying to survive in adverse conditions, but we were wrong. Evans probably knew the truth and it's a pity she wasn't able to note it down   anywhere..."

He sighed against his will. He was still affected by Silvana's death and blamed himself for not being able to protect her, even though there was nothing he could've done.

I looked at Kensell. I don't think he was older than Chris. He looked like a young man from a good home who thoughtlessly involved himself in criminal activities, and by the time he realized it was already too late. From the entire hunched body emanated boundless despair and embarrassment, so much that I felt sorry for him.

"And what did you need all that for?" I asked reproachfully.

He shrugged silently.

"Repeat what you said at the interrogation," Cavanaugh said sternly.

The boy swallowed his saliva and stared at the desk top.

"Sidney Glory doesn't pay his employees," he mumbled. "We have not been getting a salary for two months. We're living on savings, and the bosses only keep promising that we'll be paid soon. They said that it's a temporary difficulty, but..."

"But what?"

"I saw the papers. Someone bought out all the shares we had available on the stock market and took over the loan we took to build new mines. Usually an investment like that returns itself in the span of a year, so it's worth it to take a loan, and banks are eager to give one. However, for everything to go well, work must be completed. Meanwhile, the one who took over the company's liability blocked the payment of further tranches of the loan on the pretext of having to re-evaluate the project. We worked for what we had on the Sidney Glory accounts, but we couldn't complete the investment and stopped. Now we're in ruins, and what's worse, the company no longer belongs to the Australian Consortium of Natural Resources."

"Who does it belong to then?" I asked.

"That's what nobody knows," Sue said. "In the banking system he is listed as William Maximo Perez, but I already checked that, it's false data. The whole operation was illegal and I had a lot of problems before I could figure out how. Someone cheated the bank, depositing money as a private sponsor of Sidney Glory. He presented some perfectly counterfeit documents confirming the arrangement with the company management, and when he had the pledge in his hands, the misfortune began."

"Have mercy, what pledge?" I moaned.

I was not familiar with banking or stock market matters, which for my friend had no secrets.

"A loan this big requires a pledge," she explained to me like to a child. "As is customary, these are securities, stock exchanges of the borrower, deposited with the bank as collateral for loan repayment. Such documents are not personal, so even the fact that they were obtained dishonestly does not affect the possibility of a trade."

"But that's a legal absurdity!"

"Sure, in a way, but it would be quite difficult to find a solution to that. Let's suppose that Perez falls into the hands of the authorities. He gets at least ten years imprisonment for fraud, but he can still trade shares because the bank has been repaid and he has not received equivalent of value from Sidney Glory. In addition, the law states that no one can be forced to make a transaction against their will, so if Perez was to be unwilling to sell back the shares, he has the right not to. And so, as it stands now, we've hit a wall."

I sat helplessly on the nearest stool. I became dizzy from all these revelations, and Sue probably noticed it because she stopped her disquisition.

"You don't have to know all this," she said reassuringly. "It's enough for you to know that it came to a very serious crime, threatened by long prison time. Someone got stubborn about it and in a hell of a clever way. That someone is here in Lunnar, and we must find them."

Hundreds of thoughts flew through my head.

"There were no identifiable traces?" I finally asked.

Kelley shook his head and looked at the held pod. He quickly warmed up to this invention and used it with such nonchalance as if he had been doing it since childhood.

"We have fingerprints, a DNA sample and a retinal scan taken from the bank," he said. "The problem is, they belong to two unrelated people, a man and a woman, both of whom are long dead. I confirmed it. The DNA sample also failed. I replicated it several times and it did nothing. It's not in the database."

"How is that even possible?!"

"I don't know, apparently it is. On Earth, something like this wouldn't have happened, but in the local branches the comparative system sometimes has delays of several hours. Of course, clients don't know about this... but this particular one, as you can tell, did."

The puzzle became more and more complicated. How did this relate to our previous discoveries? I looked at Scott. He seemed unimpressed as usual, even the large implants were resting calmly in their housings. When he was nervous, they protruded against his will like ancient telescopes, which terrified the interrogated more than screaming and threats.

"Is this somehow related to Romain Corporation?" I asked.

"That's what I'd like to know," he grunted. "Miss Herefort is looking for connections, but I haven't allowed her to use the Integra program again, so she hasn't been able to find anything so far."

"Well, that's how it is when you demand miracles without the right tools," Sue pursed her lips in an angry grimace. Given how her previous experiments with the Integra program ended for her, I was grateful that Scott didn't allow her for that again, but she clearly didn't appreciate it.

I turned again to the arrested boy who was fidgeting in the chair, not knowing where to direct his eyes.

"Why didn't you contact the management of the Mining Corporation? If you had made a formal complaint there, you would have received benefits and tried to resolve this situation as soon as possible. Why instead of following the legal route, did you try to scam at the casino?

Alexander Kensell look at me pleadingly, as if I was able to do anything for him. His lips trembled like a little boy's who had just done something bad and was afraid of the punishment.

"If this plan was successful, I would have enough resources to satisfy at least some of the employees' demands. It would give the company some time and maybe we'd be able to come up with something. If the Corporation finds out about everything, it will temporarily take over management and the stock market value will drop significantly. As one of the CEOs, I swore to look after the prestige of Sydney Glory and couldn't just settle for a complaint."

"How do you know Bertie Szeskpir?" Cavanaugh asked sharply.

"I was buying fortestim from her. Sometimes it's hard to endure my job without an afterburner, and Bertie always had the best stuff."

"I don't doubt it, but she won't be doing that anymore. She will be answering for an attempt of fraud, a plot to the detriment the casino owners, and resistance to arrest. What you will answer for is up to you."

"What do you want me to do?"

"You should testify before the main management of the Corporation."

Kensell shook his head miserably.

"Do you know, Inspector, what that means for us?"

"I don't care. As long as I am responsible for order in Lunnar, a crime will remain a crime which must be prosecuted ex officio."

Scott picked up one of the photos lying on the table. It depicted an elderly man signing a dimly visible document next to a table with the logo of the Bank of Besserheim.

"I handed this to the patrol, but more for order than with any hope," he murmured. "A false identity and a false face."

"I uploaded the photo to the web, but didn't find anything," Sue testified. "I think we are dealing with a single-use doppelganger. Some scum are desperate enough that they'll be hired for that role. It's well paid."

I knew what she was talking about. A 'disposable doppelganger' is a man who agrees to two plastic surgeries: one before the action and the other immediately after. Of course, such a procedure is illegal, and the object of substitution in case of being found goes to prison for many years, but as it always has been in this world, the perspective of criminal liability doesn't deter everyone.

And one more thing: the brutal takeover of Sydney Glory corresponded oddly to the aspirations of Romain Corporation. Just as did the fact that some they've used some unknown method to fool the retina scanner. It would've been easier to comprehend if it was the fingertips, or even a DNA sample – probably all you'd need there is some dexterity. The whole manipulation was carried out extremely skillfully. I was would be willing to bet everything that behind the problems of the Australian company are the same people who have already slipped away from us once. As it turns out, they didn't cease operations, they continued their plan, not being too concerned about a police investigation. We already knew that they wanted to take over the Corporation, have control over all companies and mining, but was it all for the sake of some predictable greed?

Questions, questions, questions and not a single answer. I wanted to make some genius guess, show off to Scott, but nothing came to my mind. I sat silent like a pole until the inspector spoke again.

"Let's get to work. Before we leave, we have to develop all evidence so that it cannot be challenged. There's a lot of work ahead of us."

"What about me?" Kensell asked timidly.

Scotty looked at him briefly.

"You'll be going to jail."

I opened my mouth to protest somehow, but I quickly closed it. Just because the young man seemed like a likeable person cannot influence the judgment of the act itself. Scott must have guessed what I was thinking, because when police officer Mills escorted the detainee, he said tartly:

"Did you want to say something?"

"No, I mean... maybe it would be enough to give this kid supervision and an electronic sensor?" I said from the bottom of my heart.

Kelley laughed briefly, Sue smiled forgivingly, and the inspector nodded pityingly.

"He's not a kid, he's twenty-five, old enough to be held responsible for acts he committed. And you are not a lawyer from the 21st century."

"Who?"

"A lawyer who, for the right money, defended even the worst degenerates in court, explaining away their crimes with a difficult childhood or a temporary mental illness. He could manipulate evidence so well that without trouble he could obtain a low sentence or even an acquittal for any bandit."

"That must have been a really long time ago."

Scotty stood up and rummaged through the desk documents.

"Yes it was. After the ecological disaster, other rules were introduced and the impunity of those who could afford a skillful lawyer ended. Enough history lessons, we're getting to work. We only have thirty-six hours to make a believable report."

The work took nearly all the remaining time until the flight. I tried not to show my fatigue or weakness, but in truth I was at the end of my strength when we were finally done. My shoulder felt painful, my head ached and I had the feeling that I was about to collapse at any moment. I must have looked really bad because Cavanaugh finally took pity on me and told me to lie down in his apartment.

"Get some sleep," he said. "Then Kell will give you the right stimulant to give you enough strength to travel."

He said that as if we were planning to go to Earth on horseback, like in the movies for the youngest. In the meantime, we were supposed to fly on a cruise shuttle, without even showing a special privilege card, which would provide the four of us with a compartment separated from the rest of travelers. Scott didn't like to abuse this solution. He said it caused an unhealthy sensation among travelers, and that it didn't provide much security – unless a dangerous prisoner was being transported.

II

Chris arrived at the last minute before the lift off. Contrary to his fears, he was very calm and didn't complain. He gave me a warm kiss and said:

"Don't worry, sister. I don't blame you for what happened. I should have bitten my tong before bragging to my friends that I found my sister."

"You couldn't have known..."

"All I had to do was think. You wouldn't move to the Moon without a good reason. Either way, it doesn't matter anymore. It seems that I've lost all I have fought for."

"That's not set in stone yet, boy," Scott interrupted. "We don't know what her boss will decide."

"Isn't that you?"

"Well, I suppose, but not the only one. You'll meet the second one on Earth and better take care of what you say then, because your fate will depend on him."

He wanted to say something else, but at that moment an official from the landing pad came up, so he went with her to the side to take care of some formalities. Chris finally looked at Monty, who was standing next to me, holding a bag with clothes over his shoulder. He pointed to him with a movement of his head.

"Is this the android?"

I nodded. He sighed with delight, watching my companion closely. His face resembled the admiration of a child upon seeing an unknown toy."

"A perfect recreation. Amazing, if I didn't know beforehand, I wouldn't have realized that it's artificial."

"You would've figured it out, you're smart. And don't call him 'it'."

"Okay, okay... he talks, right?"

"Yes, of course. Ask him something if you don't believe me."

He reached out and touched Monty's face with his fingers, then his neck and hand. He looked carefully at the glittering eyes, it seemed like he would've looked at his teeth too if he could. Monty gave himself calmly to the inspection, showing no dissatisfaction, which probably every person in his place would.

"Do you really talk just like people?"

"I don't know if that is the case," Monty replied. "I don't know all people and I don't have the data to draw such conclusions."

Chris whistled softly.

"Awesome. This is not a scientific achievement but a work of art, sister. He's amazing. How did it happen that he came into your hands? You've never wasted a penny, and some insane cost must have been involved."

I shrugged my shoulders.

"It wasn't my money. Well, not exactly, and not as insane as you think."

"Do you know how much money they spent on him at least?"

"I know from an appraiser that the components themselves cost about three hundred thousand pepes. Add to this the body modelling, which was not cheap either, but I have no idea how you could calculate the value of what's inside his head. In my opinion, such a prototype brain is priceless. It cost a lot of years and work to build it."

"I can imagine. I would like to meet the creator."

"You may be able to. He will be present at the hearing. He is supposed to be a guarantee of Monty's truthfulness."

"Great! That's one good thing that can come of this situation."

I had to admit that studying had a great impact on Chris. He became serious, learned to control himself and certainly was no longer as idealist as he once was. In past times, when his plans broke down, he fell into a gloomy mood and loudly accused himself of failure, lack of luck and other such things. He seemed to have learned to react differently, and that pleased me. At the same time, there is enough of a 'big boy' in his personality that even here, on the moon, he wears the university badge pinned to his shirt with childish pride.

Inspector Cavanaugh returned after a few minutes and in a rough voice told us to get into the shuttle. I saw that he was nervous even though he was trying to hide it. I didn't know whether it was the necessity of his testimony that upset him or the fact that he had to leave Lunnar for that, even if it was only for a short time. Or was the idea of meeting Hakat the worst thing? I couldn't rule that out either.

An unpleasant surprise awaited us on the ferry. Instead of sitting in our designated places, we had to quickly move to the service section. From there, through the emergency hatch we went down with a specially mounted sleeve to the patrol shuttle, one of those that constantly scans the space around the Moon and helps to determine safe flight forecasts for passenger vehicles. Usually these are unmanned drones controlled from the control tower, but in this one we ran into two military pilots.

"Put on your masks and hang onto whatever you can," said one of them commandingly, without even looking in our direction.

I looked around. No seats or belts, only four oxygen apparatuses and bent rods protruding from the sloping walls of the hull – a type of handrail, or rather – what I understood after a while – stabilizers used to secure cargo. Luggage space, barely enough for the four of us. With a trembling hand, I removed the motion sickness medicine from a handy first aid kit, swallowed one and offered the other to Chris. Scott shook his head in refusal when I offered him one too.

"Will you be able to reach Earth with this scrap?" he asked the pilots.

"Only the orbit. There, the guys from landing will take over. One of them replied and began to switch the indicator lights on the control panel. "The T50 patrol ship is not intended for entry to the atmosphere. You there, big boy, put on the face mask!"

"Monty, they're talking to you," Scott growled and helped the android put on the completely useless to him device.

I realized that whatever the plan was, the pilots were uninitiated. Their only task was to deliver us from the Moon to Earth's orbit like sacks of mineral samples, they didn't care about anything else.

The oxygen apparatus was new to me. The mask made of nanite rubber closed around my face as if it was alive, and for a moment I felt fear. Fortunately, a refreshing breeze of clean air soon filled my mouth. Almost at the same moment, the ship twitched and I felt an increasing heaviness.

A flight in a small vehicle, designed for two people plus cargo, is quite different from traveling in a passenger shuttle. Most of all, it was shaking us as if we were pushing through an avalanche, and the inside was cold. Although that's not surprising, since there was the absolute zero of space vacuum outside. The heating devices couldn't keep up with the temperature equalization for so many passengers, they were not calculated for that. The pilots were protected by wetsuits, while we with only plain clothes. Soon my teeth started chattering like in a feverish attack.

"Scotty, you could have told us, we would have dressed warmer!" I finally shouted into the microphone built into the apparatus.

"I know what I'm doing. We couldn't arouse any suspicions," he replied with full calmness.

As usual, he was acting completely unemotional and reminiscent of Monty. Me and Chris were shaking, we were nauseous and could barely hold onto the metal rods.

Weightlessness is a very unpleasant thing, especially when you haven't had the time to get used to it. Your stomach starts turning, your head is throbbing with pain, and you can only breathe through your mouth, because the nasal mucosa swells as if you had a severely runny nose. I don't know why this happens, I have no medical background, but it is a fact and I have already felt these symptoms during my first shuttle flight and skimmer ride through the surface of the moon. Only it didn't take so long then, and now I had to muster my strength to hold on until the pilots could safely leave the patrolled area. Chris was a little better – space engineering classes include zero gravity training – but I could see that he was feeling miserable too.

I don't know how long we circled around the Moon because I couldn't look at my watch. To occupy myself with something, I looked at the tiny window, behind which I saw the endless black of the cosmos, and the relatively close, furrowed and crusted surface of the Moon. And in the distance – the Earth, big and blue like a glass ball on black velvet sewn with zircons. Finally, one of the pilots lit a yellow light under the vault and called out:

"Careful, we'll jump forward now! It'll get unpleasant!"

At first, I didn't understand what he was talking about, but it then became immediately clear. Despite the compensation systems, such a small vehicle cannot provide comfort to casual travelers, and in order to reach Earth relatively quickly, high speed is needed. This is associated with heaviness, which literally pinned us to the floor. I had the impression that there was a mountain of stones lying on top of me and I could hardly breathe. My ribs and shoulders ached, the areas I was injured the most, everything in front of my eyes blurred and darkened. It all went on and on, and it felt like it would never end, but finally the longed-for moment came when the pilots began to slow down. The overload slowly disappeared, I didn't have to fight for every breath and I regained my ability to see normally.

"Scotty, I think I'm going to kill you," I choked out as soon as I managed to get my breath out. "Why the hell didn't you tell us about how it'll be like?"

"Don't ask stupid questions and you won't hear stupid answers," Cavanaugh snapped, his voice distorted by the oxygen apparatus. "I didn't know anything, it was only at the landing strip that I got the instructions from the headquarters."

"The central, damn them," Chris groaned. "This was worse than a practice decelerator. I bet that we were in at least four G."

"It was even five at the peak," the chief pilot cut in over the radio. "Get ready, we're about to dock at the 'Strogoff' orbital station."

He switched to broadcasting and we heard him call air traffic control. After a moment a woman's voice spoke, telling him to direct the vehicle to dock number three. The ship turned, we heard a knock that shook the vehicle, and then the engines went out. Everything was still.

Flaps closed, oxygen phase, said a voice from the console. *It is now safe to leave the vehicle.*

The insane flight was over – we were at the orbital station. The co-pilot turned to us.

"Get out now," he said. "And remember, we've never seen each other."

"I swear on my honor," said the inspector sourly, pulled the apparatus mask off his face and rubbed the red marks on his forehead and cheeks.

I tried to follow his example, but I didn't know how to unblock the seal, and it was Chris who helped me get this thing off. I breathed in the foul-smelling chemical air inside the patrol ship and felt dizzy.

My brother supported me.

"You're bleeding," he said with concern. I looked at the blouse and saw a red stain under the collarbone.

"The wound must have opened under the gravity load, that's some luck."

"Stop whining," Scotty said harshly. "I'm sure there's a medical point at the station. Let's go."

The hatch released. We went down the gangway to the docks, where two people, a woman and a man, dressed in guard uniforms were waiting for us. They immediately approached us and pulled out their badges.

"Leo Jones and Viola Rasmunsen from the government intelligence agency," the man said, showing the ID. "Chief of Arms Hakat sent us. Please come with us."

The woman looked at me.

"Did you run into some trouble along the way?" she asked.

She looked at the blood stain on my blouse and a slight frown appeared on her forehead, which was decorated with the mark of an A3.

"The wound opened as the gravity on the patrol ship increased," I replied. "I got hurt two weeks ago. Nobody warned us that we weren't taking a cruise ship."

"That's none of our concern. Our job is to escort you. Let's go, we're wasting time."

Scotty grunted something incomprehensible. By the tone of his voice, I concluded that it must have been a curse. He only used them when he was really nervous or angry, but his repertoire was very rich. I was glad I couldn't hear the exact words. Cynthia Lara taught us that the use of foul language is as much a disgrace to a civilized person as taking care of your natural needs publicly, and none of us – with the exception of the eternally rebellious Mia – even in adulthood used anything worse than 'damn it'.

Inspector Cavanaugh was brought up differently, however, and the environment he had been in since coming of age was hardly parlor. I suspected that most of the people he dealt with at work wouldn't understand words anything other than really thick phrases. His disapproval of our current situation, however, he expressed only with this curse and with a movement of his head told us to follow the unexpected escort.

We left the dock through a floodgate and into a wide corridor, which must have been the equivalent of a pre-takeoff area at a standard airport. There were mechanics in gray-blue overalls, security soldiers and air traffic control workers in uniforms resembling those of the old navy. Among them, we saw some civilians, although rarely. Jones and Rasmunsen took us through several checkpoints to the inner part of the station. It looked like... a shopping center and, despite my will, I looked around for the ice cream parlor. Only there were much fewer people here than in a regular gallery.

This isn't how I imagined the orbital station. I didn't think it would have shops, service points and colorful decorations. It took me a moment to realize this was a dock zone after all. It was used by people visiting the permanent residents of 'Strogoff' – mainly scientists – and those who were transferring through here onto heavier ships, traveling between research stations on Mars, the orbit of Venus and the moons of the gas planets. In further sectors there were probably laboratories and company apartments.

"Hold on," Scott growled, stopping abruptly. "Where are you taking us? I thought we were only changing the means of transport here."

Jones also stopped and turned.

"These were our orders, Mr. Cavanaugh," he replied stiffly.

"Inspector Cavanaugh, if you please."

"If you say so, inspector. I'd like to ask you to not protest. We all answer to one boss."

"And that is all the misfortune. Oh well, let's go."

"Where's the doctor?" Monty said suddenly.

We all looked at him with surprise. He had been silent since we got into the patrol ship, as if he had suddenly forgotten to speak.

"Leeta is bleeding. She needs a doctor," he added in a tone of explanation.

I couldn't help smiling, I was so touched by his care, or whatever it was.

"Don't worry, I'm fine now," I said. "It's just a few drops of blood. The scar ruptured during the overload, but only at the top. I just need to change my shirt."

"Yes, please do that now," Viola Rasmunsen interjected. "You can't stand before the Chief of Arms looking like that. There's a bathroom over there. We'll wait for you."

I took the bag from Monty and locked myself in the bathroom and changed my blouse to a clean one. I didn't have a first aid kit in my bag, so I put a folded handkerchief under my bra. The fresh crack stopped bleeding, but I didn't want to risk it starting again.

The agents took us to one of the closed offices, but they themselves did not enter. After the passwords were exchanged via the electronic panel, they lined up on both sides of the door, which slid open, inviting us to enter.

The office turned out to be a well-equipped conference room, designed for a dozen or so people, and therefore intended for board meetings. In the center of the room stood a heavy table, with a hologram display device mounted on top of it, screens hung to the walls, currently turned off. In the corners there were vending machines with drinks and a wide selection of snacks. I'm certain no one has complained about the lack of comfort here

At the head of the table sat Citizen Hakat, dressed in black clothes resembling a soldier's uniform without insignia, browsing data on an old generation pad. As the door closed behind our backs, he looked up.

"Sit down," he said. "If you'd like something to drink or eat, you can help yourselves."

"We didn't take the hellish road here to gorge ourselves," Scott growled. "We were supposed to go to Earth, and instead they brought us here. What is going on?"

His implants twitched and popped out of his eye fittings, signaling difficulty in controlling his emotions. Chris looked at him, then at Hakat, finally shrugged and walked over to the soda machine.

"I don't know about you, but I for instance could use a decent latte right now," he said. "Who else wants some?"

"Make one for me," I muttered resignedly.

Everything indicated that the conversation would not be easy and that the Chief of Arms had a rather unpleasant surprise for us. Once again, I felt like a pawn on someone else's chessboard.

Chris whistled this year's hit of the band Pocket Quasar and after a while he handed me and Scott – even though he didn't ask – a plastic cup with a hot drink.

"And you, Citizen?"

"If you feel like it, boy, you can pass me one too. The atmosphere will clear up a little if we have a drink together."

"You would need good brandy for that, and in large quantities," the inspector was still intransigent. "Can we finally find out what's going on?"

He sipped his latte greedily and sat down on one of the cushioned chairs. Hakat, unmoved, took the mug from Chris and took a sip too.

"I do owe you some explanations," he said. "You see, I couldn't bring you to Earth, not even to the Central Island. As you can imagine, you have a lot of enemies when you're in my position. Mine are very powerful and very well organized. They have their own intelligence, so I assumed that they would know when to expect you. The events at Lunnar are closely related to them, and you have evidence that will overwhelm their bosses. You wouldn't make it to the seat of the Supreme Court alive, and believe me, the guilty ones would never be found."

Scotty choked on his drink and slammed his fist on the table.

"So you're saying that our investigation was to protect your private business?!"

Hakat laughed heartily.

"It's not that bad, please calm down. These are not my private adversaries, if that is of any comfort to you."

"Wait a minute," I broke this exchange, feeling that despite good air conditioning, sweat was rolling down my spine. "How are we supposed to testify if we can't appear in court?"

The Chief of Arms looked at me with an understanding smile.

"You won't be testifying," he replied. "You'll stay here. Only the android will go to court with me, and of course I'll take the material you brought here."

"Monty? I'm not letting him go alone!"

I raised my voice a little more than I intended, scaring even myself.

"Calm down, Leeta. He will be with me the entire time and will come back to you right after he is questioned by the attorney general. The thing is, in the event of an assassination attempt, Monty will have a chance of survival. You don't, and neither does the inspector."

"We don't know that for sure."

"You may not, but I do. Engineer Karpinsky said that the shells of the androids he constructed were as resistant as a protective vest for a member of the intervention brigade. He specially uses plastic masses made of super-durable materials. And your sweet little body could barely handle the stupid overload in a standard patrol ship."

"And if they target you?" Chris asked ironically, staring at him with innocent blue eyes. He was leaning back in his chair as easily as if he were in a university cafeteria with a fellow student in front of him, not one of the most important people in the world.

"That's my problem, young man," replied Hakat coldly.

"I'm not talking about the attackers," I felt an agitation rising within me, no worse than that of the inspector. "You want Monty to testify by himself. I don't know how he will act then. Please understand that this is not some anthrobot, but a conscious being. He can be unpredictable. I really should be there with him."

Hakat finished his latte, got up to his feet, and took a batch of butter crackers from the machine.

"I won't risk the life of one of my agents recklessly, much less one as valuable as you," he said firmly. "You can consider this robot as equal to a human being, if that is your whim, but to me it is a machine and cannot be valued higher than a person. For your sake, I'll do my best not to damage it, but you will stay here. That's an order."

"Here? What am I going to do in this place?"

"Rest, and so will Inspector Cavanaugh and Mr. Nikanov. I'll be back in two days at most and then we'll talk about the rest. I would like your material from the investigation, please."

Scott puffed up another curse in his mouth and pulled a few small media carriers framed with a police logo from his belt pocket. They differed slightly from the regular ones, having the form of a flat, transparent crystal with a spiced adapter for plugging into a computer. When they came into common use, it was joked that you only need to look at them against light to read the data. This is obviously impossible, from the outside you can't even see if something has been encoded in the crystal, but the new carriers were so different from the old ones based on microprocessors that they were a great attraction for people. The police ones were dyed dark blue with cobalt salts, and their adapters only fit police computers with non-standard outputs. Attempting to use an adapter or replace the tip resulted in the data being blocked, so it was a rather safe solution.

"Everything's in here," he said. "The results of the investigation, testimonies of witnesses and defendants, complete photographic documentation and the formulation of the thesis by my team. Every possible piece of information."

"Let's hope that's true," Hakat took the items. "We've known each other for a long time, Inspector Cavanaugh, and I know you are extremely diligent at your work. I don't know if what you gave me is enough to convince the Attorney General, I can't know, but I'll do my best."

"Who's the prosecutor now?"

"Esther Bjork. She was nominated at the end of last year."

"You don't trust her?"

"It's hard to say. I believe that is honest, incorruptible and tries to be objective in every matter. However, this may not be enough. I don't how open-minded she is and whether she will be able to accept A.I. as credible, even if Henry Karpinsky vouches for his truthfulness. Yet much of the findings are based on what you discover with his help. For example, the identity of Peter Johnson and his unmistakable relationship with the mysterious Mr.Brel..."

Scotty nodded. Suddenly, the feeling that the two had something in common deepened decisively – they became similar in some elusive way while standing here, in deep thoughts. Finally, Hakat shook his head and exclaimed imperiously:

"Well then! Rasmunsen and Jones will take you to the quarters. You have all boarding paid until my return. Then we will talk about the future of Mr. Nikanov and other pressing matters. Agent Ankes, please instruct the robot here to obey my instructions until we return.

I struggled to refrain from protesting the term 'robot'. However, this was not the time to argue about semantic matters. I got up and walked over to Monty, who was standing against the wall, as if in an incomprehensible rebellion to indicate that he was not taking part in the conference.

"Monty," I began hesitantly. "You must go with Mr. Hakat and do whatever he says as if I were saying it. This is very important."

"Are you giving me away?" he asked. Though his voice was not emotional, I thought I could sense an unease in him.

"No, don't be silly. It's only two days, maybe three. You must give them your testimony. Tell the prosecutor everything you know, answer every question. Nothing bad will happen to you, and engineer Karpinsky will take care of that anyway. I'll wait here."

Monty was silent. If it were possible, I would have decided that he didn't like this whole thing, but to ask about his personal attitude to Citizen Hakat's ideas would be pointless. He probably wouldn't even know how to formulate the answer.

"Tell me, do you understand what to do?"

"Yes, I understand. Until my return to this place, I am to belong to Citizen Hakat and carry out all of his orders."

"No, damn it, not like that!"

"Then like what?"

"Nevermind. Just listen to him until you get back. Now take off those clothes and put on the formal suit, I won't let you go looking all casual."

Monty took his 'formal outfit' out of the bag and, not embarrassed by the presence of strangers, changed into elegant fashion clothes. I helped him tie the bow tie and cut the tags with the manicure scissors I had with me.

"Be careful. I don't want anything to happen to you."

"It'll be as you wish, even if I am to belong to someone else temporarily."

"I told you it's not like that…"

"Enough," the Chief of Arms interrupted. "If that is how he understands the situation, so be it. It's important that I don't have problems with him."

"You shouldn't have," I growled through my teeth. "Not any that I could predict, at least. On Earth, you'll be able to consult Engineer Karpinsky if necessary."

Hakat nodded imperiously at Monty. The android looked at me again, and when I nodded, he walked over to the Chief of Arms. I felt an overwhelming urge to kiss him goodbye, but I couldn't help but feel embarrassed. Chris would probably be able to understand it, but Hakat? He would mock me mercilessly.

The quarters were located further inside the station, in the residential section. Scott barely glanced at the room. He was clearly not interested in the interior design, as he only took off his uniform jacket and immediately lay down on the unmade bed. He didn't say a word, but we realized that he wanted to be alone, so we left quietly.

"You want to get some sleep too?" Chris asked, pausing in front of the wall mirror and smoothing out his hair with the movement of somebody used to taking care of his appearance. Following his example, I also looked at the smooth surface to see if any blood had soaked through the makeshift dressing.

Beauty was never something I cared about, unless I was going to a dating center – you always want to look good there. At the root of this attitude towards appearance was my belief that there isn't anything you can do to improve it that much anyway. Not that I was unattractive, but from my childhood the mirror revealed an ordinary and average-looking person. I got used to it, and despite Cynthia's suggestions, I didn't even try to learn makeup techniques, which could slightly increase my attractiveness. Maybe if I fell in love with someone for once, it would be different. Now, after the reconstruction treatments, I looked better – I had a narrower waist, nicer breasts, thicker and redder hair, and my nose also looked better. But I still didn't see anyone in the mirror worth paying attention to.

"No, after all that happened, my blood pressure is through the roof," I answered my brother's question. "Scotty already experienced much worse, so he won't be affected by anything, but I need some time to calm down."

I looked around.

"You know what? I never thought an orbital station would look so ordinary on the inside."

"How did you think it'd look? After all, station employees spend years here, they must have the right conditions."

Chris tucked his hands in his pockets and looked at me with a mischievous gleam in his eye.

"There is a public computer in the room we passed. Wouldn't you like to find out more about that Hakat of yours?"

"Are you crazy?"

"You said you didn't know anything specific about him. You're not curious?"

"Who wouldn't be," I admitted reluctantly. "But what you're implying is complete nonsense, do you think you could get information about such a titan on some random computer?"

He smiled broadly and patted me condescendingly on the shoulder.

"It's not the type of computer that matters, but the access to the network, sister. And whoever is connected to it."

"Could you do it?"

"I'm not worse than a professional virtualist, only that I didn't have to take the oath, thankfully. A candidate for a cosmotronics engineer must be au courrant in these matters, which is a basic requirement of the profession."

I hesitated. The prospect was devilishly tempting, but dangerous. If we were caught...

"You're surprisingly calm. I thought you would lament more over your current situation," I said to save time.

"How would that help me?" Chris snorted. "You have no idea what studying in a department of space engineering is like. Right from the first year, you have to pass through such a thrashing that you either quit or learn to accept everything with a distance. It simply can't be otherwise. I know there is nothing I can do about this, so instead I'll do something until that freak returns. I'm not going to sit around and cry like a two-year-old over a broken doll."

He looked at me differently than before, as hard as someone twenty years older.

"I see," I muttered. "You want to get busy, so you've decided to investigate who Citizen Hakat really is. Such knowledge can be dangerous."

"Yeah right. Don't worry about it anymore."

He pulled me into an open room. It was a small room with several stations, clearly for general-purpose computing. Looking at the old-fashioned wall clock, I understood why no one was working here now

– it was currently night-time in the living area. The clock had a 24-hour dial and the hand showed 1.35 a.m. The division into work and rest time happens in all such facilities. It keeps people in good shape.

Chris turned on the computer, went online, and started typing.

"I have to create a firewall first so that they can't detect me," he explained lightly. "Have to be extremely careful when entering government territory."

I raised my hands in mute terror. He glanced my way and laughed.

"Relax, I know what I'm doing. Although coding will take some time. In the meantime, tell me about your android. I can divide my attention, so go ahead."

I pulled up a second chair and sat on the other side of the table.

"What do you want to know, little brother?"

"Everything."

I told him briefly how Monty came into my possession, trying to avoid anything that might have been a classified for the investigation. He listened carefully, while his fingers danced across the keyboard as smoothly as Sue's. Columns of multi-digit numbers scrolled across the screen that I couldn't understand, but which clearly had meaning to   Chris.

"Quite an interesting story," he said when I finished. "And does... I don't want to sound like a buffoon that asks stupid questions, but there's one thing that I'm curious about."

"What is it?"

"I've read hundreds of fantasy books and watched those old movie programs. Even the very old ones, those remade many times. Many of them carry the theme of the rebellion of artificial intelligence against its creators, especially when they realize that they are superior to humans. There are even novels and movies in which androids create their own civilization. Are you not afraid of that?"

I shifted in my chair. How could I summarize in short words all my conversations with engineer Karpinsky, in which this extraordinary man passed on to me the knowledge he had acquired at the cost of many years of work?

"It's not a stupid question. In order to answer it, you have to go beyond the anthropomorphic way of thinking."

"Which means?"

"The thing is, we know only one species of rational beings so far, that is, us. We necessarily measure hypothetical extraterrestrial races by our own. We ascribe to them our own characteristics, though often perverted or exaggerated, and fail to take into account that they may be too different to even understand them."

"We're not talking about aliens right now."

"I know. I had to start somewhere. Androids are a product of humans, so we feel even more so that they must be similar to us in every aspect. The thing is, they aren't."

Chris gave a short whistle.

"I thought that they are."

"You're wrong. They look like us, but that's just the packaging. It's the mind that counts, and their mind works differently. Curiosity is the basic human trait. That's what pushed the explorers to the seas, and then to space. Artificial intelligence is devoid of it – what it cannot see and cannot reach is indifferent to it. An android has no imagination, is alien to empathy, has no gut feelings, and never dreams of what may be. He may as well be the perfect worker, but he will never be a creator. Human progress has always been based on searching for things that at the moment didn't seem absolutely necessary or even attainable. An android wouldn't attempt inventing them, moreover, it would not even occur to him to replace what is good with what is better."

"I think I'm starting to get it. To change anything, you first have to imagine what you're doing it for."

"Exactly."

He nodded, his eyes never leaving the computer screen. I'd probably have to give everyone else a two-hour lecture and answer a hundred questions, but Chris always got it all in an instant, and I was sure he understood the main idea correctly.

"Isn't this lack of imagination somehow a result of their construction?" he asked after a moment.

"No," I said. "It's more because androids don't arise as a result of natural evolution, so they don't need what we inherited from our animal ancestors. If it weren't for the traits I talked about earlier, we might have survived as a species, but we wouldn't have built any civilization. We would be sitting on trees to this very day."

"It would've better for the planet," Chris tapped the Enter key, pursing his lips as if he wanted to blow into a triumphal horn on the occasion. "There we go. Now no one can catch me unless I mess up and get caught in one of their traps. Relax, I'm not planning on doing that."

"Be careful, they could put you in jail for hacking."

"Don't worry, no one can track me now. I can search for whatever I want."

A graphic grid entry signal appeared on the screen, then successive gates began to cascade. I had no idea how Chris could navigate all this, but he skillfully moved the cursor until he reached a point of interest.

"I'm at a government base," he said, with a tone as if he was just ordering some fries. "Wait a minute, I need to activate an additional personal firewall. We'll have no more than an hour, then I have to close everything down and erase the tracks."

My throat felt unbearably dry and I glanced nervously at the door. What my brother was currently doing might could bring us both to the chair of the guilty, but I get myself to stop him from going any further, as I once used to stop him from fights with his friends. Curiosity was biting me as well. As long as I thought that there was no way I could find out anything, I just didn't think about it. Hakat was a mysterious figure and he was to remain so. Admittedly, Sue knew a bit about him, but this information was limited to her childhood, when Hakat wasn't yet working for the government – at least not officially. As for what he was doing now, she knew about as much as me, or maybe even less.

"Government database. Chief of Arms," Chris paused, then moved his lips silently, as if trying to remember a forgotten phrase. "Everything's encoded. I'll try to get something out, but I'm afraid we won't get far without the key. I should have expected this."

He plunged into the work, his left hand operating the cursor, while the right entered data into the handy minipadd. I peeked over his shoulder, but all I saw was a series of mathematical signs I couldn't understand. I got up and locked the door so that no one would enter unexpectedly. I felt more and more nervous, my blouse was sticking to my sweaty back, and my teeth were clenched as if I was expecting physical pain. I bet that my blood pressure was higher than after a few caffetinos with double the caffeine.

"I have to log out, the firewall is about to go down," Chris said finally. "I'll cover the tracks and delete the logs, then we'll take a look at what we've got."

"I hope you know what you're doing."

"You could bet your year's salary on that."

It was past five by the time we stepped out into the hallway – too late to go to bed and too early to bother the cafeteria staff. So we took from the vending machine two large cappuccinos and a few vacuum-packed buns with pudding, and went to the room assigned to me. First of all, Chris took a small device from a bag over his shoulder, set it on the table, and turned it on.

"A professional jammer," he explained. "Places like these are usually tapped and monitored. Safety precautions."

He sat down on the made-up bed, drank greedily, and unpacked one of the buns.

"What do we have here?" he raised the mini-padd to his eyes. "Let's see... Citizen Hakat, current position Chief of Arms. Original name Karl Pulasky. Age: Fifty-two, sworn in as a member of a government group at the age of forty. Earlier, head of military intelligence... I'm not sure about this one, this term could also mean the head of the military police. I didn't have time to look into it deeper. Personal property... listen to this, that's interesting. Control package of the Extraplanetary Mining Consortium."

"Not the 'Lunnar' one?" I frowned?

"No, I am sure of that. Extraplanetary Mining... I heard the government had plans to mine asteroids, but so far the costs have been too high. Same goes for mining on other planets in the system or on the moons of the gas planets. Until they solve the problem of cheap logistics, there is nothing to even talk about."

I thought deeply, searching my memory for any scraps of sentences I had heard that might match this discovery, but found nothing.

"Maybe they're just far-reaching plans," I said finally, hesitantly. "For now, the program covers only the exploitation of lunar deposits, and the Company consists of supposedly independent partners. What does it mean that Hakat has a control package?"

Chris smirked sarcastically.

"I think that is in the context of at least 51% of shares. No wonder he became so interested in the events at Lunnar. It's about his fortune."

"Hold on.... someone is buying shares of companies that make up the Mining Company. We figured it out during the investigation. It's likely that this someone is trying to harm the entire organization. I admit that I don't really understand this. I mean, our saboteur also incurs losses in this way."

"It makes sense. This someone wants to shake the market and cause stock prices to fall. They will buy them cheaper afterwards. It seems to me that your boss has a formidable enemy on his neck. You have to have a lot of money to do something like that."

"You think the action is aimed personally against him?"

"That I can't know for sure," Chris looked at the padd again. "It can only be business, but on the other hand, I wouldn't be surprised if it was about personal revenge. I wonder what Citizen Hakat has behind his ears..."

I shrugged helplessly.

"I don't know."

"I suspect that it's unlikely. From what I noted here, it appears that he is playing not only a political game, but an economic one as well."

"What else did you get?" I asked.

"Hmmm... he has an estate in Las Palmas. He was married twice, he was a father once, but the wife and child were killed in the accident. Siblings: sister Carim, deceased. Distant fa..."

He paused for a moment, staring at the padd with his mouth half open.

"Talk," I encouraged. I unwrapped the pudding roll and began to eat.

"He has a brother-in-law. Guess who it is."

"Don't make me solve riddles. Not at five in the morning after a sleepless night and that hellish flight."

"Inspector Scott Cavanaugh.:

I really did not expect such a bomb and I froze with a bitten roll in my hand, staring at my brother with wide eyes

"Scotty?!"

"It says so right here," Chris tapped the padd's screen with his fingernail. "It's his wife's brother, the one who died with the child."

"Holy...!"

"Now I understand why the inspector hates him. He must have been able to get to know him well."

"It could be worse. For a moment I thought Scotty was Hakat's sister's husband and Sue's father.:

"You watch too many soap operas."

"Okay, what else do you have there?" I drank down the bite of the roll and reached for another one.

Chris moved the notes on the pad.

"There is also data on his education and political career. Do you know that he refused to run for the position of Number Three twice? His party was almost on its knees pleading with him, but he insisted."

"He's aiming higher."

"Without a doubt. Number Three deals with economic matters, but only planetary. Everything about non-orbital exploration is in the hands of the Chief of Arms, who is responsible for decisions only before Number One."

"So Hakat became what he wanted to be from the beginning. I aided him with that, I'm such an idiot."

He patted my knee.

"You had no choice, sister. People like him don't tolerate opposition, and you'd be bad for a rebellion. Fortunately, you've always been amicable."

I looked at the jamming device. My younger brother was well prepared – was he planning something else? I never suspected he could be so cunning. In childhood, he was a straightforward little boy, and later on in life I could still read him like an open book. I always knew what he was thinking, and he couldn't lie to me even if he wanted to. Now he presented a completely different face.

"What are you going to do with this information?"

"I don't know yet," he replied. "But I prefer to have it."

"For what?"

He looked at me. He really has changed since entering university, and perhaps the biggest change has happened in the way he looks at things. On one hand, I liked it – he must have lost his old illusions and learned to stand firmly on the ground, and that was very good for him – on the other hand, I felt a longing for the Chris I loved as a child. He seems to be gone for good.

"That Hakat of yours likes to control everything and everyone," he said. "I bet that he destroys anyone who stands up to him and treats other people as objects dependent on his whims. I don't like it, and I'm not going to let him run my life."

I was terrified. The tenacity in his voice was also something new. It felt as if an evil wizard had transformed the gentle boy he used to be, and I shivered at what that might lead to.

"I'm begging you, don't do anything stupid!"

"Don't worry, I always know what I'm doing. I mean, I'm not going to throw a glove at his face and challenge him to a duel! However, you must know that information is the most powerful weapon, and it's good to have it."

"And if someone takes your padd? It's an outdated device, it has no security."

"Oh boy, how wise you are. Data protection methods were invented before anyone even dreamed of electronics. I have everything written in code that I developed myself and that no one but me can read."

He put the padd and jammer in his bag.

"The surveillance equipment will be operational again in a moment. Everything will look like an overvoltage fault on the record."

I shook my head in silent admiration.

"Chris, you've become a dangerous man."

"No, just a predictive one. I concluded that in a world divided into predators and prey, I prefer to be a predator."

"I don't know if I like that."

He put his arm around me and sat me on the bed. He acted as if our roles were suddenly reversed – I used to be the one to take care of him, and now... I felt like a little girl when he started explaining to me:

"Don't worry, I haven't forgotten Cynthia Lara's teachings, I'm just trying to modify them. I'm not going to attack anyone, but if somebody attacks me, I know how to defend myself. I was taught how. Space engineering is not only a field of knowledge, but also a lifestyle that requires special skills. One of them is adaptation to every situation. The second one is to adapt situations to yourself, to bend even the most hostile circumstances to your advantage."

He paused for a moment. Snuggled to his side, I waited for him to take up the topic, and after a while he started talking again:

"Don't think that I want to blackmail the guy. Blackmail is a slippery slope, especially when dealing with someone so influential. But I'm not about to just let him ruin my life. I don't know yet how I will use what I have, but I will come up with something. I didn't fight so hard to be where I am right now. Even if I was a little foolish, it's not a crime."

"Are you afraid that Hakat will send you somewhere far away, just like me?"

"I wouldn't call it fear. I'm just getting ready to fight for what's mine, dear sister. I might lose, but I won't give up easily."

He fell silent again. We were both silent, as I somehow couldn't think of anything to say. My beloved brother grew up and became independent, he no longer needed the advice or support of his older sister. He had changed too much to hide behind my skirt again. If we were to use poetic comparisons, we could say that not a butterfly hatched from its cocoon, but a predatory dragonfly.

Tired and cuddling, we finally fell asleep until Inspector Cavanaugh woke us up, concerned about our absence from the lounge where we were supposed to meet before lunch.

*****

Two days is not enough to get to know the orbital station well, but I looked around as I could. Chris accompanied me eagerly explaining the construction details of 'Strogoff' which were something completely unknown to the layman, we were also followed everywhere by one of the agents, either Jones or Rasmunsen. The second was keeping an eye on Inspector Cavanaugh, who didn't want to partake in our tour. I got the impression that he was not interested in this station or what was happening on it. He spent all the time at the computer, talking to the Lunnar headquarters or browsing through the documents Kunch had sent in. However, he didn't mind treating my stay in this sky town as an extra vacation.

With his approval, I ran around the dock part, the service part, where shops and workshops were located, I also managed to visit the 'institute', in other words the sector of the station where scientific experiments and long-term research programs were conducted. Although I wasn't allowed into the section where research on plant organisms was carried out in a zero-G. However, I was able to obtain a pass to the hospital section, where me and Chris were shown around by a young nurse, assigned by the ward.

"We treat here mainly severe forms of cancer and rehabilitate difficult neurological cases," she explained eagerly. "We have excellent results. It's even possible for us to achieve effective improvement in patients with locked-in syndrome, who before were subjected to euthanasia."

"What's the locked-in syndrome?" Chris asked.

Medicine was not his hobby, he knew very little about it. I had a memory of something, but I also looked at the nurse with curiosity.

"It's a very serious condition where the brain is separate from the rest of the body," she explained. "The brain works fine, but has no effect on the body. An unimaginable torment."

The mere thought made me shudder.

"It's incurable?"

"There have been occasional cases of treatment, too rare to be any argument for extending the lives of such disabled people. However, we managed to improve the condition of three patients with the locked-in syndromed. It's a great thing, don't you think?"

"Of course," I admitted.

I felt glad that I lived in a time of such medical advancement, and not back when, in many cases, they plugged hopelessly ill people into machines and awaited their death.

We weren't allowed to disturb the patients, of course, but we were shown around the equipment and rehabilitation rooms – a room with a swimming pool, a large hyperbaric chamber and a zero-G exercise room, where gymnastic equipment was attached to the walls and the ceiling. The water in the pool, as we found out, came from a closed circuit, drinking water was supplied from Earth. I didn't ask how that was done, but probably not in the same way as it was delivered to the Moon – towing frozen, hundreds of tons of blocks of fresh water through a vacuum. Here it was only going into orbit, so there was probably no point in freezing it.

Our visit to the workshops and repair docks we decided to do on the third day, although we had to give up on this activity. When we arrived in the morning at the dining room, we found Hakat and

Monty there. The Chief of Arms ate a serving of corn ragatto, while Monty stood beside his chair, hands behind his back. He raised his head slightly at the sight of me, and the silvery eyes flashed noticeably. Was he glad to see me? Was joy something he could feel?

"Hello Monty," I said.

"Hello, Leeta," he replied. "Is this the end of the case because of which you ordered me to go to Earth? Do I not need to listen to Mr. Hakat anymore?"

"Yes, it's over. You don't have to listen to him anymore, lucky for you."

Monty looked at Hakat, who was eating, then removed the badge attached to his jacket, set it on the table, and walked over to me. The Chief of Arms took it with indifference, as he continued his breakfast.

"Sit down," he said. "Breakfast is the most important meal of the day. Eat, and pretend I'm not here."

"Let's just say that it's possible," Scotty muttered.

He looked as if he had lost his appetite. As a matter of obligation, he forced himself to eat two toasts and drink some coffee, and we followed his example. Rasmunsen and Jones, who accompanied us as usual, didn't dine with us – I have no idea when or what they ate. Truth be told, what was served cafeteria didn't inspire much enthusiasm, and without the company of Hakat, only the toast and pre-packaged food from the vending machines tasted relatively normal.

After breakfast, we all went to the conference room where the station management meeting was taking place, but at the mere sight of Hakat, they all got up and went elsewhere. Agents stayed in the corridor, guarding the door. Hakat, using the remote control, turned off the surveillance system and sat down comfortably at the table.

"Sit down," he invited us with a broad gesture. "We'll talk."

"I hope so," Scotty kicked one of the chairs away from the table, then sat down looking as if it were studded with spikes. "How did the questioning at the general prosecutor's office go?"

"Unexpectedly good. The prosecutor turned out to be an intelligent woman, and Karpinsky had no problems convincing her of the essence of artificial intelligence. She asked Agent Ankes's robot a few tricky questions and decided she could tale his testimony at face value."

"Perfect. So there's nothing left for us here, we're going home."

"Not so quick," Hakat poured himself some water with an artificial lemon from the flagon standing on the table, and drank it. "The investigation will be continued by the economic police. The entire squad is now on its way to the moon, led by Detective Rosanda Merrick, a stock market crime specialist. They will be quartered at Lunnar's main police stations, and local policemen are to give her help and all the materials."

"What?!" Scotty jumped up from his chair as if he got burned, and his visual implants sprang to their maximum length. "By what right are you taking the case away from me?!"

"By the right of your supervisor. Sit down, Cavanaugh."

The inspector sank slowly into his chair, never taking his eyes off Hakat. I felt that he was keeping himself in check with the remains of his strength.

"What about us?" I asked.

The Chief of Arms glanced at me.

"I have a task for you," he said. "It's related with the person of Mr. Nikanov, who was involved in our matters in an unfortunate way."

"Exactly, about that" Chris muttered.

He sat down in his seat, and after folding his arms on his chest stared at the Chief of Arms with cold, appraising eyes. He seemed as emotionless as Monty at that moment.

Hakat looked back at him with complete calm and a sense of his own strength.

"I believe in the opinion that human talents are as much of a natural resource as coal or metal ores. They must be exploited, not wasted."

"Where did that come from?"

"I've read your file. You are an extremely talented and energetic individual. You won a student index in a national competition, and your accomplishments earned you a scholarship for your second year of study. You have mastered virtually all theoretical knowledge necessary to obtain a diploma, you only lack the credit for all required internships. That makes things simpler, since I'm sure you've figured out already that you can't return to Earth."

My brother smiled sardonically, in a way that made me shiver.

"And how will you convince me not to?"

The Chief of Arms turned on the projector attached to the table and slipped his own carrier into it.

"Do you see these plans?"

Chris leaned forward a little.

"The design resembles Lunnar..."

"Correct. Later this year, a large construction will begin on the Moon. A recreational and sports center will be built next to Lunnar. An increasing amount of people wish to visit the Moon as part of their vacations and holidays, especially since travel prices have gone down. Such a snobbish fashion. The hotels in Lunnar can only accommodate a small number of vacationers, so it was decided to build a second city. Due to the specificity of the place, it will be a colossal engineering project, not only in its construction, I mean, the masonry kind. I hope you understand what I mean."

"Of course!"

"I have made the decision to place you in the team responsible for the fixture of the city, that is, the entire apparatus system that creates the life there. If the chief engineer gives a good opinion of you, you will be admitted to the diploma examination without any additional formalities. I have no doubt that you will pass it in the top five. First of all, however, I warn you that you will face hard and responsible work before that."

Chris nodded approvingly.

"That's before, and what's after?"

Speaking these words, he glanced at me, and I could swear that we both thought the same thing: what is Hakat's involvement in this to be created Moon city, which is to be named Riviera. He certainly wasn't doing it selflessly. He was doing it according to plans. Even if he had nothing to do with sending his brother-in-law to Lunnar, he had deliberately placed me by his side. He also had the goal of transferring his niece to the Moon, who was a virtualist, and not just any, but having the power to operate the main data stream. She could get the information and documents he needed at any moment.

I was aware now that the Moon wasn't only important for political reasons. Either way – is it possible to completely separate matters of economy from matters of politics? Perhaps my protector needed a lot of money to implement his plans.

"What's after, we'll see," he said calmly. "A lot can happen until the construction is finished. For now, I have a different task for the three of you, or the four of you, rather."

"What is it?"

I groaned on the inside. Predictably, Citizen Hakat was always hiding something up his sleeve. Scotty didn't seem surprised either. We looked expectantly at the Chief of Arms, who took a drink again and began speaking:

"As you may know, for the past year they've been building another station in orbit. The 'Strogoff' has become too tight, so there are plans to move non-medical research laboratories to a new location, and to turn the local institutes into a hotel for sick families, or at most weirdos who want to spend their free time exploring orbital laboratories. The construction was going well until last month. Although the team was already complaining of malaise and strange, inexplicable events before, but a few weeks ago the problems escalated. In short, people have abandoned the construction, claiming it's...   well,   haunted."

The word was so unexpected that we burst out laughing against our wills. Hakat didn't seem offended and continued:

"The technicians and engineers were questioned, of course. They all testified the same. They heard whispering voices, had a strong feeling that there was someone invisible in the room, said the tools broke for no apparent reason, electricity punctured wherever there were relays. And that's not all. People also saw strange, inexplicable phenomena. It must be true, because they were so scared that they didn't even want their paychecks. This is an unprecedented event, at least I have never heard of anything like this."

"Collective psychosis?" I risked.

He shook his head negatively.

"Our psychiatrists have ruled out that possibility. There really is something going on there, although I would bet on sabotage, rather than ghosts from fairy tales."

"Send another team, then. I can't believe that you have only one at your disposal."

"That's something we can't do. The news have already spread, and the professionals in this industry are superstitious. Nobody's going to go there until we solve the case."

He paused for a moment, drumming his fingers on the table.

"That station is a very important project," he said finally. "A prestigious one, I'd say. It has absorbed a lot of resources and we cannot afford to lose it."

"What do we have to do with this?" Cavanaugh asked roughly.

"That's obvious, isn't it. You're going to find out who or what is haunting it. You are the dream team for this job: two detectives, a talented engineer and an android whose most important advantage is that it cannot go crazy. Of course, I could send a commando squad there, but the agency cannot afford such an embarrassment. Do you have any idea what people would say about that?"

"Did no one try to examine the construction site after the team left?" Chris asked on point.

"I sent Detective Paul Rainer there, my best man. He didn't come back and hasn't contacted us."

Scott smiled slightly, and the implants, so far extended, retracted a bit.

"Then it could be a missing case, accidental death or even murder."

"Absolutely," confirmed Hakat. "Rainer knows the rules, one of which is keeping in touch with the headquarters. If he's silent, something must have happened. You'll have to figure out what. The station is at most half completed, but the shell is sealed, the air purification apparatus and heating circuits are operational, and the artificial gravity system is on. At an appropriately advanced stage of assembly, it's necessary to avoid accidents. There are also supplies of water and food. According to unwritten contracts, the food provided to the construction team is part of the salary, but our employees didn't take anything."

I got up from the table and poured a full glass of water. I drank it in one breath and then asked:

"When are we going?"

Hakat stood up as well.

"In half an hour," he replied. "I've already arranged your transport. I also prepared a portable laboratory and, of course, communicators. I will make connection once per day, so don't neglect that. Reports can be short if there's nothing new, but they must be broadcasted."

"I know the rules no worse than you do," Scotty grumbled. "Although I've never hunted ghosts before, I been fulfilling other duties flawlessly. You don't have to lecture me like a rookie, I know my job. But let's assume that there will be no reports for a longer time, then what?"

"It's better that you don't know."

"That bad?" the inspector raised his eyebrows.

The Chief of Arms looked at him as if he wanted to say something, but remained silent. Now that I knew what the two had in common, I better understood their relationship and the problems they must have had with each other. It was certainly not easy for them, but when operating within one service they had to get along somehow.

I looked at Chris, who sat still, running his fingers through his pale curls.

"So, what do you think, little brother?" I asked.

"Nothing. I don't believe in ghosts," he replied indifferently. "If I have to go to this construction site, then I will, why not? However, I doubt that we can find any evidence of supernatural forces there, mainly because such a thing doesn't exist on Earth or anywhere in the cosmos."

Hakat looked at him sarcastically and softened his stony features with a slight smile.

"You don't think that I actually believe in ghosts haunting the extraterrestrial stations myself," he said pityingly. "I just want to know what's going on there. I'm sure you understand, when pictures fall off some wall or glass vessels suddenly burst, you can either blame it on ghosts or try to eliminate the real cause. I'm betting on the latter."

"Me too. At least we agree on that."

"We don't have to agree. All I demand is obedience and results."

"Yes, yes, I know that I'm forced into this situation and..."

"I beg you, end with this discussion," I interrupted desperately.

Knowing my brother, I was afraid that he would lead into an argument and scream out everything he learned to Hakat. I didn't even want to think about how that could end.

Chris paused, his lips frozen in annoyance. I knew that the capitulation was only temporary, but for now the storm had been averted.

III

The 'Hoover' station from the outside looked like an enlarged disk, similar to those used in sports competitions. It was completely finished from the outside, which made sense. When building in a vacuum, you need to have a cover in front of it first, only after can you install the equipment.

The construction site was lit only by positioning lamps. The station windows were covered with armored plates, and of the six docks, only one, automatic, operated with a remote and which was really a hangar lock, was in order. The shuttle pilot opened the hatch, lead the vehicle inside, closed the entrance, and positioned the shuttle so that the automatic containment sleeve could latch on to the hatch casing. The remote control system was not yet finished, so the regular procedure couldn't be started. The hangar was unheated and airless. We had to go through the sleeve to the internal airlock, and through it to the interior of the base.

As we closed the last airtight hatch behind us, Scotty signaled to the pilot that we were inside and that he could return to Strogoff. After a moment, the shudder of the walls let us know that the shuttle was departing the station, and then a single jolt announced that the hangar inlet hatch was closed. We were left alone in an abandoned, only half-finished station, lit only by emergency lamps. It gave a gloomy orange light, adding to the awe of this place.

"I hope we haven't forgotten anything," Scotty said tartly, breaking the growing, dangerous silence. "Let's count the packages."

We had with us a laboratory kit in four backpacks, luggage with sleeping bags and hygiene supplies. Suddenly I felt like we had ridiculously little, although I realized that we probably won't be staying here too long. I shivered involuntarily.

"Everything we took with us is here," Monty said.

The station didn't leave an impression on him, just as even the most beautiful place in the world would not. I've noticed it before. My companion flawlessly distinguished what was nice and elegant from what looked bad, and yet was completely indifferent to what kind of surroundings he was in. I think that he would even live in a landfill if I moved there and he would feel as comfortable there as in the most expensive apartment.

"Let's get to work, then," Cavanaugh picked up the assigned to him part of luggage. "We have to find some social room where we can sleep, and another one where we will set up the laboratory. Then we'll come up with a plan of action."

One of the social rooms was rather close. Finding it was made easier thanks to the illuminated arrows with markings, placed in the corridors by workers. What we were looking for was marked with the symbol of a steaming cup, just like the door of the room – they were of an old type, opened and closed by hand. I haven't seen ones like those in a long time, maybe only in historical films, but here they were probably mounted only for the duration of the construction. The photocell circuits, just like other small things, were always mounted last, when everything else is finished.

We put the sleeping bags on the floor and looked around. The room was large, with a portable stove in one corner and an inflatable couch with a backrest in the other. There was a second door on the wall opposite the front door, leading to a storage room full of cans and bottles.

"I guess we won't be starving in here," Chris said. He uncorked one of the bottles and took a sip. He gave me the second one, and third one to Scott. It could also be carbonated if one wishes, I see a few packs here.

The inspector took a drink and wiped his mouth with his sleeve.

"This is pretty good. Let's leave our things here and do our first inspection. First, we need to find a second room to set up our lab. Secondly, it's necessary to establish what happened to Detective Rainer."

"True" Chris agreed. "He could be anywhere, though. The station is pretty big."

"That's why we have to start as soon as possible," Scotty cut off. "Take some water with you, you may need it. And a first aid kit."

I opened one of the backpacks and took out a small bag with a long strap, marked with the Aesculapian snake. I put the water bottle in one of the overalls' pockets and the other in the haversack with a basic set. We all wore the same outfits, the so called travel overalls, comfortable, strong and sewn with a lot of pockets. It's a very functional outfit that doesn't restrict your movements and allows you to carry a lot of necessary small things. Ours were additionally equipped with a thermal insulation layer, which we fully appreciated now. It was cold in the station, the heating was working poorly, all the necessary cells must have not been installed yet, and the ones that worked could not suffice for such a large space.

"Monty, look and memorize everything," I said to the android, who followed us silently. "Remember the way so we can go back. You will be the guide in case we get lost."

"Can people not remember the way?" he asked.

"We have to focus on something else. It's hard to do two things at once," I replied evasively. I didn't want to explain that human memory can be unreliable. The conversation with Chris, even though I presenter engineer Karpinsky's arguments during it, caused a certain anxiety in me and I preferred not to make Monty aware of how imperfect his creators are.

"Which way are we going first?" I asked.

Scott looked around, but he was looking not at the hallways but at the walls. After a while he decided:

"This way."

We started walking. Our eyes soon became accustomed to the emergency light and we could make out every detail without any problems. The corridor we walked along was only roughly finished. There was no carpeting or wall cladding, and the we passed didn't have any doors, not even makeshift ones. Inside some of them were discarded materials and tools, others were completely empty and dark. We looked into each one, not finding anything supernatural anywhere, which was to be expected. It took us a long time, as we also examined dead ends that were later to be made into separate galleries.

I was already quite tired and hungry when the corridor split into two, then into four. Neither bore the symbol of a trowel to denote expansion, and none ended with dead ends, at least as far as we could see. Chris looked at Scott.

"Where to now?"

The inspector looked around. I noticed that he was sniffing searchingly, and involuntarily I started to sniff myself, but apart from the smell of metal and oil, I couldn't smell anything unusual. Scott must have had a better sense of smell than me if something alerted him.

"There," he decided, pointing to one of the corridors.

"Boss, have mercy!" I groaned. "My legs are already numb. Let's rest for a moment."

He looked at me searchingly and waved his hand.

"Fine."

He pulled a folded blanket from the bag over his shoulder, spread it on the floor, and motioned to us to sit down. I did it with enormous relief. I don't think I've ever walked for this long. Our civilization did what it could to make long walks no longer necessary, and they only became entertainment for the 'healthy lifestyle' geeks, which were not that many. Despite the obligatory use of the gym and attention to physical fitness, we are not as good walkers today as our ancestors were.

Scotty sat down beside us, grabbed a tin of food from his bag, which he had taken from the storeroom, and opened it. There was something inside that resembled pieces of meat with vegetables, covered with a kind of hard jelly. We had only knives for cutlery, so we used them as substitutes for spoons. The canned food had a nice, salty taste and immediately calmed my twisting stomach.

"What exactly is this?" I asked after my hunger had been satisfied.

"Assignment rations for C-class workers," Chris replied. "When I was on my internship, we ate ones like these, too. It's a custom that everyone at the construction site gets them, that is, those who work physically."

"University apprentices are hired to do physical work?"

"Of course. A future engineer must be familiar with everything, starting from the basics. During the first practice, the most demanding and the most spoiled ones crumble. They give you a good beating there."

"But at least they feed you well."

Scott quickly finished his portion, took the communicator out of his breast pocket and made a short report, "We've started our investigations, nothing so far." I admit that I completely forgot about it.

I took another piece of canned food. Chris did so as well.

"Many people turned their noses at such food," he said. "They said it was a disgrace to give them such a thing to eat. It's not meat, or even a commercial substitute, but a mass of basic protein. Immediately after the ecological catastrophe, they made rationing cubes from those things. Either way, I'm fine with them. It's usually eaten hot, like a soup, but it tastes fine cold too. I have no prejudices there."

I didn't have them either. We mainly owed it to the upbringing of Cynthia Lara, who for years instilled in her pupils that they eat in order to live, not the other way around, and was a fierce enemy of the so-called 'refined gastronomy'. It's hard for me to define her attitude towards kitchen matters, but she believed – I think – that excessively sophisticated and expensive dishes are a 'sin' to all of mankind, doomed to poor-quality rations for so long. A word like that escaped her one time. As a kid, I didn't really understand what a 'sin' was, only later did Sean explain to me that it was an ancient word for guilt. True to her philosophy, Cynthia has taught us that eating is first and foremost the act of filling the stomach, which we must do to stay healthy. She did not tolerate any fumbling at the table, although she was sometimes indulgent in other matters.

Having rested, we moved on. We had to travel a long way before I could smell what bothered Scott – a faint, unpleasant smell. It intensified as we plunged deeper into the corridor, making even Chris, the least experienced at the job, filled with doubts.

"I'm guessing that we're about to find Detective Rainer," he muttered.

"It seems like it," Scotty agreed. "I've been around this smell too often not to recognize it."

"I thought that the air at stations is devoid of bacteria and viruses. There should be no such thing as rotting here."

"People bring microorganisms on themselves and within themselves. There are enough of them to initiate the decomposition process."

After a few more steps, we finally found what we were looking for.

Detective Rainer was lying in one of the social rooms, where he had set up – like us – temporary quarters. He was certainly not clean in life. There were empty water bottles, crumpled energy bar packages, and emptied cans everywhere. His investigation probably lasted several days, maybe even dozens, before... well, this happened.

At first glance, it was difficult to tell what actually happened here. Bending over the body, I had to cover my nose with my sleeve. The sight wasn't pleasant either. The detective's body was lying on its left side, curled up in a strange way, a solid, thick substance lying around the floor. Scott took pity on me and took the baton.

"Search his things," he said, pushing me away. "I'll check the body, since Kelley is not here. He would've been useful."

With relief I rummaged through the detective's belongings that had been casually thrown in a corner. I immediately found a typical evidence bag. There weren't many of them: bits of burned wires, some damaged cells, and a bag of grayish powder. This was what interested me the most, because it didn't resemble any building material I was aware of.

"Don't open it," Chris warned. "We have to analyze it first."

"You know how?"

"Of course. I was learning how to use a handheld spectrometer and other laboratory equipment."

"What for?"

"A cosmotronic engineer must sometimes analyze oil, fuel or grease when diagnosing a machine malfunction. I had to master the basic methods and everything that goes with it."

He put the bag in one of the pockets of the haversack, the remaining evidence from Rainer's belongings in the others. Then he walked over to Scott, who was scratching the substance on the floor with a spatula.

"What do you think, Cavanaugh?" he asked. The inspector looked at him.

"It looks strange," he replied. "Either a sudden attack of illness or poisoning."

"Are you sure about that?"

"Well, the deceased was clearly convulsing and vomiting."

"So, that thing you're collecting is…"

"Old vomit. I bet the guy's pants are full of excrement, and we have to take a sample of that too. In my line work, you come into contact with various things, usually not very appetizing."

"I'll do it," I sighed resignedly. I wasn't very keen on this type of job, but as a candidate for a police detective I had to get used to activities that weren't very pleasant.

I took the sampling kit out of my haversack, knelt beside the dead body, and overcoming a reflex of disgust, I unbuttoned the pants. Scott was right, the unfortunate detective's buttocks were partially covered with dried, distinctive yellow-brown goo. I scooped up a large portion with a spatula, put it in a plastic container and closed it carefully.

Meanwhile, the inspector also took a sample from Rainer's mouth and stood up.

"Pictures," he said briefly in my direction. I took the camera out of my hip pocket and carefully photographed the body and the entire room.

"Anything else?"

"No. That will do for the day, let's go back. Monty, lead the way."

With relief we left this room, temporarily turned into a morgue. In the long run, there was nothing to breathe with there, and the company of a corpse could put anyone into a nervous state. Monty walked steadily ahead, not hesitating or stopping, and we followed him.

"You were expecting this, right?" Chris asked after a long walk

"Sure. I had hopes that it was just a broken communicator, but they weren't too high. There are always emergency lines in break rooms, and I knew that the detective couldn't be an idiot. A fatal accident seemed most likely."

Scott put his arm around me.

"I'm proud of you, you know?"

"Why is that, boss?"

"You made it. You're starting to act like a policewoman, not like a random spectator. You wouldn't lose your temper as you did at the beginning, and that was worse than the view in Laboratory F."

"What laboratory?" Chris asked.

"We closed down an illegal research laboratory. They were doing human experiments in there. The sight was gruesome, but at least nothing stank like back there."

"Never in my life would I have thought that Leeta would end up in such a profession."

"Neither did she, I'm sure. She simply didn't have a choice. Hakat doesn't give that to anyone."

He snorted dismissively.

"You don't love your brother-in-law very much?"

Cavanaugh stopped and eyed him.

"So you've dug your way into that, congratulations. I can see tell that you like the smell of trouble."

"That's my business."

"It sure is. Do what you want with your life, but don't splash your tongue around, okay? I don't want this spreading."

"Relax, I know what's a problem and what isn't," Chris patted him on the shoulder. "Either way, you're not the one at fault, are you? You didn't introduce this guy to your family, it was your sister."

Scott nodded and continued on his way.

"I think that Betty really loved him. However, I don't know if she was happy with him. He isn't able to care for anyone but himself."

Suddenly I felt compelled to stand in Hakat's defense. Despite everything, I was grateful to him for what he did for me, and preferred to think he cared about me in some way.

"He helped me when I needed it," I said in a spicier way than intended. "I'm alive thanks to him, even though I had to give up many things. He could have gotten rid of me once I testified and he would have had me out of his head."

Scotty laughed heartily.

"Oh, you naive creature... he didn't place you on the Moon from the good of his heart, but so that he could use you when needed to. His plan was only partially successful. He gained a position he excelled at, but he also had to yield at something. He failed to destroy his enemies. You are very valuable to him as a living witness. I assure you, he wouldn't have bothered with you otherwise."

"I think you're exaggerating," Chris interjected. "If the guy wants to keep Leeta alive, then why did he place her in the police? It's not the safest place to be, to put it mildly."

Scott winced slightly, his implants twisting.

"It may seem that way. In fact, however, a police detective is less vulnerable than they appear to be. The patrol service or the stormtroopers are different. And you have to take into account that as a detective from headquarters, Leeta has unofficial 24/7 security, especially after the tragic death of Silvana Evans. You must know, young man, that this was the first case of an open attack on a detective in a very long time, and the first one in Lunnar. My brother-in-law was right to assume that within the main police headquarters Leeta would be as safe as she was on the Central Island. He couldn't have anticipated that someone like Brel would show up."

Chris agreed with him. We all walked in silence for a while, then my brother spoke again:

"So, you really don't like your brother-in-law."

"It's not possible to like him," Cavanaugh said harshly.

"You blame him for the death of his sister and her child?"

"Don't play the fool, kid. Was he the one who caused the accident? No. It was not an attack, they looked into that. No, I hate him for completely different reasons. And let's end this topic."

I could see my brother wasn't happy with this answer, but he didn't push it any further. He didn't last long in silence, though.

"I understand that you smelled decay when we were near the corpse. But it was you who chose the direction of our search. Coincidence?

I looked at the inspector curiously. I was also curious about that. Scott smiled at our stares.

"There are no coincidences. At least not in my line of work. Pay attention to the arrows with the markings."

We obediently looked in the indicated direction.

"Okay, they're there. What about them?

"Right, you don't see well in this light. My implants have a higher resolution than the human eye. I noticed that some have handwritten marks and some do not. I figured only Mr. Rainer could have done that, because workers on facilities like this follow the principle that direction signs are inviolable. Not one of them would scribble on them.

This explained what the inspector was thinking when choosing our directions. I already thought that my supervisor had a supernatural sense, while it was simply perceptiveness and the ability to analyze facts.

We ate a modest dinner in 'our' break room and then went to bed. Scott would have liked to work on the material he had found, but Chris and I were literally falling off our feet, so he thought it would be better to give us a break before proceeding with the work. Monty was ordered to stay awake and wake us up if anything unusual happened.

"Since he doesn't sleep anyway, let him stay on guard," said Scott.

"He does sleep, in a way," I corrected him. "He switches off from his surroundings when he needs to charge the battery."

"Ooh. And does he do that often?"

I looked at the android.

"Monty, how often do you need to charge the battery?" I asked.

"It's enough if I do it every ten days," he replied.

Chris, unfolding the sleeping bag, stopped in mid-movement. Professional curiosity flashed in his eyes.

"What are you charging with? Electricity from a socket, or maybe sunlight?"

Monty's eyes blinked steadily, which meant he was searching for answers.

"I don't know. I only turn off activity."

"He really doesn't know," I explained. "A significant decrease in brain potentials triggers in his body the activation of a self-charging cell, which is connected to a battery that replaces the heart. That's the whole secret."

"Clever. His creator is a genius."

"He sure is."

We stopped talking, we were too tired. We fell asleep mere moments after slipping into our sleeping bags.

I was woken up by pain. Most of all, it was my legs and back that hurt, and it was not any pain known to me. I had the feeling that I couldn't move and I was scared to death.

"Scotty!" I called. "Something happened to me! I'm sick!"

Cavanaugh wasn't sleeping anymore, he was just opening a tin of food. At my scream, he left it and walked over to me.

"What's hurting?"

"Everything. Mostly my legs. I can't move. There must be a virus here and I got infected...!"

He burst out laughing.

"Don't be silly," he said cheerfully. "You simply have 'muscle soreness', as they used to say, because you aren't used such long periods of wandering. And you can definitely move. Wake up, you'll have to walk it off."

I got out of the sleeping bag with difficulty.

"Are you sure?"

"Yes, I'm sure. As a result of physical effort, the muscle fibers attain microdamages, around which occur inflammatory reactions. It was once believed that lactic acid was deposited there, if I am not mistaken, but this has been debunked. The remedy is to massage your muscles and rest, but don't expect immediate miracles. It'll hurt for two more days, but less and less. Come on, honey, give me your feet.

I obediently surrendered to his hard hands, and almost cried out in pain. Scott knew how to massage, and with his power it was almost unbearable.

"Why did I never feel this way after the gym?"

"Because you probably followed your exercise schedule. They are arranged in such a way that the muscles get used to the effort gradually, and additionally everyone receives a tonic that protects their fibers from damage. Now hardly anyone knows what 'muscle soreness' even is. Either way, you weren't prepared for traveling long distances by foot, so your body rebelled. Besides, you've been to the gym exactly four times since landing at Lunnar, I counted. You're out of shape."

He opened the first aid kit and looked through its contents.

"Oh, luckily it's there."

He poured water from the bottle into a plastic cup and dissolved a flat pill in it.

"Drink it."

"What is it?"

"Toner A. It soothes any inflammation. Will help a little."

He handed me the cup and approached Chris, who was sleeping like a log despite my shouting. He was always that way. In the past, I had to spend a lot of energy every morning to wake him up and send him off – first it was to school, and then later it was work.

"Wake up!"

Chris muttered something and attempted to turn over, but Scott shook him so hard that he came to his senses.

"What the hell, is this the army or what?"

He sat down and yawned loudly.

"Damn, and how will I brush my teeth and all the rest? Bathrooms aren't working yet."

Scott tossed him a filled-up bottle. He caught it in the air, took a roll of towels from the cupboard, took a cosmetic sachet from his bag, and went out into the hallway. I felt that I should clean myself up too, and groaning, I dragged myself to one of the makeshift latrines. Hygienic procedures had to be kept to a minimum, but at least they could be done at all. Unfortunately, changing clothes had to remain a mere thought. Although I did take some clean underwear, I couldn't figure out how to wash the one I was wearing. Finally, I did it by hand using antibacterial gel and bottled water, then hung it to dry on a towel rail. The muscle pain subsided. Not that it disappeared altogether, but it became bearable.

Chris had to manage with the morning ablutions too, and came to the table right after me. While we were away, Scotty heated the rations and dissolved coffee tablets from the medicine cabinet in hot water. I've never had anything like this before. Pure coffee, which was once a popular stimulant, is now available only in a pharmacy as a tonic in capsules, and to be honest I wouldn't think of making a drink out of it. It was very bitter and tasteless, but I felt much better.

"Eat," said Scott, setting a plastic plate with a portion of the rations for each of us. "We don't have time to lose."

"What are we doing after breakfast?" Chris asked as he started eating.

"We will penetrate a portion of the station, while you'll analyze the samples," answered the inspector. "There is an empty room next to the break room, we'll set up the laboratory there and you'll begin your work. We need to know what killed Rainer."

Monty, who had been watching and listening to us without reacting until now, spoke so suddenly that we twitched.

"Please allow me to charge the battery. I feel that my energy levels will soon be too low for me to function."

"That's some luck," Scotty muttered. "All right, load up properly then."

"For this purpose I must enter a closed room."

"Ah, that's right," I remembered. "He has an isotope or whatever it's called. While charging, the cover opens up, activating the link, so the android must hide to avoid contaminating people with radiation. Monty, there is a kind of alcove for tools in the hallway, you can use that."

The android turned stiffly and left. Not for the first time, I noticed that in the presence of other people he behaves like a typical robot, completely different than when I'm alone with him, or when only Sue is in our company. He accepted her as a family member, so to speak, and kept his distance from everyone else. He spoke only when necessary, and kept his gestures to a minimum, as if he wanted to hide something.

After breakfast, I helped Chris unpack and set up the handy lab, then (without much enthusiasm) followed Scott to inspect the designated section of the station. Considering how much supplies we've taken, I realized we wouldn't be back soon, and I groaned at the thought of my battered legs.

"Cheer up," Cavanaugh said, "it won't be that bad. I put a roll of mounting tape in your bag. At each turn, cut a piece and stick it on the wall. It will help us get back in case we get lost."

The very thought of getting lost in this gloomy place made me shiver. I took out the roll, placed it on my wrist like a bracelet, rolling up the sleeve of my suit so it wouldn't fall off, and placed the scissors behind my belt.

The inspection of the second portion of the station was similar to our previous 'tour' – carefully examining each room along the way, which in itself is simply boring. We did it almost mechanically, stopping only a single time for a short rest and meal. The rooms, devoid of doors, were empty, with some parts and tools left abandoned. The ones marked as social rooms contained cookers, chairs, sometimes a camp bed or an old couch. We discovered the bedrooms of workers and engineers, full of abandoned sleeping bags and personal belongings.

Everything we saw had to be examined and documented. My legs and back were in pain, I felt like we've been walking for days. I gritted my teeth to avoid complaining and tried to follow Scott's instructions as accurately as possible, though I had an irresistible urge to sit against the wall and refuse to cooperate. In addition, my mood was continuously deteriorating. I felt worse and worse, and at some point I became convinced that somebody was following us. The impression was so strong and unpleasant that I didn't dare look back, and when I suddenly felt a touch of someone's hand, I screamed much louder than I should have.

"What happened?" Scotty spun on his heel, his habitual motion reaching for the gun.

"It's just me. Why are you screaming?"

Monty was behind me. Out of anger and relief, I wanted to punch and hug him at the same time.

"You nearly scared me to death!"

"Why? I didn't do anything."

"Doesn't matter. What were you thinking, to follow us? And how did you know which way we were going?"

"I've finished charging the battery. Mr. Chris said I might be of use. I was guided by the tape stuck on the walls. It's fresh and hasn't quite cooled down from the touch of human hand, so I knew you were leaving it."

The inspector snorted slightly.

"All right," he said briskly. "You are here, so be it. We'll take this opportunity to eat something, get some decent sleep, and I will send a message to the headquarters. It's about time, because according to the clock it's already evening. And you, kid, don't scream like you're possessed for any dumb reason."

A break was a good idea, since we were both tired, and my entire body was hurting nearly as much as in the morning. After we slept, we ate something resembling a breakfast, and Scotty gave me another painkiller. Either way, I felt a bit better than the day before. After breakfast, we continued our search. In my *pod*, I described every checked room, while Cavanaugh was drawing something in his – I had no idea what. I tried to be calm and professional, but something was bothering me.

Although it turned out that it was Monty who was following our trail, and now he was walking right next to me, the strange feeling never left me. I felt watched, I would even swear several times that something was moving between me and the wall. I tried to convince myself that it was just my wild imagination, but it was getting more and more difficult. At one point something brushed against me. I couldn't stand it and screamed again.

"What?!" Scott exclaimed sharply.

"There's something here. We are not alone. Some animal rubbed against me."

"Nonsense. There aren't any free-living animals here and I'm sure no one has tried to smuggle a pet to the station. Get it together."

I tried, but it wasn't that easy. The atmosphere thickened imperceptibly, even the emergency lights dimmed. I noticed that Scott became restless too. He looked around a few times, his implants extended to their maximum length and literally 'poked' around as if they had a life of their own. He must have felt what I felt, too, though probably not as strongly. He was keeping it together somehow, while I was shaking with some strange, pointless terror, and it felt as if something was pressing against my chest, preventing me from taking a deep breath.

No wonder then that when suddenly something slippery, wet and heavy fell on my back, wrapping its soft limbs around me, I let out a scream that I would never have expected myself to make in my lifetime. I screamed and screamed in fear and disgust and didn't stop until Scott shook me so violently my teeth rattled.

"Stop yelling, right now, or I'll give you a slap so hard that you'll never in your life forgive me for it!" he exclaimed angrily.

Monty grabbed his hands and forced him to let go of me.

"This is not allowed, inspector. This is physical violence."

"Get it off me! I wailed hysterically, crouching on the floor and covering my head with my hands. "It's on my back!"

"Let me go, you mechanical son of a bitch!" Scotty broke free from the android, who was not holding on too tightly. "Listen to me, Leeta, there us nothing on your back and no one or anything but us is here. It's all happening in your head. Tell yourself you're in an amusement park, tunnel of fear or something like that, and you'll be fine."

I fell silent obediently and tried my best to take control of myself. The sensation of something clinging on my back has eased, but hasn't gone away completely.

"You don't feel anything?" I stammered, looking questioningly at Scotty. Maybe if he had normal eyes, not those goddamn implants, it would be easier for me to see what he was thinking.

He shrugged.

"I do," he admitted reluctantly. "A couple of times something rubbed against me and I still have the feeling that we are being watched."

"Exactly."

"It's exactly nothing! I knew immediately that it was just an illusion."

"Or ghosts."

"Don't be an idiot. There is no such thing in the world. Ghosts are not real. Do you want proof? Fine, then."

He turned to Monty.

"Look around, android, and tell me if there is any living being here besides us."

"Here, do you mean on this station?" Monty asked.

"In the part of the station we're in now."

The android obediently looked around.

"I don't detect the presence of any protein entity."

"Ghosts aren't protein," I groaned. "Maybe you can see their plasma cloud or energy?"

"I don't see anything abnormal."

A strange split occurred in my mind. One part still cowered in fear like a caveman terrified by lightning, while the other began to think logically. If artificial intelligence cannot perceive something, it must really not exist. It was the only conclusion that could be drawn, and therefore everything that terrified me was actually born in my mind and could not have been otherwise.

"I'm sorry," I mumbled.

The inspector patted me on the shoulder.

"Don't apologize. Since I have these symptoms too, they are not the result of your weakness or excessive imagination. There is really something going on here, though it is not the result of paranormal activity. I'll never believe that."

He marked something in the diagram on his *pod*'s screen. Then he looked at Monty again and tapped the stylus on his chest.

"You really don't feel anything?"

Monty didn't answer right away. He seemed to hesitate or pause before answering.

"Vibrations."

"What?"

"Vibrations. Twitching. Low frequency. And something else."

"Be more specific."

"I'm not able. I don't know what this is. I am... uncomfortable with it."

Inspector turned the implants towards me.

"You see for yourself. I bet the explanation of the phenomena happening here will be simpler than we think and one hundred percent materialistic. But right now I think we should go back and consult your brother."

"You think Chris will solve this mystery?"

"He's an engineer, and not just any. Cosmotronics know about every possible mechanism."

I took a deep breath and let it out slowly. I felt a little better.

"Do you think these phenomena are caused by machinery?"

"It's possible. Perhaps someone wanted to scare people away and came up with some sort of a virtual reality projector for this purpose. They must done a good job at hiding it. The two of us are unlikely to find it, but Nikanov has the skills. All right, turn back, my dear. We're heading back."

As we moved away from the place Scott had marked on the diagram, the unpleasant feelings faded and finally stopped completely. Now I was convinced that Cavanaugh was right. There aren't, and never were, any ghosts on this station, at best there was an exceptionally sophisticated sabotage. I was ashamed of my reaction. I acted like a woman from an ancient primitive village, not like an educated representative of the civilization of a New Age and a government agent. I should be smarter, more reasonable. Maybe the specificity of this place influenced me in that way.

Our journey back was stretching unbearably. Ashamed of myself, I trailed behind Scott, increasingly tired and discouraged. My self-esteem had dropped to almost zero and I only thought about finally leaving the station and going back to a more civilized location. Monty must have somehow detected my mood, because at one point he took my hand and wouldn't let go. I needed that touch badly, and I was grateful for it, though I couldn't understand how he – an artificial mind – knew what I was feeling. In Karpinsky's words, androids did not understand empathy and could not, like humans, 'put themselves in someone else's shoes'. Meanwhile, the behavior of this particular 'copy' was at least ambiguous. I didn't feel like thinking about that right now. All I needed was the touch of a steady, cool hand, the comforting thought that there was someone to lean on.

When we finally got back to the docks section, I was completely exhausted. Cavanaugh didn't seem to pay any attention to it, and himself looked as if he'd spent the last three days not on the road, but behind the desk. The man was truly admirable. He didn't mind the ghostly lightning of this place, the canned food or the inability to meet higher hygienic needs. He was not afraid of any known and unknown phenomena. He was able look at things objectively in every situation. I was sure I would never be equal to him.

"Can I wash up a little?" I asked in a defeated tone.

He turned his implants on me.

"Of course. You know where the water is. Hey, Nikanov!"

He was answered by silence. Concerned, I went to the makeshift laboratory. There was no one there, just samples spread out on the table and the equipment turned off.

"What the hell?"

Scott was the first to spot a scrap of computer foil tucked under the rack with containers. He pulled it out and unfolded it.

I have to check something. I'll be back soon. Chris, he read. "That fool!"

"Where could he have gone?"

"How would I know? Go wash yourself if you want to be clean so badly. We'll wait for your brother, and if he doesn't come back, we'll look for him. If he could've at least left the result of the analyzes, but he wasn't that thoughtful."

With the help of bottled water and paper towels, I cleaned myself up, changed my underwear to the ones I washed earlier, which had already dried out, and lay down to rest a bit. My muscles didn't hurt as much as before, but as I fell asleep I felt that painful blisters were popping up on my poor feet. The field boots were firm and comfortable, and I was given a pair a little too large. I didn't take them off for over three days and that was enough to scrape the soles of my feet.

When I woke up, I realized that I couldn't get up. Despite my protests, Scotty cut the blisters and smeared them with first aid kit ointment, then bandaged my feet. After that, I somehow managed, with Monty's help, to hobble to the latrine, but it was clear that for the time being I would be of no use to further penetration of the object. I could only take a few steps with the android's help. I washed myself with difficulty and returned.

"Sit on the couch," Cavanaugh said. "I found gel inserts in the local medicine cabinet, I'll fit them to your shoes in a moment. We'll take off the bandages in a few hours and you'll be able to walk again."

"In just a few hours?" I was surprised.

"Yes. It's not called quick-healing ointment for no reason. It's a hell of a good specific."

"I didn't know such a thing existed."

"For use in closed medicine only, but the police have special privileges."

He handed me some biscuits, which Chris must have found in the canned storage room while we were gone, because they were now on the table in an open box. In addition, I was given some hot water with dissolved coffee capsules.

"Would be nice with some sugar," I muttered, taking a sip.

"I couldn't find the sweetener, and we didn't take any from the station. Don't be picky."

"I'm not picky. It's just a shame we don't have anything sweet…"

Footsteps and whistling in the corridor interrupted our further conversation. Chris walked into the room shortly after.

"Oh, you're back already?" he said merrily at the sight of us.

"Where the hell have you been?" Scott asked strictly.

My brother didn't seem to feel guilty about it.

"I was looking for the last piece of the puzzle," he replied. "If you wait for one more hour, I'll show you all the arrangements."

Not waiting for an answer, he grabbed a few biscuits and disappeared behind the door. The inspector didn't try to stop him, although I could see that he wanted to. Chris's behavior must have irritated his disciplined nature.

"All right, an hour it'll be," he sighed. "At least we'll get the chance to eat something and I can change my socks."

We ate, then Scott left, taking with him bottles of water and clean underwear found in one of the 'bedrooms', which he presciently put in his bag during our search. Even he must have been annoyed by the fact that it was not possible to use even some simple disinfecting spray, not even mentioning a shower. The only one not bothered by the horrible hygiene conditions was Monty, whose artificial body functioned without excretion systems or sweat glands.

Chris managed in the promised time and showed up in the break room just as Scotty was trying to understand something of the station diagram he found in a drawer under the table.

"Oh, so did you manage?" he asked. "Can you understand the technical diagrams?"

"Honestly, not one bit, but I wanted to at least try. Our problem is not supernatural, it comes from engineering. We'll talk about it in a moment, but first tell me what you discovered."

My brother threw a bundle of lab printouts on the table.

"As I thought," he said, pouring water and coffee powder from a jug into a mug. "I preferred not to say anything until I was sure. Detective Rainer's death was completely accidental. No ghosts had their finger in it, and no enemy of flesh and blood."

"So why did he die?"

"Because he was careless, that's why. The powder he had in his sample bag is mercury azide. It is used in sensors for additional shock absorption. It's a very durable compound and it works even when exposed to water."

"How does it work?" I asked.

"It bursts on impact. That way, it activates emergency cushioning when all else fails. The problem is, it's also a strong poison. The technician who mounted the sensors must have scattered it before escaping. Rainer collected it into a standard sample bag, guessing that it must have been an important clue, but he wasn't careful enough. The bag leaked. Some azide got on Rainer's hands and on the canned food he was eating. It's hard to wash your hands here, so he must have neglected his hygiene and that had its effects. I found traces of this stuff on his clothes and in the secretions of his body."

Cavanaugh made a sound that meant he was appalled.

"It's that much of a rotgut?"

"All mercury compounds are poisonous. Moreover, I suspect that our unlucky guy died not so much from the action of the toxin itself, but from dehydration caused by violent vomiting. I wouldn't bet my life on that, because I am not a doctor or a biologist, but that's the most likely."

"Very unfortunate," sighed Scott. "Well, we can at least close that case. Now it's time to focus on the ghosts."

Chris grinned broadly. He was just washing his hands, pouring water from a bottle over them and rubbing the gel meticulously.

"So, what apparitions did you find?"

"Some zombies and two poltergeists. What a stupid question."

Scott took the dirty dishes off the table and spread the computer foil with the technical diagram of the station on the table. He then turned on his pod and, looking at it, moved all the markings onto the foil. Chris wiped his hands and walked over to the table.

"Somewhere over here," the inspector tapped the foil with his stylus, "there must be a machine producing all these strange phenomena."

"What did you see?"

"That's the thing, basically nothing. But we felt a lot of things. Even the android said he felt discomfort, though he couldn't say what it was."

Chris looked at me, then at Scott, and began nibbling at his lower lip with his fingers.

"What kind of impressions were they?" he asked after a moment.

"Mainly tactile illusions and... a strong feeling that someone who is not there is following us step by step."

Doth walk in fear and dread, And having once turned round walks on, And turns no more his head; Because he knows, a frightful fiend, Doth close behind him tread,[1] Chris quoted turgidly. "During the first

---

[1] Poem "Ancient Mariner", quote.

year they taught us about this type of special effects. They've been already doing experiments with a magnetic field and a specific frequency of vibrations during the twentieth century. The volunteers examined said exactly what you're saying now."

"What's the conclusion?" I asked.

He looked at the diagram. He picked the foil with both hands and examined it in the light.

"There must be a system producing artificial gravity in the immediate vicinity of the marked area," he said after a moment. "That's a logical place to put it. In that case, the possibilities include an accidental failure which caused the whole confusion, or sabotage. Personally, I would bet on the latter option."

"Me too," Cavanaugh muttered thoughtfully. "But why do you think so?"

"That's simple. As far as I could see, there were no cosmotronics at the station at that critical moment. They did their job and flew away, planning to return at the end of construction to check on everything. They were not necessary at this stage of the assembly. But they left behind two specialized gravity technicians. They should have understood what was happening. Why didn't they check everything?"

Scotty snapped his fingers.

"Interesting that you say that. From the description of the incident it seems that the psychosis started from these technicians. Are you sure that ones the same education as them have to be aware of the source of such effects?"

Chris shrugged and set the diagram aside.

"But of course," he said irritably. "It can't be otherwise. However, it's hard for me to accuse anyone without seeing the apparatus."

"So it's decided then. We're both going there."

"What about me?" I squealed with a fear that I couldn't hide.

Scott snorted.

"You'll stay here. You wouldn't be able to walk far anyway."

"And you want me to stay here by myself?!"

"What do you mean, by yourself? Monty will stay with you, we don't need him. You're not going to be scared of ghosts now, are you?"

"Well, no. It's just creepy in here. I'd rather come with you."

Unfortunately, Scotty was right. Though the miraculous ointment quickly reduced the abrasions on my feet, I wasn't in the condition for long walks, and the elevators weren't yet functional. There were only technical cranes, but the chief engineer removed the code card from the reader before he left the station, so we weren't able to start them.

And so, the men left me in the workers' social room and left. When the sound of their footsteps had faded for good, Monty sat down next to me, put his arm around me, hugged me, and asked:

"Can you tell me something?"

He seemed freer now, much more human. Now I thought that my previous suspicions were correct. In the presence of other people, my artificial companion behaved completely differently than when we were alone.

"Yes of course. What do you want to know?"

"What are ghosts and apparitions?"

Just my luck! That's some topic he found to talk about. But, thinking about it more, the question was completely logical from his point of view.

"You see, for millennia, people believed in what could be called the projection of a dead organism. Science has ruled out the possibility of such manifestations, but it's difficult to get rid of the innate belief in superstition. It's part of our genetic memory."

"I don't understand."

"I guess it's hard to understand with a logical mind and without the influence of subconscious memory. Humans are not like androids. Sometimes they see and hear things that don't really exist. If we could act the right way on your brain, you would have hallucinations like this, too, and I'm sure that engineer Karpinsky knows how to achieve that."

Monty nodded that he understood the explanation.

"If you know where it comes from, why are people afraid of these phenomena? They know they are not real. They are created within their brains."

"Oh, Monty," I sighed. Thinking about it, I started my lecture by trying to choose my words the best I could. "You were created on the assembly line, you have no ancestors. And we do. Every human is made up of billions of carriers of gene information, and a lot of this information comes from the time when we were still animals."

"Ones like Sid?"

"Roughly speaking, yes. Humans are a result of millions of years of genetic selection and the exchange of information on the basis of which the biological body is built."

"Who is building you?"

"You don't need a team of scientists for that, the body is built as a result of processes initiated so long ago that we don't even have evidence of what happened back then. All we have are leads. How it looks right now is that two cells, each from one donor, come together to form one and start multiplying. The genetic material they contain is like a computer program in a 3D printer. The cells divide and differentiate, and as a result, a new human is created. However, the program, which caused it to come into existence, has a part from animals that has been passed down through countless generations. This part commands us humans to believe our senses uncritically. In the past, it's what we used to avoid the dangers of the primitive live, such ancestry can be troublesome, however, when something from the outside influences the sensory experiences. We react automatically to many things."

"What does that mean?"

"It means that... our bodies are kind of switching to automatic control. A thing like this in animals is called an instinct. Logic ceases to influence what we feel and how we behave, the patterns fixed in the subconscious memory operate. It's like a second, emergency control center. You don't have that."

"Yes, I know. Don't worry, I can understand that we are different," Monty stroked my head. "That doesn't mean that either of us is worse, right?"

"Of course not!"

He was silent for a long moment, still stroking my hair in a measured motion. I remembered that this is how Sue once stroked and hugged me, when I was struggling with a relapse of lunar depression. I caressed Sid in a similar way. Monty noticed when we do this type of behavior, like many other ones. He learned from examples, just like a child learning about the world from their surroundings.

"Mr. Hakat said that I am merely a servant and that my role is to obey orders," he said finally.

I straightened up sharply and looked into his silver shimmering eyes, calm as ever.

"That isn't true," I said emphatically. "You must never believe something so absurd. I forbid you from saying this nonsense again."

"Don't be mad."

I realized that I had accidentally raised my voice and tried to calm down. Monty wasn't guilty of anything, but I felt a growing resentment towards my boss. I felt respect for him at first, with a lot of gratitude, then I started to fear him, and now... now I just felt angry. My respect for Hakat was slowly vanishing, and so did my fear of him, but instead I was beginning to realize how dangerous and selfish he was. Scotty was right. The only reason I was alive is because at some point the Chief of Arms might need a live witness to the attack, which meant that he was planning his next step. Although, it might even be a good thing that he treated Monty like a machine.

"I'm not mad," I assured him. "But I have a request. I'm sure you remember everything that happened when Citizen Hakat took you for questioning."

"Yes, I remember everything."

"In that case, don't forget any of it, but don't talk to anyone but me about it. When the time comes, your photographic memory may be needed. If, however, someone else asks you about something that happened during this journey and interrogation, reply that I told you to forget it, and you have complied with my request."

"As you wish, Leeta."

I don't even know myself what I was thinking at that moment, but it was probably on that day and at that hour that I felt, for the very first time, a determined impulse of rebellion. And it made me a different person.

My brother and Scotty returned after a few hours. Judging from their unclear expressions, I immediately realized that something was wrong.

"You didn't find the apparatus?" I asked.

Chris shook his head and removed his helmet.

"We don't have access. The technical elevators are down and the only emergency channel we found was blocked over with remnants of building materials. The magnetic field next to it is so strong that we almost lost control over ourselves, so no wonder. The workers must have thought that if they fill in the tunnel, the strange phenomena would stop."

He sat down on an overturned box and ran his fingers through his hair.

"What now?"

"I don't know, sister. We could risk opening the tunnel with explosives, but first of all, we don't even know if there are any here, and second, it's damn risky on an orbital site. One of the walls could leak, and then say your goodbyes..."

"We've got to get the maintenance elevator working, no doubt about that," Cavanaugh interrupted, opening a can of cheap beer that he found in one of the cupboards. "I mean, you're an engineer after all, aren't you? You were picking at that shaft for over an hour, I think you've learned something."

He took a drink and handed the can to Chris.

"I sure did, I found out that we're in a dark ass," he pushed the inspector's hand away and stood up heavily. "These types of passenger-freight lifts are operated by voice control via an interactive module. And these modules have been removed from all of the elevators. We could search the station for parts, but it would take weeks. We can't start them manually."

"So then, engineer?"

"And so all we've got left is the cave method. We need to open the emergency hatch in the floor and go down the rope to the engine room."

"Within higher intensities of the field, we could fall, since our minds will be playing tricks on us," I noted.

They both looked at me simultaneously.

"Will you even be able to come with us?" Scott asked, and Chris said almost simultaneously. "Not a stupid remark. Give me some time. I'll look through the electronics inventory and make us shielding caps. I don't know if they'll eliminate the impact of the field completely, but they will certainly weaken it."

I assured them that I would be able to. Under the influence of the ointment my feet nearly healed in front of my eyes, and besides, I was very reluctant to get separated from the group again. As I managed to find out, Monty's company – in such an unusual situation – could not replace the company of people made of flesh and blood.

"So what else do we have left?" Scott muttered after some reflection. "Look around then, in the meantime we'll connect to the 'Strogoff' station and submit a report. They must be wondering what has happened to us."

Only now did I realize that since we began feeling sensations connected to this station, we didn't think about making contact even once. The Chief of Arms and those who, apart from him, knew about our mission must have felt very tense during that time. The construction designer, chief supervisor and, of course, the investors. I knew that they're on 'Strogoff'. Hakat didn't have to tell me anything, everything indicated that they've been meeting in the conference room for several days. I've already learned enough about the police work to recognize obvious traces.

"Damn it," I muttered.

"Agreed," Scotty commented.

The station didn't have autonomous telecommunications circuits installed yet. For communications, we could use our own device, or – if that one turned out to be damaged – the one that was used by the tragically deceased Detective Rainer. We didn't expect any failures either way. Our subradio was checked four times before we were given a bag with this precious cargo.

In that case, I don't need to describe how great our disbelief was when all attempts to connect with the scientific station failed. We've tried everything. We even took the telecommunication device apart to check for damage and put it back together, but that didn't help either. There was only white noise and slight crackling in the receiver, while two messages blinked on the screen: "Message sent" and "Confirmation of receipt not found" flashed on the display.

"Let's get Chris on it, he'll fix it," I suggested

"There's nothing to fix here," said Scott irritably. "Just look at the controls. This piece of crap is working perfectly fine, only the signals aren't getting through. Something is cancelling them out. Rainer must have been broadcasting an SOS, but no one ever received it."

"That poor man," I whispered sympathetically. I couldn't even imagine what this man, who was in great pain, was feeling when he realized that no one would come to help him. How long was he alive, dying by himself?"

"Maybe so, but we aren't in a much better situation either," Scott muttered. He tried to send our message again, then cursed in impotent anger, "What do we do now?"

"I told you, let Chris take care of it. Neither of us know anything about this stuff."

"Good point. Let's wait until he's done assembling our magnetic shields, then we'll give him a new task."

He made up for it with his expressions, but I could tell that he didn't like any of this. Suddenly a nasty thought occurred to me.

"What if they come to the conclusion that something extremely dangerous has taken over the station and," I loudly swallowed my saliva, "they decide to destroy it?"

He looked at me.

"It's unlikely given its cost and its importance to Hakat, but... who knows? Either way, we'd better hurry up. Let's find Chris."

He was easy to find as the location beepers worked just fine. Chris was in one of the workshop rooms, two hallways away. He was sitting amongst opened electronics boxes, fiddling around eagerly. One of the 'caps', that looked like a medieval torture device, lay finished on the floor, my brother was working on another one.

"Did you send the message?" he asked, hearing our footsteps.

"We can't," Scott replied. "Something's blocking our signal. That would explain why Rainer didn't call for help."

Chris looked up from his work and looked at me. I would give my head that we were thinking the same thing.

"Let's take care of the generator first, after that I'll check what's blocking the communicator," he muttered after a while. "For now, find some rope, as thick and strong as possible. We're going to need to ensure out safety."

I thought that my childhood hobby of climbing, which I used to practice for years, would finally come in use. Although it's true that I've never been faces with such a challenge, I think I should be able to deal with the delusions caused by the sabotaged apparatus.

By the time Chris finished assembling the protective devices, we've managed to procure an entire coil of good quality rope, as well as a bag with a set of precise tools left by one of the evacuated electronics. We took it with us, which Chris reacted to with full approval. He was probably the least concerned about our situation from all of us. Perhaps he didn't even consider the possibility of failure, the same way he never did through his entire life. We, on the other hand, didn't feel such comfort.

Once our blockers were ready, we headed for the chosen elevator. I immediately understood why Chris picked this one in particular – because it wasn't fully completed. We got to the screws holding individual panels without any trouble and removed the floor paneling. The sight of the dark shaft, of which I couldn't even see the bottom, made me feel faint, but Scott didn't pay attention to it. First he shone his flashlight to see if the shaft was clear, then he tied the rope with a solid knot to one of the supports. And then he turned to Monty:

"Stand here and make sure the knot does not come off and that the rope does not rub against the edge of the shaft. If someone down there jerks it three times, pull them out. Do you understand?"

"I understood every word, Inspector," Monty replied stiffly. He looked at me at the same time, so I quickly confirmed the orders he received.

"And did you understand the point?" Scotty continued, skeptical of AI as ever.

"I am to ensure your safety. If necessary, remove the one holding the rope. Signal – jerk three times."

"Well, good enough," Cavanaugh still looked unconvinced, gave in.

Amongst the rubble covering the floor, he looked for a large rectangle of insulation paneling, carefully wrapping it around the rope in the area where it would touch the edge of the window, and secured it as tightly as possible with technical clamps. Then he rubbed his hands together.

"Here we go," he said. "I'll go first. How are you feeling?"

"Great," we assured him. The caps which Chris constructed, although must have made us look ridiculous, fulfilled their role. Despite the proximity of the generator, we felt nothing but a slight anxiety and we had no delusions.

Scotty was the first to disappear into the darkness of the shaft. We waited, listening diligently, until we finally heard his call from the depth:

"All clear! Come down!"

At the same time, we saw the glow of the flashlight turned on by the inspector. He wasn't able to light it earlier since it was a carried one, not a head-strap kind, and it would interfere with his descent. The light revealed walls encased in security from within the darkness. Not it was my turn.

Chris was the third to descent, carrying the bag slung over his shoulder.

"It's all good," he said cheerfully, brushing off his hands scraped by the rope. They burnt him pretty badly, just as did ours. "Well, time to look around."

He reached into his bag and pulled out a detector which tracks down working electronics and quickly tuned the signal while we looked around the engine room.

It was enormous. Filled with some apparatus, of which name even I didn't know, entwined with kilometers of thick as my hand cooling pipes, unfinished in places and scaring with exposed integrated circuits. It smelled like metal, grease, burned rubber, and varnish. The smell was so strong that it made me cough. It was freezing cold and dark everywhere. Even the emergency LEDs dimmed so heavily that they barely glowed on the walls, not illuminating anything.

"I have signal," Chris said, staring at the detector screen. "We have to go there, into the depths."

He waved his hand more or less in the direction.

"Let's go then, smart guy," Scotty grumbled.

He dutifully led the way, plunging without hesitation into this mechanical forest which made me feel an unknown kind of fear. The electronic caps continued to block the magnetic field's effect on our minds, though as far as the vibrations were concerned, through the bottom they could finally be felt by the soles of our shoes. I don't have a thorough neurobiological background and I don't know exactly how this type of vibration affects the human nervous system, but the tickling in my feet was really irritating me. The whole floor vibrated slightly, steadily, incessantly, and I could feel it all the way through my teeth.

We stayed as close to each other as possible. We didn't want to risk any of us getting lost in these mountains of machinery, so large that we seemed like ants crawling inside of a computer. We didn't feel any admiration for this work of human ingenuity, although we probably should've, instead we only felt crowded and an indescribable fear.

"It's really big, all this," Scott said finally.

"I mean, you need a lot for a large station designed as a recreation complex," Chris didn't even glance at him. He still didn't take his eyes off his scanner. "It would be hard to fit its machinery inside of a matchbox."

"Yes, but…" I don't know what Scott wanted to say, but he didn't finish.

Right above us, there was an inhumane howl, and something leapt from above at Cavanaugh and Chris, knocking them both to the floor. The precious detector fell into the corner with great force. I gripped the flashlight tighter, shining the beam of light into the tangle of bodies that was swirling on the floor. My companions, although surprised, didn't panic, and I didn't feel any fear at that moment. However, overpowering the attacker turned out to be extremely difficult and only succeeded when Scott, level-headed as usual, wrapped his own, scratched and dirty sweatshirt around his head.

"I think this must be one of the fitters," Chris grunted, struggling to his feet.

He was bleeding from his split lips, and his left eye was disappearing within a rapidly increasing swelling. Nevertheless, he didn't lose his composure. He quickly found his scanner and picked it up.

"I think it's undamaged."

"Good," the inspector was just finishing tying the attacker with rags he picked up from the floor, while he kept howling constantly at a high note. Finally, he tore the sweatshirt off his head. "Who are you, buddy?"

It was hard to tell whether he understood the words. In the light of the flashlight, I saw ragged and stained rags, bared teeth and restless, completely demented eyes – a terrifying sight. Only now did the fear hit me, and I began shaking.

"Who could it be?"

"A worker, as I said," Chris replied. "They mentioned something in the main report that they were a few people short, but the evacuation was so chaotic that they weren't sure of anything anymore."

"Isn't that great," Scott picked up his flashlight and started shining it in the corners. He moved away from us, and after a long while we heard him shout:

"Come over here!"

Both me and Chris tied the hapless madman to the coolant hose and walked towards the voice calling us. I was still shaking like a leaf and felt like a sitting duck.

Scotty was standing in the doorway of a small storage room. Inside, we could see packs of drinking water placed against the walls, various scattered objects, splashed with dried liquid, black in the light of the flashlights, and... bones. Raw bones, as if eaten by an animal. The head and one hand were intact, and in the corner there was also a bundle of dislodged viscera. There was an unbearable stench in the room. We would probably have sensed it sooner, if it were not for the intense smell of oils and burnt plastic that suppressed everything else. I felt sick.

"That's some sight," Chris muttered somberly, finally losing his good mood.

"We'd better be careful, there might be more of them here," Cavanaugh scanned the surrounding area with his beam of light. The field here had to be extremely powerful.

"The generator is really close," my brother reported, looking at the detector readings.

"Let's go then. We have to turn it off, as soon as possible."

We didn't have to go far to find another unlucky victim. This one was not aggressive. He was curled up in the fetal position, pressed into a corner, moaning softly.

Scott didn't allow me to pause in front of him.

"We'll be of most use to them if we turn off the generator," he said curtly, "and fast. Else, if the field overloads our caps, we'll also go crazy and everything will be damned then."

I shivered at the very thought and touched the electrodes that were wrapped tightly around my head. I had no idea how they worked, but that didn't matter to me. The only thing that mattered was that they work and protect me from the terrible fate that befell these workers.

The floor suddenly broke off, turning into some kind of a wide panel with a handle on one side and hinges on the other. The men immediately found a crowbar, which they used to pry open and lift the hatch. We stood on the edge of a square recess, about a meter deep. Inside, the LED lights flickered and the small, flat structure hummed softly, perfectly fitted into the structure of the artificial gravity circuitry. It was the generator.

Chris jumped to the bottom of the alcove, inspected the machine, and quickly decided how to approach it. He sat cross-legged on the floor, unfolded the tools from the bag in front of him, and began working. This time he was not whistling, and that alone told us how serious he was. He couldn't violate the integrity of the gravitational systems, else we'd launch to the ceiling. He also had to avoid current leakage to the housing at all costs. It would fry him like a vegetable on a grill, and trap us in an electrified trap. The rubber soles of our shoes would save us from instant death, but what next? It was terrifying to think about.

The generator didn't have a typical switch, it had to be dismantled piece by piece, and very carefully. After all, we didn't have a schematic diagram of the device, so Chris had to think about every move he made first. Me and Scott stood still, shining flashlights into the 'operating field', afraid to even breathe loudly, so as not to distract him. Finally, something clicked, the camera lights went out and the hum stopped. Another thing that stopped, as if cut off with a knife, was the constantly accompanying us howl of tied up worked.

"Done," Chris said proudly, standing up and wiping his hands on his pants. "So who's the genius here, huh?"

"You, it's you of course," I said. "Just let us send the message to 'Strogoff', and I'm sure Hakat will personally give you a medal."

"What, is the transmitter not working?"

"Oh, it's working. It's just that our messages won't reach outside of the station. That's why Rainer didn't call for help."

Chris kicked the now harmless, disassembled apparatus.

"Local shield," he said scholarly. "This contraption gave the shell of the station a charge that blocked out communications. A bit like the Earth's magnetosphere that reflects the solar wind. Now there should be no more problems."

"This station is just one big problem," Scott grumbled. "Now we just have to get out of here, and also take those two weirdos with us. I'm interested in whether they've come to their senses yet or not."

No, they did not. The one in the corner had stopped moaning, but his eyes were completely empty. He didn't understand what we were saying to him, he didn't react to anything, I don't even know if he could see us, but he obediently got up and trailed behind us. His friend, still tied to the oil pipe, no longer howled or tugged at the bonds, but instead fell into total catatonia. It wasn't hard to get him to the shaft, where our savior rope awaited.

Even if Monty felt any surprise at the sight of the two men, he didn't show it. I still didn't know whether androids could feel surprise at all. He pulled us out one by one so that we didn't have to struggle to climb, after which he methodically rolled up the rope as if it was going to be needed for something else. Scott, without bothering to explain anything to him, first of all checked the ties binding the rescued worked in a relatively normal light.

"Let's not take any risks," he muttered, meeting my gaze.

Both men looked terrifying. Ragged, covered with dried blood and grease, they looked more like the living dead than anything else. At least they calmed down now.

"What do you think, will they get better?" I asked.

"Maybe," he replied without conviction. "All right, Chris, go get the transmitter. Monty, go with him. We won't be wrestling with these two, we'll wait here.

IV

We sat stiffly still, with our backs straight, on the chairs in the office of the director of station 'Strogoff' and stared at Hakat. He was wearing a brand new, personally fit uniform with ribbons of decorations, and his stern face reminded me more than ever of a statue of Julius Caesar. The dark eyes looked at us without blinking. The mission reports we had written were on top of the desk behind which he was sitting.

"Do you put your reputation behind every word in this report?" he asked sternly.

He was looking at Chris while speaking these words, who had done the hardest part of this job, not only dismantling the generator of the field and vibrations, but also detailing how it worked.

"If I wasn't sure, I wouldn't have said anything at all," my brother replied coldly. "I've been suspecting this kind of sabotage from the very beginning, but just in case I didn't say anything, to not make a fool of myself, just in case. I became convinced when Monty described some disturbances in his mind to me. He experienced them as he approached the source of the disturbance. If the phenomena at the station were supernatural, they wouldn't have had any effect on the artificial brain.

"I see, so you were considering the possibility of a 'haunting'?"

"Please, no need for the sarcasm, Citizen. The world still has a lot of secrets up its sleeve and things that would surprise us should be taken into account."

"That may be so. In any case, the case is now closed. Thanks to all of you, we'll be able to arrest the guilty parties and resume work," Hakat now looked at me and Scott. "You have my gratitude."

"What about the ones we found in there?" I blurted out.

This case kept me awake at night. All the time I was thinking about forgotten by my colleagues fitters, trapped in an unfinished engine room for so many days that, under the influence of madness, they turned to cannibalism. They must have gone through incredible psychological torture to find themselves in such a state and my heart contracted with pity at the very thought.

"They are under the care of doctors," the Chief of Arms replied dryly. "There is a chance that they'll recover their mental health. Those who failed to see them evacuated will be brought to justice. In any case, your role ends there."

Scotty, who had been silent so far, cleared his throat.

"We can go back, then?"

Hakat eyed him up.

"For now, I am sending you to rest, while Mr. Nikanov will be going to the personnel training facility where the Selenoport Project engineering team is currently staying. Fortunately, it's not full, and there is a shortage of specialists, otherwise I would've probably had to find you a job washing up in some kitchen. I wouldn't allow for you to ruin my plans with your talkativeness."

He spoke his last words with peculiar pressure. We all understood what he was trying to say. It was easy to guess when we knew as much as we did."

Chris narrowed his eyes like a cat.

"What if I don't accept your terms?"

Hakat rested his elbows on the table and placed the tips of his outstretched fingers together, like Sherlock Holmes in an old engraving.

"I believe I should have no difficulty in obtaining an order to deport a political suspect to a designated location," he replied. "In fact, I am the one who issues such orders."

"In other words, I will either either accept your terms or you'll do me in?"

"If that's how you want to see it, Nikanov, I don't have the authority to forbid you from that."

My brother pursed his lips and then nodded.

"I just like knowing my position, that's why I asked. I was sure I had no choice anyway, but I wondered if you had the courage to say what you were thinking."

Hakat didn't seem offended, although his interlocutor's tone was at least impertinent.

"I got to where I am because I've never succumbed to cowardly reflexes. When a person sets the highest goal for themselves, they must be able to control their emotions, otherwise it will be unobtainable. In my adult life, I allowed myself to succumb to them only once, and more precisely at the funeral of my wife and child. Never before and never after. You will not be able to provoke me."

"I'm of the same opinion. No need to worry, I will accept your generous offer. First of all, because I have no choice, and second of all... because it's a great opportunity and I'm not going to waste it just because I have my own opinion about you."

"It's always better to have your own opinion, rather than someone else's. Pack your bags please, Nikanov, we'll be traveling together. I need to do an inspection of the facility, so I'll introduce you to the rest of the team while I'm there. The government shuttle will be here in two hours. That should be enough time to say goodbye to your sister and make sure you haven't forgotten anything."

Two hours isn't that long when you have to do at least a minimal amount of 'shopping' and discuss current affairs. It was only when the government vehicle started and the blue light on the control board announced that it had taken off the station that I felt sad, and nearly started crying. Chris's presence, always happy, lively and so close, was like a return to the old, more carefree times, and now that he was gone, I felt I came back to reality. I turned away from the barrier separating the airlock lane from the waiting area, and walked back to the living section, with my head down. Scott also seemed moody, walking alongside me without saying anything, so much that it worried me.

"Why are you so quiet?" I asked.

He threw up his arms.

"Do you like him?"

I stopped in amazement.

"Who, Hakat?"

"No way! The blonde stud."

My eyes widened. I was slowly starting to understand the point of the question, and I didn't know whether to laugh or kiss Scott.

"Chris? Come on, he's my brother!"

"Your social brother. That doesn't mean anything. Not from the point of view of moral law."

"So what? We grew up like real siblings and never treated each other differently. Scotty, you're jealous…"

He cleared his throat in embarrassment and looked away. The melancholic mood vanished without a trace, to be replaced by a tenderness I had not experienced in a long time.

"Give me a break," he gasped. "That's some idea. I wouldn't even have the right to be jealous of you."

I stepped closer and moved my hand across his cheek.

"Don't be embarrassed of it, Scotty. It's… very nice of you."

"Very stupid, I'd say. I'm too old for you and I look what I look like, while that boy has everything a girl could want. Handsome, young, with great prospects…"

"But he's just my little brother," I cut him off. "It never even occurred to me to look at Chris that way. You are different."

"Stop it. I won't believe you fell in love with my scars, let alone all the rest! Sorry, I shouldn't have started this conversation."

I hugged him, feeling the tensed-up muscles through the fabric of his freshly washed uniform. How was it possible that a man for whom risking his own life was a daily routine now felt and acted like a schoolboy on his first date?

"Or maybe you should have? Forget about the prejudices and let's give it a try," I said softly. "What's the harm in that? We both know what to expect, we know each other and we trust each other. If you want, we could just hang out at the dating center like two strangers for now, and we'll see what comes of it."

Cavanaugh was silent for a moment, then forced himself to hug me as well. I could see how much it cost him to show any affection, even if it was reserved. What was he afraid of? Losing control over his life, or maybe that he would be ridiculed, or – worse – getting hurt? Someone must have hurt him before, maybe more than I thought, and that's why he wrapped himself in such a thick shell. But I never thought meeting at the dating center meant so much to him. He disguised it perfectly, pretended very well... until today.

"You're so young," he whispered. "On top of that, I'm your supervisor. It wouldn't be right."

"It's not forbidden by law, so it would be fine," I disagreed strongly. "I know that at some point in the past, such a relationship would have been considered something unacceptable, but we are modern people. Scotty, let your heart speak at least this once. I already know how you feel, and I... want to try. I believe we have the right to do so. We're both lonely. Maybe even too lonely."

He nodded slightly, though he didn't seem convinced. Something was bothering him, he was clearly afraid of what I was proposing. And yet, I wasn't that convinced either. How could I be? We were faced with a tough trial, perhaps more complicated than our entire investigation, than any investigation in the world. For the first time in my life, I felt a joyous excitement at the thought that... something extremely difficult was awaiting me. And I didn't feel like stepping back.

I've never been to any of the 'orbital cities' before, as the great orbiting objects were called. Some were science stations, while others acted as holiday resorts, mainly for wealthy snobs. Even richer ones came to the moon, although so far – to tell the truth – there wasn't much there to see. The only thing is the fact that you could later boast 'I spent my holidays on the moon'. I'm sure that after the construction of Selenoport it will be different, but as long as Lunnar remains an industrial city, it won't offer any real entertainment, only very expensive accommodation in a rather luxurious hotel.

I had some difficulty persuading Scott to take advantage of Hakat's generous offer and spend these two weeks at station 'Colchis'. I was initially planning to take Monty along, but after some thought, I decided not to. I wanted to spend this time alone with Scott and make sure we got along together. I called Sue and arranged for her to pick up the android from the landing port, then placed him in the care of a flight attendant from the cruise ship, introducing him as a policeman in plain clones. Of course, that required a small lie.

"Please take care of him. He has recently been injured in action and has undergone neurological rehabilitation, which is why he may behave and express himself in a slightly odd way."

The flight attendant smiled sympathetically.

"I understand, ma'am. Don't worry, I've undergone nurse training. I'll take care of Mr. Romain as best I can."

All that was left was to explain to Monty how to behave during the trip so as not to arouse suspicions. He listened carefully and when I finished he asked one question:

"Why do people lie all the time?"

He really surprised me with that question.

"Sometimes it's what you have to do."

"Why? It has no basis whatsoever."

"It does," I replied. "It's related to the specificity of the human culture. We will talk about it one day, but not right now, okay?"

"Okay."

"For now, you will travel back home alone, pretending to be human. I taught you how to do it. Until I get back, listen to Sue in every case. She is a person you can trust."

And so, Monty began his flight to the moon, while me and Scotty made our way to the station 'Colchis'.

Subconsciously, I expected it to resemble 'Strogoff', but I was met with a big surprise. The station was arranged like a huge biosphere, refined by videoplastics in every detail. If someone was brought here while in deep sleep and not told where they were, they would certainly be convinced that they're on a real island of paradise. It fully deserved its name, taken from – if I'm not mistaken – Greek legends.

We could see the detailed sketch of 'Colchis' and the description of all objects in the brochure we received. The more I delved into it, the more I felt admiration for the builders of this place. The engineers here reached the heights of art, to take advantage of a relatively small space and fit all planned attractions in it. Not only the beach, but also an amusement park, a go-kart race track that encircles the entire station like the ring of Saturn, a magnificent botanical garden, two theaters, a three-dimensional cinema, bowling alleys, tennis courts and many other facilities.

All around us grew decorative trees and shrubs, amongst which soared colorful birds. Here and there the ponds glistened with a calm surface, on which hovered lotuses and lilies. There was a pale blue sky overhead, lit by an artificial sun (or maybe they've used the real one to achieve this? Such a solution would've required a system of mirrors, but it would be feasible. It was hard to tell from observation alone how this was done).

They've even taken care of ragged, white-pink cloudlets. Even the most knowledgeable connoisseur might struggle to distinguish what in here I sreal, and where the videoplastic illusion begins.

According to the map we received on the ship, the strollers were equipped with all the attractions, and in the back of the building, by the holographic sea, there was an artificial beach covered with sand. It was advertised as the perfect sunbathing spot, so a solar lamp must have been located above it.

The rover, equipped with the station's logo, drove us between all these wonders, to the hotel 'Emperia', where we had a reserved room.

"That's some decor," I whistled as a valet in a red jacket ushered us inside. "Scotty, look."

The hotel was clearly intended for extremely rich people, because it was made with great attention to detail. Even if the marble from which the floors and reliefs on the walls were made were artificial – it would be difficult to prove that without specialized research. It all looked natural. The windows were made of polished crystal at the edges, and all corners stood heavy planters with palm and rubber trees. From the ceilings hung extensive candelabra, which were purely decorative, since the hotel's lighting was modern, as were the other facilities.

A lovely girl in a costume, which must have cost four months of my salary, greeted us with a dazzling smile.

"Welcome to Hotel Emperia," she said kindly. "My name is Tawnia Baker and I will be your personal hostess during your stay. You can come to me with any matter. Let's start with the check in."

She opened an old-fashioned book with gilded edges.

"May I have your full names?"

"Scott Cavanaugh and Juliette Ankes," I replied

"I can already see a reservation of class lux. Two apartments or one?"

Scott hesitated, so I took advantage of the opportunity.

"One."

Tawnia nodded.

"Married, cohabitation or an informal relationship?"

"The third one for now," I laughed involuntarily. "But well, you know how it is, everything is still ahead of us."

The hostess looked with an almost mischievous twinkle in her eyes.

"Of course. Oh, and feel free to call me by name, that's our custom here."

Scott was silent, clearly confused, as if suddenly speechless. Only when Tawnia led us to the selected apartment and discreetly closed the door, he asked:

"Are you sure about this?"

"Are you not?"

He sat down on the wide double bed.

"I'm old, Leeta, ruined by my service, and you are so young and pretty, and in addition dependent on me for business. I feel ashamed of taking advantage of your friendship. Perhaps you confuse the feeling of a certain admiration that young cadets often have towards their superiors with something more?"

I sat down next to him.

"Trust me, I know what I'm doing," I said warmly. "I'm not a teenager anymore, prone to temporary infatuation. I understand your doubts, Scotty, they bring you honor, but you don't have to torture yourself anymore. It doesn't make sense."

He turned his head towards me.

"Do you think so?"

"Of course. You know what? This bed looks great, let's try it out. We both have a big backlog in sexual hygiene. When was this at the dating center?

- A long time, indeed.

- Exactly.

I kissed him with emotion, my mouth feeling the old scars on Scott's lips. For a reason I couldn't pinpoint, it was very arousing. I began unbuttoning his shirt. He surrendered submissively to my fingers. That was something that surprised me from our first meet-up. This strong, dominant man needed someone to take the initiative in bed. This wasn't something I'd expect of him, maybe that was why it was so difficult for him to find the 'one', not because of flaws in his appearance. My problem was quite the opposite.

I didn't have any childhood trauma, and there was nothing negative connected with the planned sexual life. And even despite convictions of friends, I never took advantage of a surgeon's help to get rid of my troublesome virginity, I also didn't feel any specific kind of pain back then. There was also no shame that so often accompanies girls on this first day of their mature life. It just happened and that's it. I didn't experience any extasy, not back then nor later. In my time, I've read that there's two possible attitudes towards sex: either you like it or you're disgusted by it. It turned out that in my case there was a third option – complete indifference. I felt neither discomfort nor pleasure, I simply did what I had to according to the doctor's recommendations. And then one day, in truth by accident, I discovered that there is such a thing as bliss.

On that day, I was unable to start conversation with any of the dating center guests. I didn't feel great and I wasn't too active, but I didn't want to put things off until later. I preferred to get it over with, so I went to the third floor, which is usually the service point for the technopreferred. Despite the general tolerance towards various needs, they are still perceived as freaks. Modern medicine was able to deal with pedophilia, zoophilia and necrophilia as soon as it was established beyond reasonable doubt that changes in the brain's neurons were responsible for these things. However, no one saw a reason why the technopreferred – people who satisfy their sexual needs with various, more or less advanced gadgets – need to seek treatment. It was a type of neurosis, rather harmless, or so it was decided. After all, they weren't hurting anyone, not even themselves. So it was left to their own decision. Some people sought treatment, others didn't. With them in mind, each dating center organized a 'machine park' on the third floor, where you could make your choice.

Since I was a little afraid of having sex with an erotic apparatus (although in appearance and touch it was hardly different form a human), I selected the 'submissive' option on the control panel. It was then that I discovered what I like the most and what would lead me to a high. I was only able to achieve it when I was in a dominant position, and for this role, sexbots were better than any human being. And how is it with androids? Just as interactive, they couldn't have any sexual needs, but were they they similarly geared towards unconditionally meeting people's needs? In the end, however, Monty didn't disappoint my expectations. Was that a trait that androids have, or is it just how mine was? The answer to this was so far unknown, since Monty was a prototype.

For my entire life, I've been gentle and docile. It wasn't for no reason that Chris pointed out how I always preferred to withdraw rather than get into arguments and scuffles, no matter how much I cared about something. I let others control my fate because it was easier that way. It was only in intimate situations that I was able to take control, even more so, if I wanted something more than just following the doctor's instructions. Understanding why Scotty, the tough and hard-hitting cop, had to take the submissive position in bed, was simple. There was too much that depended on him. All his subordinates relied on him unconditionally, the environment regarded him as a man who never quits and never loses. His professional life was a constant struggle in which he could die. At least for one moment, he was able to not worry about anything and 'hand over the helm' in order to achieve a state of complete relaxation and fulfillment. Without knowing anything about each other in advance, we matched that day without unnecessary words and we really felt good together. We didn't have to pretend or act against our own wills.

******

"Tell me something, Scotty," I said.

We were lying amongst the scattered sheets, cuddling, overwhelmed by the most pleasant exhaustion in the world, a feeling known to every pair of lovers. Scott reached for the bottle beside the bed, opened it, and poured the carbonated, yellowish liquid into two cups. Champagne! I've only read about it before, or at most saw it in a movie. It must have been available at Miraton's menu, but I didn't have the chance to try it during my stay in that hotel.

"Is that for us? For free?"

"Deluxe service. My brother in law went all out, although it's all not from his money anyway."

"He didn't have to do that, so that's nice."

"Dummy," Scotty laughed affectionately and ruffled my head. "He did have to, that's the point. He's a master of using the carrot and stick method. He knows how to control events so that the people he unscrupulously exploits do not rebel, are grateful, even. That's a great art. Try some wine."

I took a sip cautiously.

"Not bad. And what's that in the can?

"Caviar. Not real, of course, because the fish from which this delicacy was obtained are long extinct, but as inventive as people are, they came up with the 'substitute goods'. The production is expensive, so the cost is close to the ancient caviar. Would you like some?"

"Maybe later. I'm not hungry."

He laughed.

"You don't eat caviar to fill the belly. It's a gourmet snack. It tastes best with some toasts."

I shifted on the bed and, closed my eyes and leaned against the inspector's bare chest. I was feeling unbelievably good.

"You know a lot about elegant cuisine, especially for a police officer. Is it because you are Hakat's brother in law?"

He poured himself some champagne.

"I accompanied him to banquets when my sister was still alive, I won't deny that," he admitted. "However, after her death, I chose to cut myself off from the guy."

"You could've been the Chief of the Central Island Guard today."

"Could be, especially if I was faithful. As you can imagine, I didn't want to do that."

"You don't know how to set yourself in life. Think about how much good you could do if you had more options. Pour some more."

I put my glass closer. Scott complied and put the bottle back in the ice bucket. Then he put his bent arm under his head

"There are simply tools too dirty to use even for the most righteous cause. The end doesn't justify the means, contrary to the proverb. I cannot deceive, exploit and destroy others, and what's worse, I cannot tolerate such behavior."

I raised my head, moved by understanding.

"You spoiled his plans, that's why you were sent to the moon!"

He smiled at the corner of his mouth and shook his glass, watching the bubbles from the bottom of the glass to the top. Then he took a sip.

"I helped in the escape of a man whose destruction he really wanted. This tarnished my brother in law's reputation, so he made sure to pay me back with interest."

I sat down, wrapped in a soft blanket. Through the panoramic window of the apartment, I saw a garden decorated with a fiber-optic fountain and Chinese lanterns. The artificial sky, visible above, was velvety, deep in color with an incredible shade of blue, turning into soft green. I looked at these miracles with a strange feeling. Only after a long time did I define it as happiness.

"May I ask you something? It's a rather indiscrete question, so feel free to refuse."

"Ask away," Scotty poured added some wine again and took one of the multi-colored cookies lying on the plate.

"Don't get the wrong idea. I'm not intending to change you in any way, even the smallest, but I just wonder, why do you complain about scars and wrinkles but at the same time do nothing about them? It's odd."

He drank champagne and took a bite of cookies.

"You aren't the only one wondering about this. The entire Lunnar team is gossiping about it as if it were the most interesting topic of conversation in the world."

"So why?"

He delayed the answer for a long time. I looked out the window without persuading him and watched the colors flicker in the artificial sky. They were not motionless, they waved, turning into each other, like the northern lights.

"It costs money," he finally said. "And most of the salary I received goes into something that I don't want to disclose yet. Not because I don't trust you," he added quickly. "I'd just prefer to wait with it."

"That's okay."

"Besides... you know, these scars are me. Each one resembles something, same with the wrinkles or folds in my body. Today the streets are full of people without history, artificially tweaked, smoothed out, changing passports, addresses and names, running away from themselves. All of it is useless. It's childish. I can understand actors, they are paid to stay young and beautiful, but not me. I'm a policeman, I don't make money with my body. I don't need to look like a display mannequin. I hope you can understand what I'm trying   to   say."

I gently put my hand on his, the one with which he held the glass. The ring finger bore a wide strip of discolored skin. It has already caught my attention earlier.

"You had a wife," I more stated than asked.

He moved the visual implants slightly.

"Yes, I did," he admitted. "We broke up."

"Did Hakat make sure of that?"

"In a sense, yes. He knew that Brenda would never agree to leave Earth and live in Lunnar. I suspect that he said something to her, either way we didn't even talk. She took my things, left a short letter, divorced in absentia without demanding anything back from me, and a month later she got married again. She married a small entrepreneur, a decent and calm person. I think she's really happy."

"And what did you do?"

"What could I do? Sometimes all you can do is come to terms with fate. I sold the house and sent the full amount to her account. Flying to the moon, I left nothing behind for me to return to."

"Have you thought about starting a new family?"

"Thinking won't help here. There's something completely different that's required."

He drank his champagne to the bottom. I did the same and put the glass on the nightstand. Now I knew I had to say something like, "That's horrible." Or "I would never leave you," but Scott Cavanaugh was the type of man who liked listening to sympathetic groans of a girl, as Chris used ti call any of my attempts to console him. Suddenly I realized that the sweet, sleek, doll-like boy who had been assigned to me as a social brother was only outwardly different from Inspector Cavanaugh – inside the beautiful paint job was an equally cool and perceptive person. That must be why Cavanaugh seemed so close to me from the very beginning, as if I had known him for a long time, almost from birth.

"You know what? Let's go eat something at the restaurant and then we can go sight-seeing," I suggested cheerfully. I hoped Scotty didn't feel the artificiality in my voice. Even if he felt it, he didn't show it.

"You know that you're right? I'm hungry. Just let me take a shower."

He jumped out of bed gracefully like a young man and went to the bathroom. I thought his movements were not appropriate for his age.

He's fifty-five years old, I knew that from the record – nowadays it's barely middle-age, a long time ago he would've been considered a grandpa, but even today it would be difficult to call him a 'boy'. And yet he moved nimbly like a cat, I also had the opportunity to see how strong he was. My man... do I have the right to think of him that way yet?

I shook my head. What are these stupid thoughts? I should just enjoy my vacation and forget about everything else. Take my time and let the relationship grow at its own pace.

I waited for Scott to leave the bathroom, then took a shower and put on clean clothes. I looked in the mirror. Maybe for the first time in my life I thought that I wasn't that ugly. The shadow under the eyes, which I have always considered a lack of beauty, merged with my dark eyelids and made my dark gray irises shinier. Freckles on my cheeks made me look younger than I was and accentuated my fair skin. My hair, once brown, and now red, lay smoothly over my head like a shiny helmet. As to my figure, in fact I could not find any fault with it, maybe only that my hips were a little too wide. Why have I not noticed that before?

The beauty of a woman is born in the eyes of a man, just like music is born in the ear of the listener. I don't remember in which book did I read these words, but I was reminded of them now. They were written by a wise man. His book must have had medical aspects to get into the library of the Academy. Who was it? No, I couldn't remember, but either way, that wasn't so important. It was something else that mattered. Never before had a man shown as much interest in me as Cavanaugh did, and that is probably why I now looked at myself with different eyes.

We walked down to the reception and asked for Tawnia Baker. The girl appeared a dozen seconds later, dressed in a clean pantsuit and professional in every detail.

"We'd like to eat something. Where is the restaurant?"

"In the second building. Should I show you the way?"

"That's not necessary... why is the hotel restaurant located not in the main building, but somewhere nearby instead?" I asked.

Tawnia smiled indulgently.

"Emperia is, after all, a high-class hotel. We can't let the kitchen smells spread into the rooms like in a cheap motel. Guests pay for the elegance and romantic atmosphere, but could that be possible if you smelled fried vegetables from the window?"

Scotty laughed.

"Sounds smart. Thank you, miss Baker."

"Call me Tawnia. You are welcome. How about I show you the amusement park later? I am available twenty-four hours a day."

"Thank you, miss Baker, I mean, Tawnia, but we'll be fine. We can handle it ourselves."

The restaurant turned out to be no less exclusive than the hotel. Taught by my experience at Miraton, I chose one of the simple dishes from the menu, avoiding expensive snacks and things I didn't understand. Everything here had different names, like the ykante leah, which I in truth wanted to eat, at least for its funny name. I've never heard of such a thing in my entire life, and it didn't even make me think of anything. Scott, who was more experienced, suggested what to order, and he himself decided on an elite dish – real meat cooked with dark wine sauce and cognac.

I was also curious about how one pays here, but everything turned out to be simple. All this was included in the general costs, as evidenced by the hotel's platinum laminated card. I didn't even want to think about how much the Chief of Arms paid for our vacation.

"You don't like real meat?" Scotty asked as he ate with a healthy appetite.

"I tried it once and I didn't like it," I explained. "I prefer substitutions."

"Give it a try," he held out a fork with a piece of roast.

I hesitated, but, encouraged by the inspector, brought the meat to my mouth. The taste was... excellent. Either Miraton had bad chefs, despite its well-established reputation, or I was unlucky and experienced a spoiled dish. What Scotty ate was tender, salty, slightly spicy and sweet with a hint of caramel at the same time. The thick sauce was like nothing I've ever eaten, and suddenly my ykante leah was no longer tasty.

"Order some for yourself," Scott advised. "Don't worry, you won't waste anything, everything here, as elsewhere, will be recycled."

"That's not the point. Cynthia Lara, the social mother of our brothers and sisters, didn't let us be picky with food. This attitude stays with you for life."

Although, despite the feeling of guilt, I ordered a fillet done in porto, as they called it, and unashamedly enjoyed it. For the desert we decided on some ice cream with fruit and chocolate sauce, then went for a walk.

"That was delicious. I love chocolate," I admitted, sighing at the mere memory. "It's a shame that it's so expensive in production."

"I like it too. Did you know that chocolate used to never be made in laboratories before?" Scotty asked.

He walked next to me with his hands in his trouser pockets, and for the first time since I knew him, he seemed completely relaxed. After a while, he even gave me a hug. Some of the tourists turned around cautiously after us, and I heard them exchanging amusing remarks in tone. I don't know if they were about such a visible age difference between us, or rather about my friend's implants.

"How did they make it then?"

"Seems like it was some fruit. It grew on trees, or maybe bushes? I don't remember, either way the plant went extinct, like many others. If you like, we can order something with chocolate for dinner. During these two weeks, let's have fun without thinking about anything."

I thought that he was right. Who knows what awaits us when we return to Lunnar? Maybe one of us will die on the very first day, or maybe something else will happen, no less terrible. Until then, we are in an artificial paradise, so we should make sure to enjoy it.

The amusement park didn't attract us, but the 'artificial beach' advertised in the station guide was interesting. This attraction was rather far from our hotel, so we took a small autocar belonging to Emperia. Unlike Lunnar, Colchis had a service center for these machines. The control computer was equipped with a touch panel with the map of Colchis instead of the usual program. To go somewhere, it was enough to touch the corresponding button and you could even take a nap, the car did everything by itself. Such a thing was possible on the station, it was used on Earth only in small centers. In cities, cars had programs or, like in public, a computer controlled from a switchboard. I've never seen one as this. It looked like an enlarged toy from a store for little girls. It had quirky carved sides, fun colors, and pink plush upholstery that genuinely amused Scott.

"It's like a box of chocolates for Valentine's Day! If my subordinates saw me in this thing, I would have to kill them or change jobs."

I had to admit that this vehicle was extremely tasteless, but it didn't really matter. All that mattered was that it could take us to our chosen location. On the way I looked through the guide again. It was advised to take caution when trying out the 'gift of nature' and to stock up on tanning oil if one wants to take advantage of the sun's rays. I was wrong to think that this part of the station was illuminated by a suitable and safe solar lamp. As stated in the folder, the source of the sunrays was a clearwing in the dome, so it really would've been a bad idea to overdo it. In addition, supposedly the beach was modeled on the former Black Sea beaches.

When I arrived, I realized that they were not simply bragging. Although in truth I've never been to the Black Sea. All natural coastal beaches were closed due to biological hazards and could only be visited on organized excursions, avoiding bare skin contact with water or sand. I was on such a trip once, organized by an oceanology station, and the only thing I really liked was the smell of the sea, similar to the atmosphere in cooling towers. As a child, I was sent to such an object several times, so I could compare the smell of the salty waves. Apart from that, there was nothing interesting on the natural Adriatic beach, only dirty sand and rotting algae, covered with foam from microorganisms. The seagulls, looking for tiny crustaceans in the algae, scared me at the time – they were large, loud and trying to attack people.

"That's because," the guide explained, "they have little food. The only larger creatures left in the sea feed along the coast, on these rotting algae, but there are relatively few of them. Our institute regularly feeds these birds and at the same time is trying to find a way to increase the number of crustaceans."

The Black Sea was in a restricted area. Radiation levels at the edges continued to exceed acceptable levels, and there was no sign that the place would improve within the next century. I won't even mention the contamination of the adjacent lands. How was it possible that the seagulls survived and even continued to reproduce? I had no idea. However, as a librarian, I have looked through enough albums of old photographs to know what such places looked like before the environmental disaster.

The view before us upon arrival at the site was amazing. In some places, the beach covered with golden sand was decorated with slender palms, among which people rested in casual suits. There were some children playing with ab all or trying to build something out of sand – the effort was futile as it wasn't wet enough to hold, but they seemed to be having a good time. The holographic sea swayed steadily against the shore, gulls circling high under the azure sky. The square pool of real salt water was so well camouflaged that if it hadn't been for the careful marking of the area, no one would have known where it ends and where it begins. I expected perfection, after all, the reputation of 'Colchis' was undeniable, but even then I was full of amazement. I was surprised by the salty humid wind that hit us in the face after crossing the sector border. It must have been created the same way as in the Earth's cooling towers. The illusion was perfect.

"Amazing," Scotty said, impressed. "Well then, what should we do? Are we relaxing on the sand, swimming or just taking a walk?"

I looked around.

"There are hanging benches over there," I pointed to a shaded spot between the palm trees. "Let's take a seat?"

"Why not?"

We took off our clothes and put them in the autocar, remaining in just our underwear, and headed towards the bushes of palm trees. I foolishly expected the trees to be real, but they turned out to be artificial, although very well made. Looking at them, I also noticed a small mistake – they were date palms, even though coconut palm trees would've been more appropriate on such a beach. That didn't really matter, however. The visitors of Colchis were wealthy upper class people, who weren't as knowledgeable about plants as I was, unless botany was one of their hobbies.

We sat down next to each other on one of the benches, swaying slightly back and forth. It was very warm, but the light breeze cooled our bodies pleasantly. The mechanical seagulls squealed overhead just like real bird, the surrounding scent of the sea combined with the scent of fresh palm leaves. Such a place was once created by nature back on Earth, and now only the artificial memory of it is all that remains. At that moment, I wasn't really thinking about what humanity had lost as a result of stupidity and aggression, I just relished an unknown and very pleasant experience. I felt pleasantly lazy to the point where I almost dozed off when Scott suddenly shook my shoulder.

"Look."

A little girl in blue panties ran into the shade of the palm trees. She may have been two or three years old at the most. Scott jumped off the bench, crouched down and held out his arms, grabbing the laughing child.

"Where did you come from, little one?"

She laughed back, revealing tiny teeth sparkling like pearls.

"Up, up!" she demanded.

"What's this about?" I was surprised.

"She wants someone to lift her up," he explained. "Are there any adults around here?"

I looked around, but I didn't see anyone who might have been looking over the girl. No one looked around, no one called. Scott straightened up, holding the child in his arms carefully, as if she was made of glass.

"We have to find the parents. They can't neglect their child like that."

He poked her tiny nose gently with his index finger. The girl laughed and, with obvious curiosity, began to feel around the frames of the visors. She has never seen anything like it before, but she didn't react with fear. Children usually have no prejudices, unless taught about them by adults.

"What's your name, princess?" I asked.

"Eshi," she chirped.

"What name would that be?"

"Gracie or Lacey," Scotty replied. "Go to the beach and ask around, I'll stay here with the little one."

I obediently ran to where the vacationers were resting, basking in the sun.

"Excuse me, are the parents of a girl named Gracie or Lacey here?" I called, looking around. Several sunbathers looked in my direction, but without interest. One of the women raised her elbow and pulled dark glasses over her forehead.

"A light-haired one, maybe two years old?" she made sure. "That's Robelses' girl. They live in the 'Mermaid' hotel, same as me. Did something happen?"

"No, I just need to find them."

"They're in the pool."

The woman pointed to the place where the hologram merged into the reservoir of the pool. Three children and a couple bathed in it, in which, as I guessed, the girl's parents. I went to the outskirts.

"Mr. and Mrs. Robles?" I shouted. "Please come out of the pool."

"Or what?" shouted in response a young, strongly tanned man.

His companion laughed. They both looked entertained, as if they had just seen something very funny.

"We need to talk about your daughter," I said.

"No we don't! Gracie is playing in the sand. What could happen to her? It's safe around here!"

"Please get out of the water."

"We're not doing that. We are on vacation and we'll have fun until we can't anymore!"

They embraced in the water and began to kiss, while splashing the water like frisky little children. Something about their behavior seemed off. I went back to Scott.

"Gracie's parents are Mr. and Mrs. Robles. Swimming in the pool. They didn't want to leave, they reacted to my words... strangely. They were laughing and fooling around. They weren't interested in what was happening to the child."

Scotty frowned. He handed me the girl, walked over to the car and began to put on his pants.

"I don't like this," he told me. "Look after the kid, I'm going to go talk to them."

"They won't listen to you."

"We'll see about that."

I don't know how he did it, but after about a dozen minutes, when I ran out of ideas on how to entertain the girl, he returned, dragging the Robleses with him. They didn't resist too much and continued to laugh every now and then, so much that I involuntarily envied their good mood.

"They're drunk," Scott growled as he brutally shoved the young couple into the car. "Get in."

"What do you want to do?"

"What do you mean what? We're going to the hotel."

"Not the police? There should be some kind of police station here."

"We're the police. No. We're going back to Emperia."

"But they're living in the 'Mermaid'."

"So what?"

I didn't understand what was going on. Sitting in the car with the little kid wriggling in my lap, I tried to figure out what Scotty was trying to do, but my imagination was too weak for that. He was engaged in taming the cheerful passengers and paid no mind to my questions, so after several attempts I fell silent. In the driveway in front of the hotel, Scott pulled the Robleses out of the car and dragged them into the lobby in front of the astonished employees. As we climbed into the elevator, Tawnia Baker appeared, called the reception.

"Mister Cavanaugh...?"

"They're our guests," Scott snapped. "We don't need help for now, thanks, we'll ask if necessary."

Inside our suite, first he locked the door panel so we wouldn't be disturbed, then pushed Robles onto the couch and began to search through his travel bag."

"What are you looking for?" I asked helplessly.

Robles on the couch began to play with his paws, laughing to tears.

"Police first aid kit. It's always with me. There."

He took a box of disposable tests from his leather briefcase and took two.

"Get a drop of blood from each of them. It's easy, just prick the index finger, get the blood on the gray circle."

I did as he said. Although I expected resistance from our 'patients', it seemed like they didn't even feel any of the prickling inflicted to their untrained fingers. I've never seen alcohol affect someone this way before, even though I've seen drunkards where I grew up.".

I was barely able to do my task before Scotty poured some water into two cops, added five drops from a brown bottle to each and forced our 'guests' to drink it.

"What is that?" I asked.

"Preparation G65," he replied. "Instantly sobers you up. Neutralizes all chemicals in the blood. Only the police and the military have it."

"Mother of God, that's poison!"

"Just like any medicine. It won't hurt them if they drink the thing once. They'll fall asleep and wake up like newborns."

Indeed, less than a minute after drinking the used mixture, the Robleses almost simultaneously yawned and lay down, immediately falling asleep. I was sitting in a chair by the window, rocking the little Gracie in my arms.

"Now what?"

Scotty took the tests off the table and slipped them into the reader.

"At least one and a half per mil alcohol in each of them," he muttered after a moment. "And a clearly marked indicator of cocaine. Look, that yellowish spot. Someone at Mremaid must be serving Carbonet at the request of extremely fastidious customers."

"What is that?"

"Carbonet – it's a wine with the addition of synthetic cocaine, colored in a black caramel color. It's prohibited in institutions of this type, like any other hard drug, but the mere fact of the ban has never stopped thoroughbred clever people."

He took Gracie from my arms and started tossing her up. The girl was laughing again. I had to admit that I was surprised at how well my supervisor could handle children. Under the cover of bitterness and cynicism, there was a whole layer of warmth that few people knew about.

"What's next? We have to report this," I said. "Drunk parents, unattended child... it's a punishable crime."

"Am, am!" Gracie called.

My eyes widened, but Scott didn't look surprised. He took the yeast cake out of the machine, unrolled it and handed it to the girl, who eagerly began eating, smacking loudly. Then he poured some juice into a glass and held it for her to keep her from spilling it.

"How can you understand her?"

"Oh, I'm from a big family. It wasn't just once that I had to look over my young cousins, when the adults went to have fun. Have you never looked after younger siblings?"

I only shrugged in response.

"Are you going to report this?"

He looked at me, sat down in another chair and stared out the window.

"I don't know," he finally said.

"Are you serious? You're a cop, you have to obey the law."

"That's true. But I think the girl could lose her parents. If we file a report, they will take their daughter away from them and give them up to be raised in a social family. Meanwhile, I'm sure these guys will never make that mistake again."

"How can you be sure?"

"I know how life is. These two tried Carbonet for the first time. If they knew its power and action, they would have been more careful. We wouldn't find them like this in a public place."

I straightened up.

"Scotty! You want to let them get away with this!"

"Everyone does something stupid in their life! I'll talk to them when they wake up, and then I'll make the decision, but I'm confident we won't need to report anything."

I hunched over again and collapsed into the chair.

"You told me that a police officer cannot look past the law."

"I'm not doing that," he began swaying the sleeping child. "I just think that sometimes it's better to let go of a small mistake than to let it ruin someone's life. Look at this child. She is taken care of, healthy, cheerful and trusting. It's obvious that one is neglecting or hurting her. A one-time excursion should not break her apart from good, caring parents."

I looked at Gracie hugging Kavanaugh. She looked sweet and innocent, but I didn't want to touch her again. I've never felt attracted to motherhood like many of my friends did, who applied for a license from the Institute of Genetic Selection, and young children didn't make me feel any strong feelings. I never even did a preliminary test.

"I don't know much about kids," I said carefully. "Have you noticed that there is no class symbol on her forehead, only the number 2 tattooed on the temple?"

"Yes. It seems that the new appraisal system has begun earlier than anticipated. This number means, if I am not mistaken, that in the future she will have the right to become pregnant twice.

"It doesn't say anything about her IQ."

"They probably test that on subsequent tests and write it down in the documents. I'll see when we get home. Lower your voice now, the little one is already asleep."

He got up and carried the girl to the bed. He laid her on the pillow, and she curled up like Sid during one of his naps. He lightly stroked the blonde girl's head. Gracie purred softly, pressing herself against the silk sheets.

"She was so energetic a minute ago... do children always fall asleep so quickly?" I asked. Scotty smiled and looked at me.

"Only not when you want them to. There were no kids in your family?"

"Chris was the youngest for a long time. Lara's family took him in when he was almost five years old, and he acted like a seven year old. Then came Mia, but she was also older than Gracie and certainly not this cute. In fact, she was the devil incarnate."

"Every child is different."

We heard moans and shaking coming from the direction of the couch. The Robles couple began to wake up. Their eyes were both sober and full of fear. They clearly didn't know where they were and what they were doing here. Scott walked over.

"Mr. and Mrs. Robles, correct?" he asked sternly.

"Y... yes," the man muttered, looking wide-eyed. He was clearly terrified. "I am Evan, and this is my wife Lucia. What happened?"

"You don't remember what the hell you've done?"

"What we've done?!"

"Yes, you, who else," I muttered venomously.

I continued to gaze reluctantly at the half-naked couple, but decided not to interfere with the inspector's questioning. The sight of the implants didn't work on just criminals, but also scared everyone else, and Scott knew how to utilize that.

First, he handed the both of the Robles some bottled water, then sat down opposite them, pulling the legs of his pants with a casual movement.

"You overdosed on a drug called Carbonet," he began counting, bending his fingers one by one. "In that state, you went into the pool, and left your little daughter on the beach without anyone to look over her."

"Gracie!" Lucia shouted in horror. "Where is my daughter?! What happened to her?"

"Don't shout, please. Your child is asleep. Fortunately, she ran into us before any unfortunate accidents could happen."

Evan Robles ran his shaking hand through his dark hair. He was a handsome man, and his wife was a beautiful, well-groomed woman. They made a good impression, but I involuntarily thought that they were both too young to be having children. And most definitely too irresponsible.

"What's going to happen now? Are you going to report this to the police?"

"I'm a cop myself," Scott said rudely. Lucia Robles began to cry, so he added, "I didn't say I would report you. But I have to know everything. Have you ever taken Carbonet before?"

"We don't drink or use drugs at all, not even the one-hundred percent legal ones," Evan assured him fervently. "We didn't know it would be so strong. We thought it was just some light dessert wine, it was sweet and tasty."

"Why did you buy it if you say that you don't drink alcohol?"

The couple looked at each other. Lucia wiped away her tears with a handkerchief that Scott handed her.

"We were offered it. We ran into a friend who suggested a drink for the occasion. He didn't say the drink would be so strong."

"Carbonet contains an admixture of cocaine. If you've never abused any substances before, it must have had a very strong effect on you. Did you know that going to the beach in such a state and endangering your child carries a risk of losing the rights to parenthood?"

"No, please! Gracie means everything to us!"

"All right, all right," Scott silenced the unhappy father with a firm wave of his hand. "I'm willing to help, but I must be sure that I'm doing the right thing. Please think very carefully, and answer me one thing."

"Anything you want."

"If we were to assume that the whole thing was not your fault, there must be someone behind it. Someone really wanted you to lose control, and in a public place at that? Could this friend have a reason to harm you?"

Lucia's eyes widened.

"Richie? What could he have against us?"

"Maybe he was acting on someone's command?"

Her husband was deep in thought, unconsciously scratching the back of his head.

"Nothing comes to mind. Although..."

"Yeah?"

"My wife is the New Zealand chess champion. After coming back to Earth, she will take part in a very important international game. Her rival will be Frank Pierce from Latin America."

"So what?"

"I know Richie that Richie knows him, even though he denies it."

"How could you know that?" Lucia indignantly asked. "How can you blame the person we've known for so many years?"

"Darling, he deliberately drugged us, and then left us alone to be a laughing stock," her husband realized. "How did we find ourselves on the beach? We weren't going there at all. Why was he lying that he was seeing Pierce for the first time when I showed him the photo?"

"Maybe he wasn't lying?"

"You think so? After coming back to the hotel, I can show you a photograph of Pierce from a Chess Magazine from a year ago. Richie is standing next to him."

"A beautiful conspiracy theory," I couldn't take it anymore. "And all of it just to avoid responsibility. Boss, this doesn't add up. Chess and a trick straight out of a spy movie? Maybe if it was boxing or football..."

Scotty, with his usual habit, rubbed his fingers over his mouth. I could tell that he was thinking deeply.

"If Lucia Robles lost parenting rights, she would definitely not be in shape for the tournament," he said finally. "Bets for chess tournaments are made with bookmakers, just like any other championship. Eliminating or weakening one of the players is an easy way to win. Sometimes it's the work of a dishonest opponent, sometimes it is the work of people who profit from the bets."

"So you believe this story?"

"I think it's believable, let's put it that way."

He got up and walked the communicator on the wall.

"Connect me with Tawnia Baker."

The communicator creaked softly, and after a while the hostess's face appeared on the small screen.

"I'm listening, Mr. Cavanaugh."

"Send two sets of clothes to room 27. Male size... 30, and female size 26 and a half."

"What kind of clothes?"

"Doesn't matter. I'll rely on your taste."

"They'll be upstairs in five minutes."

"What are you planning to do?" I asked.

Scotty looked at the couple, then at me, and pursed his lips in an incomprehensible grimace.

"You will stay with the kid," he replied. "I'll go with Mr. and Mrs. Robles to the Mermaid and confirm their version of events. They have to dress up, of course, since walking half-naked around the premises is not the best idea."

*****

Scott was gone for a very long time. I watched the girl run around the apartment, and at the same time thought deeply. The boss's behavior revealed what he was trying to hide from the rest of the world. In truth, he could do it flawlessly, but I had already learned to think like a policewoman and put the pieces of this puzzle together.

Scott was married. His wife left him when he was transferred to the Moon as a result of a conflict with Citizen Hakat. She got married a second time very quickly. Scott, despite a good income, spent very little on himself, and his attitude towards children complemented the rest. Brenda Cavanaugh was pregnant when she left her husband, and Scott either knew it or found out later. He remained silent about it, not wanting Hakat to have a blackmail tool against him, and pretended not to know or care about it. However, he was collecting money for the child, transferring it to a separate account, most likely with a password or fabricated data. That's the only explanation that made sense. Every child reminded him of what he had lost, even the little girl from the beach.

How painful was it, that he not only couldn't take part in raising his own child, but couldn't even reveal that he knows of the child's existence? I couldn't ask, I didn't even want to say that I figured it out. It would be an awkward situation and I didn't want to cause him any trouble. I've assigned myself a different role from the very beginning, and it would be best if I stuck to it.

Caring for Gracie has tired me more than I expected. The girl constantly babbled, laughed and took turns complaining that she wanted to see her mom, that she wanted a drink, wanted to pee, wanted wa wa (I had no idea what it was, only later when Scotty explained to me that she wanted to take a walk)... I was very relieved when my boss came back.

"Come on," he said cheerfully. "We'll take the little one to the Mermaid and have dinner somewhere on the way back."

"So they weren't lying?"

"Nope. One of the waitresses remembered a man who came up to their table and ordered a Carbonet. I verified his personal information. He checked in as Jack Palmero, but his real name is Richard Bialik. He checked out and flew home, so I couldn't question him. I advised the Robleses to be twice as careful when they return to Earth, the rest is their problem."

"Are you sure that we can give them the child back?" I asked, handing him the girl.

He took her in his arms and she hugged him confidently.

"I think so. You know what? Let's have dinner and go to the theater. A good comedy is being played, an old-style farce, let's relax a little."

"Until we run into another crime."

"We won't, I promise. We'll stop meddling in other people's affairs, let the locals worry about it. After all, they get paid for something too."

We didn't return to our hotel until midnight. We were both exhausted and hungry, but our mood improved significantly. I think we were comforted not so much by the humorous art but more by the thought that there are still thirteen wonderful days ahead of us, which we will use to the best of our ability.

An exquisite dinner was waiting for us back in our apartment – snacks, tender slices in a spicy sauce with capers and fresh fruits. Plus a bottle of champagne in an ice bucket. True luxury. The first thing that surprised me was that all the delicacies that were served to us in our room were clearly OUTSIDE the food distribution. Apparently, there were places where strict rationing rules were not fully applied.

"They sure are spoiling us," Scott examined the bottle carefully. "My favorite kind. Let's drink."

"Just a little bit for me. One glass or so. The last time we drank these bubbles, I felt horrible afterwards. But I'll be happy to eat something," I put the slices on a plate.

"You don't know what you're missing," he poured himself some of the sparkling liquid and tasted it for a moment, leaning comfortably against the headrest of the chair. "Delicious. The only time I tasted this kind of champagne was when organizing security at a government meeting. Are you sure you don't want more?"

I shook my head. I was never too attracted towards carbonated drinks. Although I liked regular synthetic wine, after champagne I felt like I had eaten something indigestible. I wasn't in the mood for that.

The food was so delicious that we ate everything, to the last crumb. After that we took another quick shower and went to bed, exchanging only a few tired kisses. Then we fell asleep.

I woke up feeling like someone had thrown a blanket over my head. Nothing like that happened, but the feeling of suffocation grew. I got out of bed and struggled to my feet. I was suffocating. Something was definitely wrong. I jerked Scott once and twice, but he didn't react. He was unconscious, and I felt afraid at the thought that he might even be dead, but then I brought my hand to his mouth, feeling light breathing. What's happening here?

There was definitely no breathable air in the apartment. I tried to open a window and fought with it for a while, until it dawned on me that there were no openable windows in the premises of the 'orbital cities'. The safety rules that apply to them are similar to those of Lunnar. With difficulty I reached the door, but it didn't budge. They were locked completely. Neither the traditional lock nor the remote opening panel worked. The alarm bell button didn't cause any reaction either.

Somehow I managed to not panic. The thought of safety rules gave me a sequence of associations, and I remembered that every apartment in the hotel should be equipped with an easily accessible emergency kit in case of a collision of the 'city' with some celestial body. The drawer with the set was always in the same place, next to the bathroom.

With all of my remaining strength, I was able to pull out object with a closed circulation of air. With trembling hands, I pulled the mask over my head and turned the valve. I relished in the delicious taste of pure oxygen for a while, then grabbed another set and placed the mask on Scott's face. He was still unconscious and didn't have any reaction. I had no doubt that he was intoxicated, probably thanks to the champagne, which I barely touched. Thankfully. I set the consumption rate of both devices to the required minimum and began to look for a way out of the situation.

Someone had blocked the door, that much was obvious. That same person must have tinkered with the air purification system in our apartment. Who or why was not yet important. First I had to find a way to get out of this deadly trap. The alarm didn't work, but communication must have. The internal monitoring system is connected to the communication lines, and when one of them stops transmitting the test signal, it's then treated as a life-threatening alarm. I tried to connect to the front desk and then to local security. Both to no avail. The system was working, but only in one direction. The mysterious attacker planned our death down to the last detail.

I had to outwit them somehow. I wasn't too happy about the thought of suffocation, even in such a luxurious apartment, inaccessible to people of my social class. The adrenaline rush unleashed a creativity in me that I never knew existed. I grabbed a fruit knife from the table. I removed all the screws I could find, then opened the communication panel to reveal the interior. It was not possible to send a message because the output channel was deactivated. But I could do one thing – damage the module so that people in the monitoring center receive a signal about the loss of communication.

That's easy to say, though. What was revealed to my eyes didn't resemble anything to me. Chris would've been able to find the correct circuits easily, but I lacked the specialization. I had no idea what to do next. The easiest way would be to stick a knife between the glittering LED lights of the cell, but electric shock didn't seem like the best way to call for help.

I looked around for some isolated tool that could safely break the mesh of cables and my attention was drawn to the silver bucket that was used to hold the bottle of champagne. The ice melted and the vessel was half filled with clean water. I grabbed it and splashed the water on the exposed electronics. There was a crackling sound, a gray cloud rose from the module and then all the LEDs went out.

Now all I had to do was wait. If I was right, I just alerted the hotel security. Although, what if the attacker is one of these people? I had to somehow minimize the risk. I opened a briefcase tucked under the bed, and pulled out Scott's service weapon – a heavy energy-rounds pistol. I didn't have permission to use it yet, but that was the least of my worries. I reloaded the magazine, pulled the safety, and hid behind the door so that those who entered would not see me.

I checked the pressure gauge on the oxygen cylinder and quickly realized that I would be fine for about a quarter of an hour. I was hoping the guards would hurry – and that, in the end, the attacker would not be one of the people responsible for the safety of visitors. He won't have it written on his forehead after all, I will recognize him immediately.

My calculations turned out to be correct. For me it felt like I was waiting for ages, hidden behind the inner door, but in fact, it took maybe two minutes before I heard someone yank the door from the outside. It took a little longer to unlock them. The security service struggled to activate the mechanism, and I was sweating inside the mask, glancing at the pressure gauge from time to time.

Finally, the door opened and two men burst into the room, one in a security uniform and the other in a service suit. They stopped abruptly in the doorway.

"What's happening here? It's so hard to breathe!" the technician called.

I came out of my hiding place and pointed the pistol at them. They froze in amazement.

"Take Inspector Cavanaugh outside the room! Now! I shouted. I went with my back towards the exit, not taking my eyes off them.

"As you wish, ma'am. We will. What's all this for?" the guard raised his hands slightly in a peaceful gesture and impatiently dragged the apparently frightened technician with him.

I fell into the corridor, leaned my back against the wall and took the mask off my face with relief. I was still holding the pistol in my right hand, and whoever looked out into the corridor immediately walked back to their apartment. I must have looked very interesting – disheveled like a witch, in a thin transparent nightgown, no underwear underneath, but with an oxygen apparatus in one hand

and a firearm in the other. I could already imagine everyone who saw me phoning the hotel service in panic.

I didn't have to wait long for additional forces. As soon as the two of them dragged Scott into the hallway, put him on the carpet and removed the mask from his face, five more armed bodyguards appeared. Their eyes literally gouged out as they saw me.

"Call the police and medical aid immediately," I said sharply before they had a chance to speak. "You have some here, correct?"

"Of course," gasped one of the bodyguards, perhaps the one most aware. "We have everything here. Full service."

"And assassins too, apparently, in the premium version," I muttered under my breath and added aloud. "And let no one else enter the apartment! It's a crime scene, the evidence will need to be collected."

Without putting down my pistol, I knelt down next to Scott. He was breathing, but it was shallow and uneven. I couldn't even check his pupils because he didn't have them, but either way it was obvious that he was poisoned. I just hoped it wasn't deadly.

The police officers came along with the paramedics and immediately pointed their stunners at me. Is that the strongest thing they had here?

"Detective Juliette Anckes from Lunnar headquarters, service number LT 09786," I quickly introduced myself before they could say the standard phrases. "My boss and I were attacked. Someone reprogrammed the air control system in our apartment, turned off outgoing communications and left drug-poisoned wine on the table. I didn't drink it, so I woke up when it became hard to breathe. I couldn't leave because the door was locked."

The rescuers put Scott on a stretcher. I followed them, determined not to let him out of my sight for a second. I didn't trust anyone else. I vowed to myself that I would look closely at the doctors' hands until Cavanaugh recovered.

"Please, at least wrap yourself with this..." a dark-haired girl, daughter of a couple in the next apartment, no more than fifteen years old, blocked my way and handed me a robe. She was the only one who had the courage to approach me. How funny.

I accepted the cover with gratitude, because walking through the entire hotel driveway half-naked wasn't something on my bucket list. Putting on the flannel fabric wasn't easy, since I didn't want to let go of the unlocked pistol, but I eventually succeeded. The paramedics looked at me a little uneasily, but didn't protest when I walked into the ambulance without asking. Maybe they didn't dare, not knowing what I might do next.

The Colchis medical center was located on the outskirts of the recreation center, between it and the complex of administrative and technical buildings. It wasn't big, but the equipment was no worse than one of the EPIPHANICS clinics. Each of the machines – as far as I could tell – was of first class and was shiny like brand new. They must have regularly replaced them with newer models.

The head doctor turned out to be a woman, Dr. Rosalyn Amaretto, which was written on a plate attached to her apron. She was followed by a medical team, mostly women. Only one of them was a man, a very young man, almost a boy.

"Please hide that thing," Amaretto said sharply in greeting, nodding at my pistol. "We're not at a shooting range."

"Do your job," I said equally firmly, "and I will do my job. That is to protect my boss. They tried to kill us last night. Someone might try again."

She shrugged and began working. I sat down in the corner of the office, not taking my eyes off the doctors, and defiantly leaned the pistol against my knees. I kept telling myself that although I'm not very experienced in medical procedures, I will notice when someone tries to harm Scott. I must have been deceiving myself, but what else could I do?

The tests took a long time. Visualization, blood tests, various graphs. As the doctors moved forward, I was beginning to feel all the stress, accelerating my adrenaline, and I began to shiver. Resigned, I pulled the safety on the gun, so as not to harm anyone by an accidental shot. Only then did I realize what I had been holding back for so long, and tears gushed from my eyes.

A young medic came up to me.

"It's okay, ma'am," he took the pistol from my numb fingers and placed it on the medicine cabinet. "You need to rest."

"I'll rest later. What about the inspector?"

Dr. Amaretto turned to me.

"I just finished the tests," she said. "There is alcohol and traces of gamma hydrobutyric acid in the patient's blood. I don't know if they tried to kill you guys, but you were definitely drugged. The content of metabolites in blood cells indicates anoxia in the past. Did someone strangle him?"

"I guess you could call it that. What condition is he in?"

"Not bad. He will recover. We are taking him to the ward, he'll receive pure oxygen and an IV."

At that moment, everything went dark in front of my eyes, and I passed out.

When I opened my eyes again, I was lying in a hospital bed. Someone bathed me and dressed me in striped pajamas, and there was an IV in my forearm. A nurse sat by the bed.

"How are you feeling?" she asked.

"I think I'm alright. Scott?"

"Inspector Cavanaugh is in the next room. He is currently awake and arranging the local police in the corners," she laughed as if it was something funny. She didn't seem to realize the gravity of the situation.

I slid off the bed.

"Please unplug this thing," I pointed to the canister, "I need to see Scott."

"I shouldn't... but if that's what you want."

Having freed myself from the IV, I went into the next room.

Scott was chained to the monitors, and there were two uniformed persons by his bed.

"Hey, Leeta," he said when he saw me, "are you okay?"

"I'm okay, since I don't like champagne. And you?"

"I don't remember anything, but otherwise I'm fine. Listen to what they have to say."

I looked at the police women. The shorter one, with sergeant insignia, bowed slightly to me. She was middle-aged and looked quite attractive despite her bushy, wide eyebrows, which could use some regulation.

"We examined the bottle of wine and the glasses in our laboratory," she said. "Someone wanted to put you to sleep and suffocate you. A cylinder with compressed carbon dioxide was connected to the air purification system in the apartment, simultaneously shutting off the oxygen enrichment system and turning off the absorber of harmful gases. By the morning it would be over for you, and assuming the same person did everything they needed in the early morning, no one would know why you died."

"What about biological traces?" I asked without much hope.

"We've found one trace of DNA. It was extracted from a bead of sweat on one of the internal screws on the communications panel. But according to the police computer, this person is in jail. We checked, he really is and didn't get out of prison."

"Name?" I had a bad feeling about this.

"Johnson. Kenneth Johnson. Lunnar's former deputy chief prosecutor. But either way, you know how it is these days, detective, even biological traces cannot be fully trusted."

I looked at Scott. Barely noticeably, he shook his head in denial. It meant 'don't tell them'. I was of the same opinion.

"Send us all the data," I sighed. "We'll try to figure it out ourselves."

"And as soon as you can," the inspector added sharply. "As soon as the local quacks let me out of here. We're going back to the Moon as soon as we can. A dog can chew on all these holidays and all the paradise islands of this world."

He shifted on the bed, rubbed his temple with his hand and winced.

"And you guys put the DNA found in your database, and if you ever find anyone with that sequence in Colchis, immediately arrest him and let us know."

"Of course, Inspector. In the meantime, we're currently interviewing guests and hotel staff. Although, there is one person we are unable to find."

"Let me guess," I muttered, "Tawnia Baker, the hostess assigned to us."

"How did you know?" the sergeant raised her bushy eyebrows.

"I'm smart."

Scotty cleared his throat with obvious disapproval.

"Well, get back to work, friend. I hope you won't screw this up."

Apparently, he was already in a pretty good shape, since he returned to his usual rough self. I felt a huge stone finally roll out of my heart.

*****

Once it was our time to leave, the Robles couple appeared at the docks. This time, they wore sleek tennis suits with flat caps bearing the hotel's logo, as if they had come straight from the court. Lucia had a little girl in her arms, and her husband held a large padd in his hand, the kind for which electronic tabloids are downloaded. I was very surprised to see them, since I've managed to forget about our unpleasant business. Evan walked over and handed Scott the padd. The latest issue of the Chess Magazine was shown on the screen.

"We are eternally grateful to both of you," he said.

Scott took the device and began flipping through the pages until he found the article he was looking for.

"Listen to this, Leeta," he told me. *A famous chess player named Frankie Pierce was arrested on suspicion of attempts to forge a game. At the hearing, he pleaded guilty to gambling debts and involvement in two extortions. The main witness for the prosecution, Richard Bialik, was detained the day before thanks to the report of Evan Robles, husband of world champion Lucia Robles.* So it was what I thought it would be.

"That's why we're still here," said Mrs Robles. "The tournament is canceled, we have some time left to rest."

Evan smiled as he hugged his wife.

"If it was not for your actions, the complaint would not have been accepted, because as Lucia's husband I am a party to the case. I owe you my thanks. When Richie was arrested, he had footage from the monitoring. He could've ruined us."

"We'll never be able to pay back this debt," Miss Robles whispered.

Scotty returned the padd to her husband.

"I am a police officer, so it's my duty to serve society. If circumstances indicated clear neglect, you would be childless by now, but in this situation... Well, good luck, and I advise you to stay away from all stimulants. They won't do you any good."

"We swear we will. And if you ever visit New Zealand, we invite you together with your beautiful companion. Here is the address."

Lucia handed over a business card with a wedding photo of both spouses and a printed address. I took it hesitantly.

"This lady is not my 'beautiful companion', but my investigator," Scotty said hastily, even too hastily in my opinion. "Well, we'll visit you when we can. Although I don't know when this opportunity will arise."

Passengers on Flight 153 are asked to check in, the loudspeaker creaked. We instinctively looked up, then at each other. Scott reached out his hand to miss Robles, then her husband. I followed his example.

"It's time for us to go. I wish you good luck and many victories."

"And we wish you a good flight. Maybe next year we'll go to Lunnar, then we'll visit you."

"I would advise against it. It's an unpleasant place. Although if you still decide to do so, you're very welcome."

I slung my bag over my shoulder and followed Scott to the check-in area.

V

I've been on a cruise ship before, but this time I was relaxed and calm enough to look through the window. Scotty let me sit by the window, so I threw back the round lid and stared at the black space filled with stars. They were very distant, perhaps clearer than when viewed from the face of the Earth, but still small and distant. They didn't come closer, which I expected subconsciously, they didn't move at all. If not for the moon's disk, very slowly approaching the shuttle, I would probably have the impression that we are standing still. The shuttle's damping systems are so well implemented that the passengers don't even feel any vibrations of the ship or overloads. I looked into the darkness of outer space, wondering what it would be like to fly not to a satellite of the Earth, but far, far away, to the distant stars.

People will go there one day. I'm sure of that. Only that I will no longer be in the world by that time. A shame. I would like to witness such an expedition, and even more so to take part in it. Explore distant worlds. There are already plans for such an expedition; apparently, the first fully functional interstellar ship is already being built. And to think that not so long ago the construction of a city on the Moon seemed like pure fantasy, now we have scientific stations in orbits of other planets in the system, and we can look out much further.

The shuttle passengers were quiet and polite, and soft music played from the speakers, so it was no surprise that I finally fell asleep with my head on the window.

Cavanaugh only woke me up when the shuttle reached the Lunnar landing site. I hurriedly ran through my messy hair, grabbed the bag from under the chair, and followed Scott up the gangway.

Sue, dressed in navy blue trousers with scarlet lapels and a floral sweatshirt, was waiting for us in the guest area. From what I could tell, she either gained two or three kilograms in my absence, or her outfit was very badly fit. Next to her was Monty in jeans and a fashionable burgundy shirt with black wristbands. His hair was neatly slicked behind his ears, and around his neck, instead of a bow tie, was a narrow black velvet ribbon tied with a bow. He looked like the model for a youth magazine's cover.

Seeing us, Sue began to jump up and wave her hand with enthusiasm, and as we passed the customs area, she threw herself in my arms, almost knocking me off my feet.

"You're finally hear, honey!" she screamed. "We all missed you so much!" Sid couldn't find his place, and I from worrying ate everything we left in the closet for emergencies!"

She kissed me happily and only then turned to Scott.

"I'm glad to see you as well, Inspector."

Cavanaugh shook her plump hand as I greeted Monty.

"What's been happening on our ranch?" he asked. "Is it bad?"

Sue moved her head from side to side, as if she couldn't come up with a clear answer.

"So, so," she finally said. "You'll see for yourself."

"I hope I don't lose it immediately when I do. I couldn't fall asleep when I thought of someone else ordering my rats, and if it turns out that they fucked everything up…"

"It's not that bad," she assured him. "Captain Sirtis tempered the ones from the economics department a little, without her they would just do whatever they wanted, like a herd of wild geese. Even then it was   rough."

Monty took my bag and slung it over his shoulder. Then he hugged me protectively. I got the impression that he was trying to get between Scott and me, as if he was trying to separate us. On reflection, however, I decided that this must be an over-interpretation. Jealousy and possessiveness has to be alien to artificial intelligence. Although it would be hard to disprove that the android really cared for me, albeit in a way that is difficult for humans to understand.

Chatting merrily, Sue led us to a police off-road vehicle with a widely-grinning officer Idalgo sitting at the controls. We got in, Scott in the seat next to the driver, and the three of us in the back.

My friend didn't stop talking for even a moment:

"The guys from economics rode us like hell until Captain Sirtis rubbed their horns. The moment they called her in, she immediately said that she wouldn't be ordered by the scribbles from Earth, that yes, she could help, but she doesn't have to. And then she kicked the business director out of your office and took over it."

"In my office?!" Scott nearly jumped at that information.

"Yes, she said that only then will it stop people from coming in like into their own house."

He laughed involuntarily. The feud between two military services, the police and the army, were much less serious than on Earth. Although the garrison stationed at Lunnar celebrated its independence, it was quite willing to cooperate with the headquarters. For his part, Inspector Cavanaugh made sure that the police officers under his command did not turn to the stormtroopers and avoided arguments with them. The garrison commander, the aforementioned Captain Sirtis, appreciated this, since on Earth, fights between the military and the police were usually initiated by the latter. There was more discipline among the soldiers. They often said that the police are civilians for half a day, so various things could get into their heads, while a soldier is on duty all the time.

"Good old Lois Ann," Scott said with emotion. "What happened next?"

Sue cleared her throat importantly and continued.

"The Economic Police conducted an external audit of the Romain Corporation and the Moon Company Board. They arrested several people but were forced to release them since Mr. Slavik didn't find any legal basis for their detention. On your desk you'll probably find a complain about his actions."

"They can complain to their grandmas, losers. Did they find anything specific?"

"As far as I know, no. Their only success was the capture of Hermine Arango, you know, the one that stabbed his friend. They found him on the board of directors of the company. One of the councilors turned out to be his cousin. They took both of them to Earth. Romain Corporation is prohibited from operating until further notice, and its mines are closed."

"They played it hard. What are the legal grounds?"

"That I don't know."

He thought for a moment.

"Too bad. Slavik will explain everything to me. I believe that he has already analyzed the order from the economics when it comes to the civil and criminal codes. If something wasn't right, he would immediately object."

"And Brel?" I asked. "They didn't catch him?"

"Of course not," Idalgo said. "If we couldn't find him, then these fancy idiots won't either. Some big aces of intelligence... if not for what we collected, they wouldn't have shit, because none of them even have any idea about Lunnar and its specifics. We had to constantly monitor them so that they didn't come across something really unpleasant, else it would be all on us."

Scott bit his lips. I could see that he was thinking intensively, and I could bet what about. Idalgo, like Sue, and the rest of the Lunnar Police Department, may not have known what the economic police were actually looking for on the moon. Scotty didn't know either, but Citizen Hakat who sent them to Lunnar did. Did they find what they were really sent for?

"Paul, when the representatives of the economic sector were going back, did they look satisfied?" I asked.

Idalgo shrugged his massive shoulders.

"I don't think so," he replied. "As far as I could tell, they were rather unhappy. The whole time they were complaining that we didn't help, and yet we were doing almost all the work, like some donkeys."

"That's their model of work," Scott snorted irritably. "Put all the work on the shoulders of others and show your frenzy. They call themselves the police, but all they do is fart. Did they make a mess?"

"No, boss, we were watching over them in three shifts. Oh, and Captain Sirtis didn't let them mess around. That woman has balls of steel."

"A strange conclusion," Scott struggled to keep himself from laughing.

Paul Idalgo had the gift of making us laugh with his remarks, all the more amusing because he liked to use words that he didn't understand or understood incorrectly.

At first I was planning to go straight to the apartment, but Scott demanded that I go with him. So I asked Sue to take Monty home and prepare some nice dinner that could be reheated without sacrificing the taste, since I wasn't sure when I would be back. Scott could really keep me there for a while, especially if he found some particularly interesting material on his desk.

At the police station, the whole team assembled to greeted us, so rejoiced that it warmed our hearts. It's always a nice feeling when someone is waiting for you, and so many were waiting for us. It would be an exaggeration to say that Lunnar's headquarters team was like one big family, but they were definitely people very close, to each other, with a lot of trust behind it, knowing each other thick as thieves. The specifics of life on the Moon meant that the workplace became more like a home than a rented apartment. 'Rented', because no one in Lunnar owned their own little corner. All buildings were owned by the Moon Company, which determined the rent and took care of the entire infrastructure. Although I'm not entirely sure of this, but it's my guess that the pre-written agreements ruled out the sale of apartments to private individuals. In this situation, it was difficult to call the apartment 'my home'.

After greeting our colleagues, we went to the inspector's office – with Scotty, since it was my office, and me, because I was very curious how his interaction with Lois Ann Siris would look like. I haven't seen her before, although I had contact with the soldiers. Although I've heard a lot about her, and according to these rumors, Captain Sirtis was something like a real hero, whom you should fear getting in the way of. Even old soldiers felt immense respect before her, nay! Even my current boss, who has a reputation for being an uncompromising tough guy, has always treated her with conciliation. Understandably, then, I was very curious about what she was like.

Lois Ann Sirtis, the famous 'mean bitch', sat in Scott's chair, reading the daily newspaper on a reader, with her legs crossed on the table, wearing military boots. Scott walked over and, without a word, knocked the captain's legs to the floor with one sharp movement. She jumped up from her chair, violently throwing the reader onto the table. Now I could see the commander of the Moon's garrison up close. Mrs. Sirtis was smaller than I thought, but still impressively built for a woman. She was maybe around 6 feet tall, her muscles literally ripping through the gray-green uniform, her hips narrow like a man's, and her breasts were small, barely noticeable. The hands now resting on the table were rather nicely shaped, but terribly neglected – rough, hardened, with frayed nails. Only her head poking out in our direction, though military cut, looked a little feminine. Once upon a time Sirtis must have been a pretty girl. Even now, in her late fifties, her Greek nose, soft lips and large brown eyes left a good impression.

"You have a problem?" she hissed to Scott.

"Yes, I do. Some usurper is using my office," he fired back.

They looked into each other's eyes, as if playing tiptoe.

"Someone had to guard your yard, Stinger."

"And it was you who was so nice to do so?"

"Do you see anyone else here who could put those economics guys in their place?"

"Either way, I'm back, so go back to the barracks."

"At least you could say thank you. It's only because of me and my people that they didn't get access to your archives."

Scott took on a more friendly expression friendly.

"Thank you, Tiger Lily. I bow down to my waist. Now, would you be so kind as to clear my office."

Captain Sirtis shrugged her shoulders and left from behind the table. She moved like Cavanaugh, agile, elastic, giving one an idea of her strength and ability.

"I made a report on everything that happened here. You'll probably want to read it. I admit that I don't get this whole affair at all."

Scott unexpectedly put his hand on her shoulder as a sign of friendship and sympathy.

"You're better off not knowing too much, Tiger Lily. At least in this case."

She looked at him, her lips compressed into a narrow line, as if she wanted to spoil their beautiful shape at any cost. I had a feeling that at that moment I ceased to exist for them, and suddenly I felt jealous. They had something in common. A common past in which I had no place and which I did not know.

"If you say so. But you know, Stinger, you can always count on me."

She left, and I heard her calling in a rough voice to the soldiers from the corridor.

"Tiger lily? Stinger?" I asked when Scott and me were finally alone.

He didn't answer immediately. He took his seat, then looked out the window overlooking the police parking lot. The soldiers boarded a transporter painted in protective colors, and Captain Sirtis urged them on with harsh shouts.

"Our families lived in the same apartment building," he finally said. "We've known each other for as long as I can remember. We played in the same sandboxes, went to the same schools. The nicknames are all the way back from elementary school. Where we lived back then, strategic group games were popular, we all took on nicknames. Mine was Stinger and Lewis got Tiger."

"Lewis? Don't you mean Lois?" I asked, surprised.

Scotty was still staring out the window, fingers drumming on the countertop.

"What do you think about her?" he asked suddenly. I shrugged.

"She's pretty big. Probably even taller than you."

"That's an illusion, thanks to the thick soles of military boots. In fact, we are the same height," he suddenly looked at me, I twitched. "Well, sooner or later you'll find out anyway, since it's really not a secret."

I pulled up a chair and sat down opposite him. I was already guessing what the truth was, and experienced mixed feelings. Transsexuality faded into the darkness of history along with other genetic disorders. Once the root cause was found, the corresponding gene lines were blocked, prohibiting reproduction. From time to time, however, anything can happen, and with as many chromosomes as human beings have, it's not hard to miss something. Fluctuations in testosterone levels in the womb are not always detected in time, and at the birth of a baby, it is initially not known what is wrong with them. The problem is usually discovered rather late...

"Was the captain once a boy?"

Scott nodded and smiled sadly.

"I'm sure you'll believe me when I tell you that at the time, I was the only one who accepted it... who my friend was. Others scoffed at first, then avoided, since he knew how to respond to unexpected rudeness with his fists. He didn't change into dresses or play with dolls, but claimed that he was a girl, only that his body was wrong. Everyone was surprised when he went through the whole gender reassignment procedure, had plastic surgery and went into the army afterwards. But not me, do you know why?"

"I can guess why. In the army nobody asks questions."

"Exactly. Either way, Lois wanted to be in the army since we were kids. Back when she was still a guy. She was drawn to this life, but she wanted to go to the recruitment office as a woman."

We were both silent for a while.

"If that was her dream, why did she change her sex?" I finally asked. "I always thought that it's easier for men in such power structures."

"Lois Ann wasn't born the way she was to have an easier life. Maybe someday you'll get to know her better, then you'll understand how special she is."

"And how did she get here? For what?"

He smiled again.

"Like everyone else, as punishment. She beat up the previous deputy chief of the armed forces. He came to the barracks for a check and dared to mock her. Not everyone is as tolerant as they should be."

I wanted to say that I don't know whether I am, but I remained silent. Lois Ann Sirtis was the first person I met who was after a sex reassignment surgery, and I had no idea how to judge her case. In social studies, both in elementary and high school, transsexualism has been presented as the result of an unfortunate, almost impossible to predict and correct gene sequence error. It was explained that this was no longer acceptable in the era immediately after the ecological disaster, when natural reproduction became something very difficult and was worth its weight in gold.

This was not said directly, but I think there was an attempt to condition us to this problem as something highly undesirable, but sometimes inevitable. The fact that geneticists could not determine the likelihood of having a transgender child meant that they could not prevent it. Down's syndrome, apodia[2], tetralogy of Fallot[3], hydrocephalus, spina bifida, microphthalmia[4], sirenomelia[5], anacephaly[6] and other deformations were eliminated through careful conception planning, but the problem remained. Even then, it seemed to me that geneticists are ashamed of their impotence on such an important issue and deliberately reduce the number of 'gene errors' by giving the children an operation as soon as it's found out. Maybe they even move them to different families afterwards, to erase the tracks?

We heard a knock, and Neil Slavik entered the office, impeccably elegant as always, in a tight-fitting suit and a tie. Although his stocky figure was far from perfect, he looked very impressive in this outfit. He was complemented by dark glasses from the catalog of the fashion house Mark Versace, which he always wore. Apparently, he suffered from photosensitivity and therefore never took them off, but made sure that they were expensive and in line with the latest fashion.

"How did the conversation with that monster of a captain go?" he asked cheerfully. "You have no idea how she settled herself in here, although maybe it was for the better, because she held the economics guys by their mouths and didn't let them buzz around too much. She

---

[2] Congenital absence of legs.

[3] Congenital heart defect.

[4] Congenital disorder in which eyes are abnormally small.

[5] A birth defect, where the legs are fused together.

[6] Lack of a developed brain after birth. If the brainstem is correct, a person with anacephaly may live for some time after birth.

didn't let them put their mistakes onto us, or take credit for the thing we've achieved without their help."

"What things?" the inspector asked skeptically. "Grab a beer and sit down."

Slavik grabbed a can with a raddeberger sitting in the corner and pulled up a free chair.

"Well, first of all, the support group got that wanted miner, Hermine Arango," he announced.

He opened the can, took a long sip, and sighed in satisfaction.

"Support Group? Kravitz, Ming Chao and Kohn? They deserve applause then, they showed off. Maybe I wrote them off too quickly."

"Maybe that's a bit too far, Cavanaugh, too far. They are good at what they do, but they're not intelligent enough for detectives and lack intuition."

I already had the chance to get to know the three officers mentioned by Slavik, who remained together even after their watch. Their role was to conduct investigations 'in the field' and collect information, which they then passed on to detectives. According to Scotty, they were not good at judging the importance of what they heard or found, but they were very good at catching rumors and eavesdropping on conversations. Their help was invaluable, but the boss didn't allow them to act independently.

"If everyone does their job, everything will go as it should," as he often replied to their requests.

Now he looked as surprised as he was pleased.

"Did they arrest him?"

Slavik nodded, smiling.

"They decided that in this situation it would be for the best. The economics team wanted to immediately win all the laurels, but we stood our grand, and Captain Sirtis took our side."

"And how did Arango explain himself?"

"He refused to testify. Honestly, I thought he would behave differently."

"And how did he behave?"

The lawyer sipped his beer again.

"Like a declared criminal. He refused to answer even the most innocent questions, and nothing could make him change his mind. A strange man. He is highly educated, has a reputation for being levelheaded and responsible, but he acted somehow... Kell did a toxicology test on him, but he found no traces of drugs, legal or illegal. That's what's weird. Guy doesn't take any drugs and, for almost no reason, kills a colleague from work, runs away, and, being caught, does not even try to explain the motives of the act. That makes no sense, he could face the death penalty, after all."

Scotty was silent, considering what he heard, until he finally said:

"Yes, it's very strange. Did you send him back to Earth?"

Neal turned serious and finished his beer to the bottom.

"We didn't have time to. He committed suicide in his cell. He somehow smuggled in a thin carbide blade, possibly hidden under his tongue or in a sealed fold of skin on his stomach. To be honest, he really caught us by surprise, we didn't expect such an act of desperation from him."

"Okaaay," Scotty drew the last syllable and added, "you're right. This makes no sense. Are you sure he was clean?"

"Almost certain."

"So was he or not?!"

"You heard what I said. Almost certain. He didn't do drugs, didn't drink. However, during the autopsy, Kell discovered an implant that had been stitched in to neutralize substances from a group of drugs used as a truth serum.

Scotty got up and took a can of beer too. I thought about what Slavik said while he was drinking, and the more I thought about it, the more I felt like something here was off. Before the inspector took the vessel away from his lips, I said:

"He wasn't a miner. After all, he was in a hotel room for the office staff."

Scott smiled knowingly, but then turned serious.

"Hold on, you know what, that makes sense. Neil, what does the dossier say about this guy?"

"I certainly looked at them and I know the answers," the man ran his thumb over his mustache, then reached into a bowl of crackers and popped it three at a time into his mouth. "He was hired as a shift supervisor, but he never worked in a mine. Not here, anyway. Immediately after signing the contract, he was taken to the hospital with a severe asthma attack. The company doctor refused to sign his medical card, but a contract is a contract, so he was given a position on the surface. He turned out to be very smart and hard-working, he was quickly promoted and appreciated."

"And yet he was not a miner," I repeated confidently.

"Yes, we know that," Scotty waved his hand impatiently. "Now, a question for one hundred points: is the last name authentic?"

"That's it!" Slavik pointed his finger at him. "Many people change their last names before going to the moon, but in the case of Arango, we are dealing with the puppet master. I counted eleven changes, and that's probably not where it ends. I identified the guy by his retina, teeth, fingerprints and..." he took a deep breath here, "DNA. And here I discovered something very interesting."

"Say it."

"Remember when Kelley said that the man who organized the Sydney Glory debt collection at the bank left a sample with two types of DNA?"

"Yes."

"Well, one of the sequences is Hermine Arango's DNA. We hadn't yet figured out the female code, but the male one belonged to him."

"Oh shit! Does this have anything to do with Romain Corporation?"

"We don't know yet," Slavik finished his beer.

Scott followed suit, and I felt myself thirsty for this nasty drink.

"Is Romain Corporation still operating?" I asked.

Slavik wiped his mustache and snorted.

"I think those guys have a partnership with the devil. They fell to their knees."

Scott gasped. The lawyer hit him on the back with his open palm and explained:

"They paid a fine and are operating as if nothing had happened."

"Damn it," Cavanaugh said and looked at me. "Well, you see yourself, dear. Sometimes the cops work themselves like a herd of oxen, and nothing comes of it. Such disappointments take some getting used to."

I nodded to him silently, but felt angry. My faith in equality before the law and public order has been seriously undermined. I didn't know it was so easy to dismiss someone's obvious crime.

"Anything else?" Scotty asked after a moment.

"That's basically it," Slavik replied.

"Okay, then get back to work. And bring Kelley here."

The coroner made us wait for him for more than half an hour as he was finishing a new autopsy and didn't want to be interrupted. When he finally appeared, he was clearly angry, or rather, annoyed.

"What's the matter?" Scotty asked.

Kelley tossed a small pad on the table.

"Another murder, this time under the influence of a new drug. They call it 'golden rain'. It appeared on the market just a month ago."

"Who is the victim?"

"Mrs. Lorena Casponi. Her husband caught her with a lover when he returned stoned from a fly-away. He killed her and wounded the guy badly."

"Oh God, we were neighbors..." - I moaned. "I always thought that they weren't a good couple, but to that extent?"

"That's what happens when you get high," muttered Scotty. "We need to find out the address of this fly-away and find out why they allowed a man in this state to go out into the streets."

Yes, that's a good question. The usefulness of this type of premises lies in, among other things, the fact that a person in there may abuse drugs as they wish, but spend all the time in an enclosed space, guarded by appropriately trained personnel. The client only leaves the premises once they're completely sober. At least that's the case on Earth.

"Let's leave that for now," I suggested. "You wanted to ask about the DNA."

The Inspector nodded absently.

"True. Slavik said that you identified Hermine Arango's gene code as one of those that together make up the sample left in the bank by Maximo Perez. Is that true?

"Yes," Kelley admitted. "What's interesting about it is, as you will recall, that the 'owner' of this DNA has been dead for several years. But in truth, he was alive, living his best life on the Moon. Unfortunately, he can no longer answer questions."

"Did you find anything else?" Scotty handed the coroner a beer, but the coroner pushed the can aside. Instead, he poured himself water from a pot in the corner, took a bluish pill from his breast pocket, and swallowed it in several gulps.

"I was able to figure out how Perez tricked the retinal scanner. An old friend of mine, Stuart Levy, who works in a medical engineering institution, sent me the documentation of a certain invention – contact lenses with an electronic system made entirely of transparent components. They can be used in various ways, but right now we're interested in just one. These things, when properly programmed, can emit magnetic waves causing scan errors."

"Hmm, what about fingerprints?"

"Silicone pads used when working with thin electronics. Nowadays they make them so thin that unless you examine them closely, you won't notice anything. Theoretically, you can copy someone else's fingerprints onto them, although, I confess, I have never seen such an application. Levi is saying that it's possible, though."

He stretched in the chair, making it squeak. Cavanaugh was silent for several minutes, typing what he heard into his pod. Then he closed the device and seemed like he wanted to say something, but changed his mind. He looked at me.

"Leeta, go home," he said. "Take the Arango case file with you and analyze it. Maybe you can find some kind of connection, whatever it is. I'll take care of the rest. Kelty, you are free, too."

I accepted the order without saying a word. Obviously, my boss wanted to be alone right now. This was his style of work. He was to not be disturbed until he called for someone.

Slavik helped me upload the necessary documents into the reader, and I was finally able to return home, where Sue was waiting with some good dinner and Monty. Oh no, it wasn't just them. As soon as I entered, a ball of red fur flashed down the corridor and began to rub against my legs with a throaty meow. I sat down and scratched the cat's back. He looked at me with reproachful eyes, then thrust his head into my hand, continuing to purr.

"I'm sorry, Sid, I had to. You know I don't like leaving you."

"Why do you say that?" Monty asked. "That creature doesn't understand human words."

He got up and looked at me with his usual calmness, but his lips twitched slightly, as if he wanted to smile, he just didn't quite know how to do it yet.

"Who could know that?" I answered. "Maybe he does understand?"

"Give it a break, or we'll all go crazy, even the AI," Sue snorted. "Wash your hands and come to the table, otherwise everything will get cold. I won't heat it up for a third time. You should have been here an hour ago."

"You know what my job is like, damn it."

"Yes I do, damn it."

Only when I saw the stacked table did I realize how hungry I was. My friend may not have been a great cook, but she knew the basics and became more interested in cuisine after we started living together. This time she cooked meat substitute rice flakes stewed in spiced soy sauce. They tasted good. We ate, drank some punch, had a little gossip, and then we had to get to work. Sue went to her room, and I went to mine, where I could calmly examine the documents that Slavik gave me. The suicide of Hermine Arango complicated a seemingly simple matter – two friends quarrel under the influence of drugs, which leads to tragic results. Sure, but usually the perpetrator doesn't act in such an irrational way after sobering up.

I carefully reviewed the reports, the list of exhibits and circumstantial evidence, psychological portraits compiled by experts, and the testimony of both men. There was not a single focal point, nothing to lean on, nothing to explain the killer's attitude. When I finally I averted my eyes from the reader, tired, I met Monty's gaze. The android sat in a chair tucked into a corner and looked at me as if I were the only object of interest in this city. I smiled, and to my surprise he smiled back, although not very skillfully.

"Why are you looking at me like that?" I asked.

"I'm waiting You may need help."

I sighed.

"I would like you to help me in this matter, but, unfortunately, it's not possible."

"Why is it not possible?"

Good question, why? I could as well let him in on it, I wasn't risking anything. Maybe his logical mind would find was eluding me.

"Come here. You can read through the documents saved in the 'Arango Case' folder. I'll go take a break in the meantime."

I handed him the reader. I expected him to read the same way as me, but Monty simply flipped through the pages. His system of perception was much better than human – he didn't need to read letter by letter, word by word, he could register and process the entire text at a glance. When he finished, he returned the device to me.

"What do you want to know?"

"Is there something illogical in this whole mess that does not coincide with the rest?"

I said that and at the same time felt like I've gone crazy. How could I expect help from a being created in a laboratory and, by definition, unable to understand how the human mind works? A criminal mind even more so?

Monty tilted his head slightly.

"Statements by the people of Horus," he said. "Everyone says the same thing, and although they use different words, the content of it is the same. Good employees, loyal colleagues. Only one expressed himself differently."

"Who?" I was surprised. It must have slipped past me.

"Jerry Beckett, nineteen, administrative messenger. He said that he didn't really know them at all, except that they ordered him around sometimes. When asked if he expected any strange behavior from them, he only said: "Nobody expected it. Both of them were, as you can see, false coins. What is a coin?"

"I'll tell you later."

I jumped up and grabbed my communicator.

I'm an idiot! How could I have missed such an obvious clue?! The point is not that the guy spoke differently from the others, but that they all told us the same thing and not a word more! I should have realized myself that something here was not right.

"Boss!" I called out as soon as I heard Scott's sleepy voice. He must have been taking a nap, and I just woke him up. "Arrest Jerry Beckett, Horus's messenger immediately!"

"What?!"

"I'll explain later!

"I'm sending the patrol, and you come back to the headquarters. Now!"

Ah, me and my long tongue... I could have waited with it until morning, nothing would have changed, and I could've gotten some sleep.

I took a shower, swallowed a stimulant pill, and ran to the office. It was close now – all I had to do is cross the courtyard, go around the corner of the building, and I stood in front of the door with the sign: "Police Headquarters". Almost all of Lunnar's officers lived in the service's living quarters, located in the back. It was easier and safer, because the building had an additional security system, and the special services weren't liked by the residents of Lunnar, even the law-abiding ones.

Scotty was waiting for me in his office. He was just finishing shaving, his hair thinning with age, damp and snug against his skull, showing the scars beneath. "Sorry that I didn't wait..." I began, but he interrupted me with a wave of his hand.

"You made the right choice. That's what you should have done. Now explain to me god damn it why that kid got your attention."

In one breath, I blurted out what Monty told me. Scott listened intently as he cleaned and rinsed the razor tank, and when I finished, he said:

"That makes sense. So, you're saying that all the respondents recited the same lesson, only dressed it up in different words?"

I nodded.

"I don't know why that messenger said something different from everyone else, but I think he was considered unimportant and so no one told him anything. The rest were given strict instructions on what to say and how, but not him."

Cavanaugh put on a clean uniform jacket, ran a comb through his hair, and wiped the wet implants.

"The patrol will be back soon," he said. "Come on. You will be acting as a clerk."

Jerry Beckett, a pencil-thin, spotted boy, looking to be only fifteen at most, sat in a chair in the interrogation room and looked so pathetic that I felt sorry for him. I didn't say nothing, as my boss commanded me, and focused on taking notes. The course of the interrogation was recorded, but according to custom, everything that's possible should be recorded manually. The main reason was that vision and sound control techniques were still being improved and the interviewee had to sign his signature and thumbprint under the handwritten protocol.

I sat down to where Scott pointed, and looked sympathetically at the messenger until suddenly his hands caught my attention. All floral technicians are regular clients of beauty salons, because the work destroys the hands. During the sessions you always talk a lot, cosmetologists are unable to work in silence, and I know how to listen and remember things. They always said that hands are the hallmark of a person. The hands of a nineteen year old boy look different from those of much older people. A trained eye can easily recognize the age of the interlocutor by the appearance of the fingers and fingerprints.

Scott sat down and stared with his implants at Beckett, and I used this opportunity to take a closer look at the messenger's hands. At the same time, I tried to listen with one ear to what they were saying.

"Full name?"

"Gerald Beckett."

"Age?"

"Eighteen."

"Profession?"

"Messenger."

"Is this your only source of income?"

"Yes. I didn't have time to finish university."

"Do you have unusual interests?"

"No."

"Are you sure?" I blurted out. I should have been silent, but I couldn't bear it. He looked at me reproachfully.

"Of course, ma'am! I don't have time for such things, I work for one and eight-tenths of the work time to make money for the university."

"What do you want to study?"

"History of art. Is that so important?"

"Someone else will decide that."

I wrote everything down on the form and told him to sign it. He did so, and then Scott growled impatiently.

"Now, talk."

"I don't understand, why am I here," Beckett began, stuttering slightly under the inspector's gaze. "I didn't do anything."

"I'm not saying you did. I just want you to tell me what was really going on between Germin Arango and Marco Landis."

"But I don't know anything. I'm just a messenger in the office."

Scott let out a short, evil laugh. I've had the opportunity to see how the implants, stretched out as far as they can go, combined with that laugh scared people much tougher than some errand boy, so I wasn't surprised to see Beckett huddled on his chair as if expecting to get hit.

"Don't take me for a fool, kid. I've never met a messenger who wouldn't know more about his company than the CEO himself. Even our Hallie is no exception."

Hallie Novak comes from Little Poland, an enclave of European refugees in New Zealand, the same place that our penal law expert came from. In fact, they arrived on Lunnar at the same time. The girl played the same role in the headquarters as Jerry had in the headquarters of Horus. Quiet, dexterous and smart, she was a veritable encyclopedia of information on every current case. No one knew where she got her knowledge from, but she was always up to date.

"But... I..." Beckett muttered, unconsciously clenching his hands into fists. I wondered if he was thinking about attacking Scott – that would be a desperate response that would nevertheless require a psychiatric evaluation. Did he count on that?

"What, you?!" Cavanaugh rose from his chair. "You've been lying through your teeth from the start. Everyone we interviewed told us the same fairy tale, but you didn't. Why?"

"What fairy tale?"

"You know what exactly! Stop pretending to be an idiot!"

"I swear I don't know anything. What are you torturing me for?"

"I haven't even started... you haven't gotten to know me yet! Now talk!"

He slammed his fist on the table and Jerry began crying. He covered his face and sobbed like a frightened child. I was beginning to feel tired of this."

"Boss, can I have a word with you?" I asked.

Scott looked at me in surprise, but without a word, walked out into the hallway.

"He's lying, it's obvious," I said as soon as the door closed behind us. "But that's just one thing. Second thing is, he is not who he claims to be."

Scotty snorted angrily.

"And who here is? Very few. Do you have anything specific?"

"His hands."

"What?"

"He has the hands of a man... well, I don't know?... maybe forty years old?"

Scott's visors extended again to their full length and immediately retracted.

"Are you sure?"

"I can't explain everything to you now, but trust me, I might actually be right. He has some strange looking hands. Is there any way we could quickly check whether I'm wrong?"

"Let's ask the source, but be warned, you must explain what you mean."

Summoned to the office, Kelley listened to my chaotic talk about the Madame Chang beauty salon and regeneration sessions, then nodded.

"That actually makes sense. Hands age quickly, especially in the case of physical workers, and men rarely take care of them. However, a nineteen-year-old shouldn't have the hands of a forty-year-old."

"Can we figure this out quickly? Horus' lawyers will be on our asses soon. If we don't present convincing evidence, they'll take him away like their property. No time for DNA testing."

The doctor smiled.

"In the past, they didn't have sequencers, but still determined people's age. A simple X-ray machine is enough. Hand the boy over to me, and we'll find out soon enough. Lying to the police is a crime for which he could be held back for longer."

"What do you want to x-ray?" I asked.

"His left hand. There's a method known for hundreds of years. Ossification points, the condition of the joints, thanks to all that you can determine someone's age with high a..."

He was interrupted by a call from the communicator. Scott pressed the button.

"What is it?"

"The lawyers of the Horus company are waiting for you at the main office," we heard Slavik's voice. "They have an official release demand for Gerald Beckett, composed lege artis."

Scott looked at Kelley and me, then nodded towards the door of the interrogation room.

"Tell the lawyers that I'll be right there," he said into the communicator's microphone.

It was a decided-on code that meant "talk to them and delay for at least ten minutes". So we didn't have much time, but at least we had any at all.

I opened the door of the interrogation room.

Jerry raised his head and looked at us hopefully.

"Mr. Beckett, there has been a misunderstanding," I said, hoping he didn't notice the insincerity in my voice. "We'd like you to sign this protocol and place the tip of your thumb in the lower right corner. You will be examined by a doctor in order to get evidence that you were not harmed at the police station, after which you can leave."

"Really?" he asked incredulously.

"Yes," Dr. McCave held out his hand. "Please follow me. It will only take a minute."

"Will I be needed again?" I asked.

The doctor shook his head.

"I can handle it."

I went to the office, where our lawyer were talking to Horus's lawyers, a man and a woman. Both were completely nondescript, in almost identical suits and even with the same hairstyle: cut short, sleek. I bet they were the same age too. Neil, as always eloquently, pulled out new documents, showed them, and each time gave a speech to which our guests responded, scattering paragraphs and precedents as if from a sleeve.

I smiled inwardly. I got to know Slavik well enough to know how he liked such challenges. When necessary, he could talk to anyone so well that he almost always achieved the desired result – most often it was delaying a trial, restricting a witness, or persuading the prosecutor to issue an authorized court order. I was very curious about what a man of his talents was doing on the Moon instead of pursuing a career with a respected earth law firm. I'm sure he would have told me the reason if I asked, but so far I have simply had no opportunity to do so.

It suddenly dawned on me how little I know not only about him, but about all my work colleagues in general. Cynthia Lara always said that there is nothing worse and more disgusting than poking my nose into someone else's life, so I automatically skipped personal topics in my conversations. I knew a little more about Scotty and Kelley, since they told me out of their own free will – I didn't know much even about the tragically deceased Sylvanas Evans.

I sat in a corner and watched as Neil argued with Horus's messengers. They were good, for sure, but they were clearly not used to such tricks and unknowingly allowed themselves to be drawn into Slavik's game. As far as I knew, he could have delayed it for any amount of time. He glanced at me from behind his shaded glasses occasionally, clearly letting me know: "I've got them now". I got the impression that even Scott, standing next to me, was a little dumbfounded, although he was already used to the way our carnist works.

The fun ended when Dr. McCave entered the office with Jerry Beckett, clearly relaxed and at ease. Scott interrupted the Karnist's speech with a short hiss and turned to the doctor:

"And?"

Kelley placed a medical pod on the table.

"You can arrest him, inspector," he said (by unwritten agreement, in the presence of third parties, we always addressed the boss formally). "He lied at the hearing. He is at least thirty-four years old and shows signs of prolonged contact with chemicals on his hands."

Beckett's eyeballs quite literally left the eye sockets, when police officers Jamal and Mara twisted his arms behind his back and handcuffed him.

"What are you doing?!" he screamed shrilly.

Horus's attorneys began speaking the traditional protest formula almost simultaneously, but fell silent when Scott glared at them. The sight of protruding implants was not the only thing that worried the criminals.

"Doctor, are you sure?" I asked.

"Absolutely. Bone age doesn't lie and I am very well versed in chemical-induced skin discoloration."

Horus's lawyer whispered for a moment with their colleague, then turned to Scott.

"Inspector Cavanaugh, what charges are you going to bring? That the messenger, in addition to carrying documents, sometimes used harsh chemicals to clean the offices? That maybe in his free time he entertained himself with experiments, or maybe that he was hiding his real age? Perhaps he did it out of shame, since even at his age he still hasn't achieved anything. Are you trying to blame him for that? This is ridiculous."

"Do I look like I'm joking?" Scotty asked dryly. "Right now, I am imprisoning Mr. Beckett for deliberately trying to mislead a law enforcement official. His fate will be decided by the prosecutor's office. Have a good day."

Slavik smiled affectionately at colleagues of same profession, who at that moment looked as if they didn't know what to say. A rare moment for lawyers.

"Sorry about this," he said amiably. "Allow me to accompany you to the exit. If there's anything else you'd like to discuss, feel free. I am on duty here every day from seven thirty to five in the afternoon."

Among many pleasantries, he escorted the Horus representatives out of the office.

I looked at Kelley.

"What do you think about those discolorations?" I asked.

He raised his eyebrows skeptically.

"One thing I can say is that they definitely didn't form as a result of contact with cleaning agents," he replied. "I would venture to say that this guy was making drugs in the privacy of his home. Maybe that's how he was making some extra money."

"Kohn!" the inspector called out. "Gather your friends and go to Gerald Beckett's apartment immediately!" Search thoroughly and take away anything that seems suspicious!

"What about the warrant?" Kohn shouted back.

Scott swore angrily and went to the office to get the appropriate form. In the meantime, I turned to the coroner again:

"What about his appearance? At first glance, he looks like a kid. Anti-aging pills are not that strong, even I know that. A thirty-year-old guy looks to be about thirty even when he takes them. They block the occurrence of typical senile changes, not the consequences of full maturation."

Kelley looked at the capsule and wrote something on it. Only then did he answer:

"Some people are this way, that they 'don't age', as they like to say. And acne that mimics youthful skin lesions can easily be triggered by the right dose of hormones. If you want my opinion, nothing here happened by chance. And I certainly don't believe that the guy pretended to be a teenager out of shame. He has the symbol of class C4 on his forehead, so it's to the surprise of no one the does the simplest of jobs. However..."

He paused, rubbing his forehead with the back of his hand.

"All this is too smart for the capabilities of a C4," he finally muttered. "Something in this damn case feels off to me. Let's wait and see what the investigation team finds."

I silently agreed with him. I was hoping there would be something interesting in Beckett's apartment that would lead us on the right track, anything at all. Just thinking about this case was making me dizzy.

Scott came back from the office and in a voice that wouldn't tolerate objection, told me to complete the paperwork. I sat down at my desk and obediently plunged into the desperate job of filling out hundreds of forms and writing reports that will likely never be read. I hated this part of detective work, but it was inevitable.

I worked in silence. Scott only appeared next to me once, looked over my shoulder at the desk and said soothingly:

"Good job. Pull yourself together and finish this, and I'm sure you won't miss a reward. Starting tomorrow, I will be taking you to the shooting range and to the police gym. It's time to learn the methods of aggressive combat."

"Will you be giving me a gun?" I asked without enthusiasm.

"Well, of course. You are entitled to it and should finally start carrying one."

I wouldn't say that I was particularly happy about this, although, on the other hand, having a weapon could help me in extreme cases. You never know what might happen. The illegally bought stunner was more like a toy than a weapon, so I didn't really count on it.

Nobody paid any attention to me for the rest of the day. Everyone focused on their own business, only Halle, even though I didn't ask for it, brought me an energy drink. At about half past five, I finished the paperwork and was able to put the pods back in the drawer, feeling accomplished. In fact, I could go home. If there was anything that was holding me back, it was curiosity about what our 'operational group' of three people found the in the detainee's apartment. Kravitz, Ming Chao, and Lucilia Kon had not yet returned to the headquarters, and I had no idea what they could possibly find.

I thought to wait for them, but Scott looked from out of his office, saw me and shouted angrily:

"What are you still doing here?! Go back home."

"I thought..." I tried to explain, but he cut me off immediately.

"Stop thinking, and go home. I'll call you if you're needed."

With a light sigh, I gathered my things and headed home. I consoled myself with the thought that Scott really won't hold himself back if I'm needed, and will immediately call me to come back, but until now I could simply relax friendly environment with the people I love.

When I arrived at work the next day, Scott was already conferring with the operatives who had not slept all night. At least that's what I figured based on the dark circles under their eyes and their tired expressions. On the inspector's desk was a bunch of small items found in Beckett's apartment. Nobody has yet had time to view and sort them by importance.

"Glad you're here," Scott said when he saw me. "We have a pretty good haul here," he turned to the policemen standing in front of him. "All right, thank you, you have a day off. Get some rest."

When all three of them disappeared behind the door, he motioned me to my seat.

"They've been looking for this trash all night?" I asked incredulously, sitting down on the chair. He scratched his head and yawned.

"Worst thing is, this is no trash at all," he muttered reluctantly. "And it took so long because they had to actually find Beckett's apartment first. No one lived in the booth he officially rented. They searched until they finally found the actual residence of this bastard."

"And what was he making in there?" I have asked.

"Nothing. But he had a lot of encrypted documents and a small laboratory, but not a production one. An analytical one."

"Why would he need that?"

"That's what I want to know. Dear, look through this stack properly, I need a shower and a nap for at least a quarter of an hour. Can you do it by yourself, or should I bring Herefort?"

"I'll try on my own. If I fail, I'll call her," I promised.

He patted me on the back and left.

I sat down in the inspector's chair, slightly adjusted its height and began to sort through the findings. At first, I had some problems with this due to the proprietary coding system, but I was soon able to customize the police decryptor installed on the table. It even surprised me how easy it was, clearly the lessons that Sue gave me were not for nothing. Fortunately, these were not originals, but copies made on ordinary computer foil. I had no idea how this even happened – theoretically, it shouldn't even be possible to produce such copies, but I left the technical details for later. Right now, what mattered was what I could extract from the documents.

After an hour of work, I could tell that all the encrypted information was about Horus and nothing else. Some were copies of company patents, others contained payroll to administration, many of which I didn't even understand. I was copying the transcribed records onto police storage, when Scott returned, fresh and clean. As he joked, he knew how to 'sleep quickly'. I don't know how he did it, but all he needed was an hour of sleep to get rid of the fatigue.

"What's the conclusion?" he asked.

He bent down and kissed my cheek, then studied the text I had just transcribed. He smelled of good cologne. The Chancellor of the Academy used a similar one, and for a moment I was reminded of my dream job in Palm Springs. Now it seemed like something from a thousand years past.

"These are internal documents of Horus," I replied. "I also found a handwritten note. They contain chemical formulas. Scotty, this is not your typical criminal case. I think industrial espionage is involved, but I can't figure out what information is involved and who's in the need of it."

"Or why," Scott said. "Come on, we need to have a talk with Mr. Beckett."

We went down to the prison compartment located in the basement of the main headquarters. It was originally designed as a refuge and was arguably the most secure residential area in Lunnar, literally packed with security. It was divided into a detention center and proper prison, where petty criminals served their sentences, ranging from several days to a maximum of several months. They had the right to be sent back to Earth, but many gave up this privilege and remained in Lunnar.

Jerry Beckett was held in a cell in the pre-trial detention area. Scott returned the weapon to the guards. I didn't have a service pistol yet, but I turned in my pocketknife just in case. This was an unbreakable rule. You were never allowed to bring any weapons to jail, since you can never know what could happen.

Beckett stood up when he saw us and greeted us with a pitiful, questioning look. He must have been a great actor, because he hasn't dropped this act for a second.

"Hello Mr. Beckett," said Scotty. "Shall we talk?"

"I told you everything I know."

"If that's the case, we'll hand you over to the prosecutor's office, but I don't think it's what you want," Scott crossed his arms behind his back and grinned. "We found your real apartment on the Kimberley Coast. You disguised it well, but cops aren't as stupid as in some childish jokes. All in all, you hid some very interesting things in that cozy little corner of yours."

The detainee rubbed his face with his hands, nervously smoothed his greasy hair and looked at us with a hard glint in his eyes.

"I'll tell you everything," he said. "But first I demand immunity."

"Why would I give you that?"

"Because there would be no point in blowing up this case. Nothing here is what you think it is."

He unbuttoned his shirt, removed the belt that stabilized his back under his clothes, and ripped one of the seams with his fingernails. He removed a thin piece of metal from this primitive hiding spot and passed it through the grate. It was a private detective's ID with five holograms and a barcode. Scott took it with an expression of serious confusion. He touched one of the LEDs on the left implant, activating the code reader. The outdated, rough visors, although unsightly, really were useful.

"Kevin Razor Winslet, Private Investigator, License No. 1096730," he read. "All right, then. So you're a private detective. Who hired you?"

"Are we speaking officially?"

Scott sighed heavily and handed the prisoner his ID.

"No. Privately."

"If that's the case, I can talk," Jerry, or rather Kevin, carefully hid the document and put on the belt again. "I was hired by the management of the Moon Company to investigate Horus from the inside."

"What for? Horus isn't doing any scams."

"It may seem so. In the past, this company really was morally crystal-clear, but lately things have been getting worse and worse. The three major helium deposits are less abundant than expected, and Khor's mineral resources are contaminated. To maintain financial liquidity, CEOs had to take out loans, and to obtain them they falsified the results of analyzes. In fact, they had no choice, the company was on the verge of bankruptcy. It can only be saved by finding new deposits. And relatively clean ones at that."

I looked at the inspector and thought that right now he looked like a cat, from which a mouse escaped. I felt like laughing, holding myself back with difficulty.

"And you can judge the purity of the samples yourself, correct?"

"Of course. I am a chemical engineer."

We looked in surprise at the vertical oval between the detective's eyebrows. He touched it with his fingers.

"It's just temporary marking."

Scotty chuckled several times, as if something was stuck in his throat.

"Of course. And how is it that you said something different from the rest of the Horus employees being interrogated? Did you want to be original or what?"

Kevin Winslet shook his head.

"No. Simply put, I hacked into the system and removed my name from the list of people selected for interrogation. No one in the company knew that you would be speaking to me, and I was sure that I could defend myself against it. I didn't think that you were already able to print your own list. I have been a little outsmarted. I hope you understand, I would've preferred to avoid the attention of the police. The board must have gathered everyone you wanted to interview and instructed them on what to say, and I was not there."

"It's like a standup, some real fucking shit... sorry, Leeta, I didn't mean to."

Scott tried not to swear in my presence, although, like other police officers, he had a very extensive vocabulary of insults and profanity. The thing was, I still couldn't get used to it. Cynthia Lara always said:

"Such vocabulary is suitable for classes D and C. We are people who are expected to be cultured, so if I ever hear such a word..."

Ever since we started trying to be a couple, Scott has been trying to keep his tongue in check because of me. I appreciated that.

"One more thing," he continued after a moment. "Do you really know nothing about Marco Landis and Hermine Arango?"

The detective put his hands in his pockets.

"That wasn't my case," he replied. "But I know Romain Corporation paid them both. I checked the payroll and compared it with the personnel expenditures, ones that I was able to get out of the system. Arango and Landis left large sums of money at the casino and the fly-away. Much more than they received from the company, and they had to be living on something."

"Maybe they were winning?" I guessed.

Winslet laughed dryly.

"There is a rule of thumb in gambling, officer – the only one who wins is the casino. Even if they got lucky, they would only win back small amounts, and they were betting really big."

"What did the Romain Corporation pay them for?" Kavanaugh asked

"I didn't try to find that out. The board of the company was not interested in such things, they paid for reporting on Horus's inner corruption."

He poured water from a pot into a mug and drank it in one breath. Then he looked at us again.

"So, what will it be?" he asked. "Will I have to sit here, or will you let me go?"

"Not so fast," Scotty muttered. "We still have to check your version of events. If everything is as you say, you will be freed tomorrow morning and receive back all the confiscated papers. I'm sorry to keep you waiting, but these are the procedures."

"At least I'll have a rest. I didn't have much time for that lately."

He stretched out on the bunk with his hands under his head. He really seemed to be relieved as he began to whistle happily.

It took Sue only three hours to establish the identity of the detainee. Officer Jones then drove me and Scott to Moon Company's headquarters for final confirmation of the information we received. We had to do it this way, since the head presidency didn't want to talk through any connection, only in person. This wasn't surprising, since the company's management was acting on the edge of the law and had to take extreme care, so that no outsiders would have any insight into it.

During our face-to-face meeting, the CEO, a stern woman who looked around forty-five, but was over sixty according to the documents I reviewed – confirmed Kevin Winslet's story. She did so reluctantly, but Scott assured her that he had no intention of harming any of the Company's board members. This was not his goal. I didn't speak at all. I accompanied the boss only to witness the conversation, this was required by the procedures and I didn't need to speak. So, I listened to the conversation between Scott and the CEO, sorting out my thoughts at the same time.

The case, which was my first in Lunnar, was finally coming to an end, but it was not how I pictured it. In light of the new facts, Hermine Arango's suicide was no longer a mystery. Industrial espionage today is punishable by death or, at best, life imprisonment, but what else to call what this person was doing? The only mystery was still the reason for his quarrel with Landis, and it will continue being a mystery, since the only people who could explain what happened were already dead. I don't know why, but when I thought about it, I felt sad. I had a feeling that in my current job, such sadness would accompany me very often.

Scott must have realized that I was worried because when we left headquarters, he put his arms around me and hugged me.

"Keep your chin up," he said. "Not every working day of a detective on the Moon is about murder, suicide and corporate fights. You might be surprised, but I can say that this town is generally quite quiet, unless the miners stab each other."

"I know," I muttered without any conviction.

I wish I could take off my uniform jacket, but in today's times the police's detectives couldn't wear civilian clothes like they used to. The material of the uniform was hard and unpleasant to the touch, and while I knew why it had to be this way, I still didn't like it.

"You know what?" Scott continued after a moment. "Let's put off work for today. We're only two streets away from the dating center. We'll dismiss Jones, go over there and relax."

"You can do that?"

"Your immediate supervisor is giving you permission."

"Wait, what about Winslet? We were going to release him."

"A few more hours in custody won't kill him," Scott bent down and kissed my neck. "So, shall we go?"

VI

Police training was something for tough people, not librarians or technicians. I was starting to realize that more and more clearly. I felt tired and in pain, but the day was not over yet. By order of the inspector, after the exercises, I had to return to the station – if I was on duty at night – or go straight from work to the gym. As a result of this routine, when I returned home, I was nearly unconscious from exhaustion, and Meesh Golloub, the head of training, was still unhappy with me.

I got the impression that this person could never be satisfied. It wasn't just about me, the new and rather unsuccessful acquisition, he had problems with everyone. He gave us grades like in elementary school, and gave us a type of 'homework' – running, push-ups, exercises for the abdominal muscles and arms, everything that we could do at home. Nobody dared to resist him. I doubted whether he could turn me into what he wanted to, but he was of different opinion.

During this time, Monty has become an invaluable assistant to me. He helped me undress, cooked for me when Sue was busy, made the bed and took care of Sid's needs. The cat, clearly missing its owner, started sleeping on my pillow, which he had never done before, and his purr was very soothing. But on that day, it was still a long way from the moment when I could press my cheek against Sid's soft hair and fall asleep.

Headquarters briefings were held every morning in the inspector's office and lasted several minutes. In fact, I don't know why we weren't using the conference room for this. It seemed like Scotty simply didn't like it. In addition to these usual meetings, we had special meetings when it was necessary to discuss a more complex issue. This time we were discussing the appearance of a new drug called 'golden rain'.

Usually such cases are handled by the sanitary inspection, but we received an official request from the Kabel prosecutor, who also happens to be the president of the city. 'Golden shower' was extremely dangerous. It had the form of a yellowish dust and was taken internally with a powder inhaler. Its effects worked after an amount of one milligram. It could easily be used to poison someone, it was enough to blow it into a person's face or... pour the drug into a container with an artificial fragrant flower and convince the victim to smell it. Thanks to this, it became not only a drug, but also a dangerous weapon. We needed to find the producer, and that's what we were going to talk about.

We were able to exchange merely a few words before we heard louds voices coming from the main office. A few moments later, a clearly trembling woman burst into the office, followed by Slavik.

"Sorry Scott, I couldn't stop her. She's unarmed, the sensors didn't detect anything."

"It's fine, don't worry," Scotty got up from his chair. "I'm Inspector Cavanaugh. How can I help you?"

At first it was impossible to understand what the woman was saying, she was hysterical and was crying so much that she was unable to speak normally. It wasn't until Kelley brought a syringe and gave her a sedative that she slowly recovered. I handed her a packet of tissues and waited. It looks like it really will be a while before I can go home today.

The woman was young, well dressed and looked good. Black hair, previously combed 'along the spine', now disheveled, her makeup was smeared, she had beautiful eyes, puffy and red. Whatever happened to her must have been serious. Her first seemingly understandable words explained everything.

"Inspector, my child has been kidnapped!"

Scott opened his mouth in surprise.

"What?"

"My child has been kidnapped! My son! My precious boy!"

"That's impossible! The hotels are secured!"

"I don't live in a hotel, I live on the Hawking Street."

"Since when?"

"For four years."

Scott slammed his fist on the tabletop, making me spring out of my chair in involuntary panic. I haven't seen him this angry in a long time. The implants were lengthened to their maximum length, the skin on his face turned red, and the veins in his neck bulged like ropes.

"Are you insane?! Don't you know the rules?!"

"I do! I... had to..."

For a moment it looked like she was going to cry again, but Kelley's medicine must have been good. She recovered quickly.

"You don't understand anything."

"You're damn right about that. Hard to understand anything here. So how about you start from the beginning, not the end?"

"Give her a break," said Dr. McCave. He stood against the wall with his arms crossed over his chest and watched us closely: "This woman is still very nervous."

"Thanks for the information. Don't interrupt us," Cavanaugh sat down in a chair and turned on the company recorder. "Please, go ahead, from the beginning."

The woman nodded and fixed her hair. She must have realized that she looked like a scarecrow and felt ashamed of her behavior.

"My name is Marika Yovovitz," she began. "I got married almost five years ago. My husband and I received a license for the child – a conditional one, since our genetic tests were on the verge of being useful. I got pregnant pretty quickly. We were so happy..."

Her voice broke for a moment, but she quickly suppressed a sob.

"It turned out that the child was going to be disabled. The pregnancy was terminated and reproductive attempts were discontinued. I couldn't accept that."

"So you fled to the moon."

"We both did. My husband got a job in a food factory, and I hid in a rented apartment until birth."

I heard Kelley gasp behind me.

"Oh my God!"

I looked around instinctively. The coroner was clearly shocked.

"How could you have given birth without medical assistance?!"

"My husband used to work on a livestock farm," Ms. Yovovitz explained. "He knows how to give receive the birth of a cow, so he could handle me as well. However, he managed to find a doctor who didn't ask questions."

"Damn risky. You could have died."

"I didn't care! I wanted my child!"

The doctor sighed desperately, and Scott advised the woman:

"Please continue."

"My son was born in our apartment. I covered my mouth with a towel to suppress my screams, since it could've given us away. Luckily, Brian was never very loud. We were able to hide him until now."

Tears ran down her cheeks again. Scotty bit his lip, a drop of blood spilling out from his lower lip. He wiped it mechanically.

"You're telling me that for over three years you've been hiding a disabled child in a rented apartment, and no one knew anything?"

Marika Yovovitz nodded helplessly.

"I didn't want him to be taken away from us. Please understand, Inspector, I love him! Brian is my whole life! I don't care if he has an extra chromosome, he's the sweetest boy in the world. If I lose him, I might as well die."

Cavanaugh looked questioningly at the doctor. The man shrugged humbly.

"An extra chromosome means Down's syndrome. Three years, almost four... how did he develop?"

"Reluctantly," the woman admitted. "But in general, he never got sick or anything."

"When did you notice that he disappeared?"

"Today, when I woke up. My husband didn't seem to understand what I was asking. He was trying to tell me that we never had a child, do you understand?"

Mrs. Yovovz's voice broke again.

"Brian disappeared and all his belongings with him. Please find him..."

Scott gave Kelley a subtle signal as he pulled the injection machine out of his pocket again. But he didn't use it. The woman cried so much that he called an ambulance and ordered to take her to the hospital immediately.

"Don't worry, we'll take care of your case!" Scott exclaimed as his visitor was raised, but I could see he was seriously confused.

"What do you think about this?" I asked the Doctor.

"I'm not sure. It's not for no reason that giving birth and raising children on the moon is prohibited. You yourself know the laws of social engineering. I refuse to believe that someone would be willing to take such a risk."

"Me too," Scotty agreed. "Come on, Leeta. I want to talk to this lady's husband. Did she say that he works in a food factory?"

There were several such factories in Lunnar. Nicolae Yovovitz worked, which we were able to quickly learn, in growing and processing synthetic vegetables. He had the duty of a quality controller. He, of course, was not pleased with our visit, although he wasn't surprised."

Hearing our story, he sighed heavily.

"I should have expected this would happen," he said. "Marika has been acting strange for a while. Lunnar's atmosphere isn't doing her much good. We shouldn't have come here."

"And the child?" I asked.

He snorted in annoyance.

"There was never any child. Marika was obsessed about that ever since they denied our license. She even bought herself an interactive doll. I threw this damn thing down the drain, it annoyed me so much. Maybe that's why she went crazy. It was bound to end this way."

I had to admit that these words made sense. But there was something I didn't like about his story. I couldn't tell what it was. There was a false note in Yovovitz's voice, and I could see Scott picked it up as well.

"We'll check your statement," he said coldly. "For now, please don't leave Lunnar."

"Where would I even god? This job is all I have."

We left the processing factory, not very convinced.

"What do you think? Is he telling the truth?" I asked.

"Not the whole truth, that's for sure," Scott grumbled. "We'll take Kelley and check the apartment. If there ever was a child in there, we should be able to find something. We just need to get a warrant from the prosecution's office."

*****

We've been working on a 'wild-goose chase', as Prosecutor Kabel dismissively said, for two days now. He was very surprised that, having so many crimes on our backs, we were wasting time on 'raving a sick woman,' but he kindly signed the warrant. This allowed us to legally search Yovovitz's apartment.

At the entrance, we were surprised by how big and beautifully designed it was. Something like that couldn't have been paid from the salary of a quality controller, especially since Mrs. Marika, as we already knew, didn't work at all. At first glance, everything seemed to confirm the husband's words, because we didn't find anything that could be associated with the presence of the child. There were men's and women's clothing in the wardrobes, and the kitchen utensils were also suitable for adults. There were no toys, pacifiers or baby food anywhere, everything was shiny clean.

"That's the thing. It's just too clean here," Kelley muttered, looking around diligently. He took samples from everywhere and carefully examined everything.

"Maybe they're just neat?"

"Come on, Leeta, the woman was clearly not mentally well. People like her aren't very orderly. Search the pockets of their clothes."

I silently agreed with him. He, of course, knew what he was talking about, and this museum-like cleanliness seemed suspicious to me. As if nobody lived here at all. Was someone this thorough in cleaning?

No, not thorough enough. From the pocket of a jacket hanging in the closet, I took out a missed holographic photograph. It depicted a small boy with blond hair, slanting eyes and a thoughtless smile, wearing a blue and white T-shirt.

"So there was a child."

The phone in Scott's pocket rang. He took it out, said "Cavanaugh" and listened for a while. Then he turned it off and turned to the doctor:

"Kell, finish here. I'll take Leeta and go to the sewage filtering plant."

"What for?" the doctor was surprised, taking samples from the couch in the living room.

"Ostronos called. My contact is at Lunwark. His colleague signaled that something strange had been found at the sewage plant."

"I have something strange here, too," McCave said, tilting one of the cushions on the couch. He showed us a piece of pink plastic, or rather rubber. He took it carefully with tweezers and placed it in a plastic bag.

"What is it?" I asked.

"A bitten off piece of an object," he replied, examining the find through the foil, "bitten off with very small incisors..."

Scott grinned sarcastically. He was opening some file that was sent to his phone and seemed to be very absorbed in it.

"This is getting interesting," he said. "This friend of Ostronos is currently a vagabond. He's living with other derailed people near the sewage treatment plant since it's warm there. They make money from time to time by cleaning sludge filters that are difficult to reach. In one of them they found scraps of cotton wool, a rather large ball."

Kelley straightened up.

"Go there now," he demanded, "bring me whatever you can find. I can handle it here. When I'm finished, I'll get Mrs. Yovovitz out of the hospital. We'll need her."

"Of course," Scott said, as if he were a subordinate and our doctor was the inspector.

A few minutes later, we were sitting in an armored all-terrain vehicle and raced at maximum speed to Lunvark, the industrial area of Lunnar, where the treatment plant was located. Constable Yamato sat at the steering, the two of us in the back seat.

"Is it so strange that they found wool in one of the filter's tanks?" I asked. "Maybe someone dropped a rag into the cleaning system or something?"

"Unlikely. This friend of Ostronos used to be a tailor before he got too into drinking, and he claims that it's natural cotton, not some synthetic, and you won't find such products in Lunwark. Clothes, cleaning products, they're all artificially made, not only because of the cost. They are simply more durable and safer to use."

I thought about this 'friend' and others like him. How desperate does one have to be to live in a factory area, sewer, or any other place like that? How can you even live there? Disgusting air, trouble getting clean water, food, or anything you need to live, and that cold. If the temperature at the sewage treatment plant was higher, then it's not surprising that it's where the homeless people resided. In Lunwark, thermostats were set to a minimum, there was no need to heat the streets – and what kind of streets are they anyway? There were practically none, only factories, processing plants, warehouses and the space between them, barely sanded lunar soil. No comparison to the smooth, friendly asphalt of the streets of Lunnar, on which the same material was poured as on the streets of earthly cities. Or maybe even better? I'll have to ask Chris.

"How do they live there?" I asked.

"Who?" Scott looked ripped out of his sleep.

"Well, those illegals. I mean, homeless people."

Scotty laughed.

"Illegals... girl, your vocabulary gives you away at every turn."

"What do you mean?" I frowned, trying to understand what she was talking about.

"A wealthy lady from a nice house who reluctantly wrinkles her prominent nose when she sees a sweaty worker."

"Give me a break. We weren't rich at all. I admit that Cynthia raised us carefully, refrained from ugly words and instilled elegant demeanor. She also taught not to despise anyone. I would definitely not wrinkle my nose at someone who sweats for a living."

He hugged me as much as the straps would allow.

"I know, you're a sweetheart. Now put on your mask, we'll be on the surface soon."

He handed me a plastic cap that goes over the nose and mouth. Given the design of the heavy rover, such caution was not necessary, but on the Moon it was always necessary to act as if we were in danger of the hull opening. In reality, it would probably need to be hit by a meteor. The T-4 rover used for such missions was designed as a miniature spacecraft. Covered in thick armor, it had tiny sights made of 'metal glass', an artificial form of aluminum. In addition, it was equipped with its own air circulation, food and water supply, and even... a toilet. Although using this smartly installed device in others' company wouldn't be very convenient, but what about when you absolutely have to?

I dutifully put on the oxygen mask. I didn't like driving in open areas. Usually, due to the reduced gravity, my belly bounced around like a ball, and the floating regolith, or moon dust, bounced off the wheels of the carriage, blocking my view. From time to time it faded enough so that I could make out the outlines of craters, the enormous steepness of the lunar mountains and the black sky above them. Spare wipers were installed only on the driver's side, who needed to know where he was going, passengers saw only clouds of gray-gray dust.

Only after entering the tunnel, which was the highway to the city, did everything calm down. Relieved, I took off my mask and put it on a shelf under the ceiling. I peered into the scope. The tunnel was decorated with the same advertisements found everywhere on the lunar trails. We were not alone. Factory transporters drove past us, drove teams to factories and took home previous shifts, supply trucks, sometimes a taxi passed by, probably called by someone from the college.

We soon found ourselves in the Lunwark area. Yamato, obeying the orders of his boss, turned the vehicle to the side. We drove to the furthest part of Lanvark, where the sewage treatment plant was located. Looking through the peep sight, I saw an indescribably gloomy, dimly lit place, the structures of which resembled the insides of an antediluvian creature. Very thick intertwined pipes ran for miles under the dark dome. Someone could get a panic attack at the mere sight of it if they didn't experience a thing like we did at the 'haunted station'.

The rover stopped in a corner which was almost pitch black dark. Scott ordered the outside lamps to be turned on, which formed a circle of light around us, and opened the swing door of the car. We got out, looking around suspiciously. It was terribly cold outside, the air smelled of chemicals and sewage, the even roar of separators and purifiers penetrated our ears. I could not understand how anyone could live in such a terrible place. Though it seems that they really could, because after a while something moved and a human figure entered the circle of light. Scott told me to stay and walked over to the person himself.

"Do you have it?" he asked.

The man nodded. I looked with surprise and pity. The man, wrapped in old and damaged clothes, was incredibly dirty, stooped, reminiscent of a homeless man from old illustrations. Behind him in the darkness hid shapeless shadows, where light could not enter – probably companions of his gloomy life. Without knowing it, I tightened my grip on my service weapon and looked around slightly. I wouldn't be surprised if someone suddenly tried to get a jump on me. This place literally smelled of vice.

Ostronos handed Scott a small parcel. I was surprised by the fact he did so while clearly being observed by his marginal colleagues – was he not afraid of them?

"Are you alone?" I asked out loud and Scott looked at me.

"Calm down," he said reproachfully. "This here is a special case. These people know that it's about a missing child. And they voluntarily agreed on a quiet cooperation."

"Which means?"

"It means that you saw nothing and heard nothing, and neither did I. We'll talk later," he turned back to the man. "Sorry, she's still green."

He lowered his voice again. He spoke to the agent some more, then returned to the rover.

"Get in," he ordered. "Yamato, to the factory."

I was still confused.

"Do these homeless people know Ostronos is an agent?"

Scott studied the package he received and didn't even look at me.

"Probably not. For them, he is a police officer who has lost his job due to alcohol abuse. They accept it as his casual contact with an ex-partner who helps him financially because they are not actually declared criminals. They've simply had misfortunes in their lives. I'd say police protects them more than purses them, because what would we need to arrest them for? For the loss of everything they had? Absurd."

"Weird deal," I muttered.

"Convenient for us. We have an observer in a place where there is a possibility of a crime... and who knows if this has happened. Coati knows how to talk to them. If he hadn't told them all at once, but had sniffed it himself, his friend would not have noticed what he found in the tank. He would simply throw into the trash bin for incineration and forget about everything."

"Do you think this is a really important trail?"

"Look at it yourself."

He opened the package. Inside, I saw a bunch of dirt and wet rags, of which the original color could be distinguished – white and blue. In my opinion, it could really be cotton, soft and delicate... one from which children's clothes are sewn. My throat was dry.

"Scotty..."

"I know. But let's not make any assumptions."

The rover drove up to the processing plant, where a T-2 with Dr. McCave, Ms. Yovovitz and Constable Maru was waiting for us. Kelley was pulling a square bag with lab marks out of the trunk. He looked in our direction as Scott lifted his find. The doctor nodded, then removed a portable DNA test kit from his bag. It couldn't be used to tell who it belonged to, but it could flawlessly distinguish between human and animal code.

I stood at the rover, holding my breath. I was afraid come closer, not wanting to see Marika Yovovitz huddled inside, who was not allowed to leave. She didn't know what Kelley was doing, although she could see him through the glass. To be honest, I didn't know either, I don't know much about such work. I just watched as Cavanaugh passed new samples to the doctor and inserted them into the blinking chamber. It seemed like a long time before Scott gave me a wave.

I walked over, forcing myself to take each step.

"There's no doubt," said Kelley. "These are not traces, but an accumulation of human tissue mixed with scraps of clothing. In my opinion, everything is clear."

"Let's wait to see what Mr. Nicolae has to say," Scott turned. "Yamato, Maru, to me!"

The officers got out of the cars and ran to their boss.

"Go to the factory and bring Nicolae Yovovitz here. If possible, don't tell anyone about the reasons for his detention. Better not call it that at all. Make the guy think he just needs to sign the evidence.

I was silent. This was one of those moments when Scott showed me how I should be working, and I just had to be a diligent observer. It was better that way. I was not yet ready to deal with such cases, mainly because I didn't know how to completely control my emotions. Feri Kunch recently told me:

"A police detective must be not only be a cop, but also an experienced psychologist and a skilled actor. If you're unable to control your expressions and tone of voice, you will get very little."

I still couldn't do it. I took lessons in shooting and hand-to-hand combat, Slavik lectured me on law, I could understand the mind of a criminal, but nevertheless I was still a newcomer to the police profession.

The police brought Nicolae about ten minutes later.

"You could have waited another hour," the man said reproachfully. "I would have finished my shift. Where should I sign?"

"Nowhere," Scott said coldly. "We brought you here for a completely different reason."

Nikolay's eyes darted blankly from one of us to the other. When I looked at him like that, I couldn't believe that this was really happening. He looked completely ordinary, innocent and harmless. All the time I hoped that he would say something that would relieve him of all suspicions. I really wanted that. He had such a clear look.

"What's happening?" he stuttered in horror.

"The torn remains of cotton cloth were found in the sewage sedimentation tank," Scott's voice sounded calm and cool, as if he were reading a newspaper. "It was white and blue. According to your wife's testimony, these were the colors of your son's clothes."

"I already told you that Marika is unstable..."

"Don't interrupt me. I admit, I doubted that this child even existed. I was willing to believe your wife invented it, but there were some signs to the contrary. Moreover, the tank did not only store cotton. Besides it, we found a lot of human tissue. Of course, we will check the DNA compatibility, but even now I have no doubts. Will you testify here or at the prosecutor's office?"

Nicolae was silent. Then he sat down on a crate dumped by the driveway and covered his face with his hands. He began to cry.

"You don't understand," he blurted out. "I love Marika. I always have. I wanted this child because she couldn't live without it. That's all she talked about, she didn't want to hear about an abortion. When started saying that she would kill herself if they didn't allow her to give birth to Brian, I decided that we should run away to the Moon. It seemed like a good idea, I was hoping that over time, Marika will understand her mistake. When the child was born, I waited day after day for her to say that she could no longer take it. But it got worse. Only Brian mattered, she devoted all her time to him, thought only of him. I only existed as a source of livelihood. I couldn't bear it."

"What did you do?"

Nicolae looked up. Kelley handed him a handkerchief.

"Tyrone Parker, the doctor who delivered Marika's child, gave me an injection and told me how to do it. I thought that if Brian was gone, I could convince my wife that everything was just a delusion, and then everything will be as it was before she got pregnant. Parker gave me several psychotropic drugs that I was supposed to discreetly add to her food. After that, she would have hallucinations and memory disorders."

"Who is this doctor?"

"He lives in the suburbs. He was forbidden from practicing his profession on Earth, but here he works as a medical assistant in a hospital."

"And he provides secret services," Scott could not help but sarcastically comment. "Please continue."

"I did it and then... I threw him in the sewage system. I knew that the grinder would grind up everything, I couldn't predict that the tank would clog..."

We all looked at Mr. Yovovitz. We didn't notice that Marika managed to open the door of the rover in which Kendra Maru locked her, and that she heard everything we talked about...

At first we heard a howl, and after a split second she flashed past us and clawed her fingers into her husband.

"Nasty case," Neil said.

We were all sitting at the reception room, drinking the cheap tequila that Kunch brought. We were in a terrible mood. Nicolae Yovovitz was in custody, we had to take his wife to a psychiatric hospital, this time for real. The doctors described her condition as very bad. The child we were looking for was dead, but the case was not over yet.

"What sentence will Yovovitz face?" Scott asked as he poured himself some tequila.

Dr. McCave handed him an empty glass. I didn't refuse one either. I hated this drink, but that day I would even drink paint thinner just to forget about it for a moment.

Slavik shrugged his shoulders and loosened his tie. His face was red and glistening with sweat. Like the rest of us, he drank too much, but he wasn't going to stop.

"I have no idea," he admitted. "I've never seen such a convoluted case in my entire life. In terms of the criminal code, Brian Yovovitz never existed, he had no right to be born, and it's hard to judge someone for killing a non-existent person. If the prosecution wanted to prosecute someone, it would be Ms. Yovovitz, not him, because she was the one who committed the crime. Through incomprehensible perseverance, she gave birth to a disabled child."

"Are you sure the child was handicapped?" I asked for no reason.

"Definitely," Kelley replied grimly. "I conducted a thorough analysis of the DNA obtained from the biomass found in the sedimentation tank. It had been crushed by the treatment plant centrifuges, it was a mixture of muscle, bone, pulmonary and brain tissue..."

"Please, Kell."

"...but from a laboratory point of view, it doesn't matter. I was only interested in pure DNA, and it was easy to get the results I needed."

I had a drink. I've come to the point where I started to taste the disgusting alcohol. And I wasn't going to stop there.

"What if we had found the child alive?" I asked.

"Well, I don't know?" he grunted. "I think they would decide for silent euthanasia rather than keeping him alive."

"Why 'silent'?"

"That's how you call situations where a decision is made without an official commission and without filling out papers. Sometimes it's easier and better that way. Though maybe they would put the child in a mental health center. We won't know anymore."

I thought that I wouldn't want to be a doctor in my entire life. And now I understood why Kelley couldn't be a 'doctor of the living'.

"Then why are we keeping Yovovitz in custody?" I turned to Scott. He grimaced dismissively.

"It's the only punishment we can give him. We are waiting for the prosecutor's decision, but we already know what it will be, since even Slavik hasn't found a starting point for formulating a motion for pre-trial detention and prosecution."

"Let's get drunk," I offered grimly.

"I think that's what we're doing."

I rested my head on his shoulder and closed my eyes. I didn't want to think, I didn't want to remember. But deep in my brain was still the image of a slanted four-year-old with a mindlessly smiling face. He was wearing white and blue clothes...

VII

That day I returned from the headquarters completely exhausted. I checked clues in the Brel's case again, which seemed like it was burying itself underground, but once again I convinced myself that it won't lead to anything. It's as if Brel had disappeared along with Johnson, who was deported to Earth, and of whom he was a faithful copy. And he couldn't have disappeared, since it was he (I was completely sure) who tried to kill me and Scott on Colchis. Now that I think about it, how did he learn where we were? Was it Citizen Hakat who tried to eliminate us?

"No, he simply wouldn't let us off Strogoff and set up an accident there," Cavanaugh said flatly when I confessed my doubts. "It would be pointless to send us on vacation for that purpose. It makes no sense and is too expensive. Either way, I don't think that Brel is working for him."

We still had no indication as to what exactly Johnson's copy was made for and what the person born from the forbidden experiment intended to do next. Several premises indicated that he had contacts with Lunnar's underworld and may have been hiding among the local scum, but there was no evidence to support this theory. Agents like Ostronos were not able to track him down, and the 'electronic spies' were also useless. One thing seemed obvious: Brel did not leave the moon. At the very least, the records of the points of contact do not indicate this. So how did he get to 'Colchis'?

All this annoyed and worried me at the same time. We didn't know what the intentions of our wanted person were and what he was striving for. Apart from reinforcing patrols, there was nothing we could do but scrupulously check all the information coming to the central computer, hoping to find any clue at all. And that's what I've been doing for the last eighteen hours – without much success.

I felt tired, depressed and useless to the world. The only thing I wanted right now was to take a shower and go to bed, but apparently, I wasn't going to get that.

"I have a message for you," Monty informed me as soon as I stepped in the doorway. "Sven Thorvald called."

I was worried in earnest. I almost forgot about the owner of the collection point and hoped that he forgot about me as well. Although everything was done in accordance with regulations, I still feared that someone would violate my right to the android.

"What did he want?"

"He did not say. He only said that you should come to him."

"When am I supposed to do that?"

"As soon as possible."

Resigned, I took out a stimulator in a disposable ampoule from the first aid kit, inserted it into a vacuum syringe and pressed the outlet to my hand. There was a hissing sound, the skin tingled slightly, as it is with injections, and after a while my fatigue disappeared without a trace. I rarely made use of such things, but at times they were irreplaceable.

I looked into Susan's room. Although she was now working for the police, she rarely used the headquarters' computer, preferring to carry out all operations on her personal one.

"I'm going to the junkyard," I told her.

She nodded selflessly, her eyes fixed on the screen. I bet that she didn't even acknowledge what I said. This was always the case when she was immersed in work.

On reflection, I decided to take Monty with me. The fact is that someone could very well attack me on such a trip, although I doubt it would be Thorvald, of course. Over time, I started to see the android as my protector, a potential bodyguard. He was very strong, almost as an anthrobot. Due to the materials used in his construction, he would be difficult to destroy. And most importantly, he was very devoted to me. He tried to intervene several times when he thought I was in danger, and I was almost certain that if I asked, he would fight by my side.

Sven Thorvald had a factory in a remote suburb, far from residential and industrial areas. It was not safe there. For this reason, I took a police bag with me and left a message on the information board where I was going. I also asked the dispatcher to borrow a police car and that's where I stopped.

I didn't know how to drive a rover. After all, such skills would have no meaning on Earth since there was central control of the machines. However, this was not the case on the Moon. I still didn't know why the construction of a central control was neglected, for some reason it did not even occur to me to ask about it. Either way, it didn't matter now. I needed a driver.

Slavik was no longer here. During the day, he was usually replaced by one of the senior constables. This time, Kendra Maru, a friend of Dr. McCave's and a good friend of mine, was on duty at the table. I liked her, and sometimes, when we were both on vacation, we would meet for a girl's conversation. In my opinion, she was too smart for the C1 class, the symbol of which she wore on her forehead, and maybe that's why I felt so good in her company. She had one flaw: she was a terrible formalist. And now I had to ask her for help, not even knowing how to explain this sudden departure.

"Kendra, I need a driver," I said shortly, standing in front of the duty table.

"Do you have a vehicle?" she asked dryly, putting off the reader with an open book.

"Yes, Lenny Halter already signed me for the equipment loan."

Maru got up from her desk and pressed the intercom button.

"Darren, get up and come to the office," she said into the microphone. "You'll replace me for a few hours."

There was a yawn and a mutter over the loudspeaker, and then a disheveled Darren Moss, constable of the Fifth Patrol, came out of the break room.

"You just had to do that, huh?"

"Don't complain. You can sleep at the desk just as well, the night seems like it's going to be quiet. We only get paid in a week, and miners have nothing to fuss about," Maru patted her colleague on the back and turned to me, "So, where do you want to go?"

"I'll tell you on the way. I don't want to lie to you. I don't know if it's a business or personal matter. I'll find out everything only when we get there. Oh, and Monty is coming with us."

Kendra froze for a moment. The police usually treated the android like a mechanical dog – some people make preferred such toys over of live pets, which are very expensive, with high maintenance cost, and are generally troublesome. Mechanodogs behave almost like animals. It runs up to the person, barks, curls up on the rug, comes when called, wags its tail, jumps and so on. But it doesn't get dirty, doesn't lose fur, doesn't need to eat and doesn't get sick. To my colleagues, Monty seemed like a different type of such a mechanodog. Only Kendra was clearly afraid of him. She tried not to show it, but I saw fear in her deer-like eyes whenever she approached my companion.

"Why are you taking him?" she asked with reproach in her voice.

"I have to. Security could come in handy, especially where we're going."

"Sounds serious. I'll take the gun just in case."

I also preferred to take my service pistol. Sven Thorvald didn't seem threatening to me, but I didn't know if we would be robbed on the way. Even the police could be in danger in remote suburbs. The lunar underworld often hosts meetings that are not watched by law enforcement or mining company security personnel. That's the kind of place the enclosed hall in which Thorvald set up his dump was.

Last time, I was there with Sue and a hired anthrobot, Kendra and Monty accompanied me. Alone, without bodyguards, I would never have dared to go to such a place.

As it turned out, Constable Maru knew Lunnar's street network better than Sue. It was enough that I gave her the name of the hall, and she immediately recognized everything.

"Ah yes, old Thorvald. We know him. He settled in that place ten years ago, I remember it like it was yesterday. The city rented him a closed hall, which no one else wanted to use. He decided to focus on buying electronic scrap from private, small suppliers, for example, a broken razor, a broken external disk, a home combo programmer... Large factories don't accept such bulk cargo, it's not profitable. Thorvald insisted that he'll make a business on that. It was hard to believe that he would succeed, but he did it.

She rode quickly, confidently and accurately, as if she knew the map by heart.

"Did he have any problems with the law?"

"No. If he even buys anything stolen or assembles some illegal electronics, he hasn't been caught yet. What impression did he make on you?"

I thought about it.

"I'm not sure? He seems repulsive at first glance, but he's likeable."

She nodded, not taking her eyes off the road.

"He was once a famous designer. I don't know why he came to Lunnar and buys scraps, because the police don't care. We don't interfere with people's privacy as long as they don't break the law. I remembered Thorvald because I wrote down his details when the company was founded, and I also brought him some knickknacks myself."

I looked at her hair, braided in dozens of braids, and at her smooth chocolate-like face with a wide mouth. How old could she have been? Anti-aging pills usually prevent wrinkles and slow cell aging, but you can guess when someone is not twenty, but forty-five, for example, by looking at the ears, temples and the perimeter of the face. This becomes even more apparent later in life, especially to the trained eye. With Maru, I couldn't see even the slightest blurring of the contours of the jaw or the sinking of the skin under the chin. The veins in the temples were not pronounced, the earlobes seemed firm and smooth, but according to her, she has been working at the police station for ten years.

I felt like I owe her some explanations.

"He called me and said that I should come. I don't know what he meant, he didn't want to say through the connection, perhaps he was afraid of someone eavesdropping. I hope this isn't some kind of ambush."

"We'll see. It's possible, though I doubt it. Even if Sven Thorvald does some illegal business, it must be in a small amount. I can't imagine him in the role of an attacker."

"Kendra," I ventured, "why didn't you try being a detective?"

She snorted like Sid when a feather tickled his nose.

"Who told you that I didn't?"

"Sorry," I muttered, detonated.

"No need to apologize. I'll tell you why I failed someday, now is not the time for such confessions. We're heading for an action, after all."

She smiled at me with a hint of mischievous mockery at the corners of her protruding, friendly lips. I used to wonder what the hell did our pathologist sees in hanging out with a woman with a C1 on her forehead – she wasn't even pretty. She had a flat nose with protruding flares, typical of the African physiognomy, a jugular upper lip and a slightly curved lower lip, and round, kind eyes. Gradually, I discovered that she was a great girl, and stopped being surprised, but began to strive for her friendship.

The enormous hall was exactly as I remembered it, gloomy and littered. Maru parked in almost the same spot as Sue did before. It was the only spot clean enough to do so. As far as I can tell, Thorvald set up his little kingdom like this on purpose. It was he who dictated where one can park, which way to go and even what to look at. He assembled the lighting himself, along with the additional air filters, and possibly an alarm system. I didn't see it, but something told me that it was hidden somewhere very well, and Thorvald found out about anyone even before they got out of their vehicle. I wondered if he additionally armed this place with remote-controlled guns or mines. I would've done so if I was in his place.

"Monty, you stay in the rover," I said, handing the communicator over to the android. "If anyone shows up, let us know."

Maru grimaced skeptically.

"Do you really think that such a sentry will be helpful to us?"

"You underestimate him."

"And you overestimate him. In any case, it's your business. Let there be an oversized doll on the watch. I won't let you go by yourself either way."

She checked the service weapon and I did the same. We walked into the office decorated with a 'RETAIL ELECTRIC SCRAP PURCHASE' sign, stumbling across various trash along the way. If it was me, I would never want to live in such a terrible environment, and I secretly wondered how anyone could even tolerate it here.

Light fell through the slightly ajar office door. When I called for the owner of the shop, it opened full width, inviting us inside. The small room was just as messy as when I first visited Thorvald, and he was sitting behind his desk, swaying in the chair like a student tired of his lessons. Each time he moved, the furniture bent so strongly on its hind legs that it threatened to topple over. My first impulse was to warn the engineer that he might get hurt, but I held myself back. After all, he was an adult and knew what he was doing.

"I'm here," I said.

"I see that," he grumbled and pointed his thumb at Constable Mara. "Why is she here?"

"You can talk in her presence. Unless you have a dirty conscience."

He shrugged his broad shoulders.

"It doesn't bother me that much, but someone is here waiting for you, and only you."

"A man?"

"A woman. She's alone and scared, you don't need an armed bodyguard."

Kendra found a three-legged stool in the mess of the office and sat down, crossing her leg on top of the other.

"I'll wait here," she suggested, "and you go talk to your secret guest."

"She's waiting in the back," Thorvald pointed to the plastic sheeting separating the office from the other rooms.

I hesitantly approached, opened the curtain and found myself in a rather cozy apartment. It was as cluttered as the office, but still cozy. There was a thick foam mat on the floor, a TV screen covered one of the walls. The furniture was solid and even beautiful, albeit unsuccessfully chosen in style and color. A wardrobe, a bookcase for various knick-knacks, a sofa, several armchairs, paintings by famous artists on free walls, an unknown keyboard instrument in the corner. Could Thorvald have a love for art, and played some instrument?

It took me a while to notice a small, curled up figure next to the sofa. It was only when she jumped off the carpet crying, throwing herself into my arms, did I recognize that it was Mabel, which left me speechless. I have never seen her like this. Even when she was a young girl, she carefully monitored her appearance, always having clean clothes and not pulling her carefully combed hair. As a floress, she bloomed like the most beautiful flower. She was always cheerful, courageous and full of energy. And now I was embracing her, a trembling, frightened creature in tatters, disheveled and dirty to the point of fear.

"Calm down," I finally shook her. "What happened? Why do you look like this? How did you even get here?"

Mabel sobbed for another moment, then took a deep breath and sat down in one of the chairs. They were dusty, but it didn't even matter as my friend was already dirty like a miner.

"I ran away... I ran away from Hakat," she confessed desperately.

A cold shiver ran through me. Ran away? Why? How? I sat down next to her.

"Tell me everything."

She shook her head.

"I can't tell you everything. It's too scary and too secret. I could no longer endure what I witnessed, let alone what I learned in secret. One day, Hakat went for a checkup and left me by myself since I pretended to be sick. In his absence, I forged the order to leave and lied to one of the pilots. He brought me to the mainland and left me. I cut my hair, dressed up as a miner and joined the transport."

"Oh my God!" I blurted out.

This spoiled, used to luxury girl, amongst ordinary workers of the lower class!

"At night, when everyone was asleep, I wanted to get through the high-speed tunnels to Lunnar."

I groaned again. Didn't she understand how far the road went and what the conditions were in the tunnels? Mabel looked at me apologetically.

"I was desperate. I thought someone would give me a lift..."

"You don't get lifts here."

"Yes, I know that now, but I got lucky. I was walking along the side of the road when a supply car pulled up. The driver stopped, surprised at my sight. I told him that my co-workers pranked me to 'welcome the newbie' and asked him to give me a lift to the collection point of Sven Thorvald. I remembered that you bought your android from him, the driver agreed, and that's how I reached the suburbs."

"Why not directly to me?"

"I was scared! I mean, when Hakat starts looking for me, he will definitely think of you, and Sue is his niece. She won't cover for me."

I had to admit she was right. I trusted Sue, but not that much. In a situation where she had to choose between loyalty to me or her uncle, she would be unlikely to choose me. Even less likely Mabel, whom she hardly knew. I looked at the crumb of misfortune that the dazzling floress turned into. What could she have found that scared her so much and made her go on a crazy expedition? I tried to think clearly and accurately, but everything I came up with was not even worth the proverbial pound.

I decided to focus on the current issue, and that was Mabel, and more concretely, her safety. Citizen Hakat didn't seem to be been a man willing to forgive such defiance, and then there was another matter. What could Mabel know? What secret information did she obtain? And what now? I was overwhelmed with the urge to call my boss, but after a little thought, I decided it would be better to speak to him in person.

"You have to stay here," I said firmly. "At least for now. Nobody can know who you really are. From now on your name is... let's say

Tanita Mae Norris. I'll talk to Thorvald right away. I'll tell him that you are an important witness who needs to be hidden from the Mining Company until the investigation is complete. I know that this isn't the company you'd want and that this place doesn't look like a fancy hotel..."

"I don't care!" she interrupted me abruptly. "As long as I'm away from Hakat, I could be living in a trash can and eating the cheapest canned substitute."

She wiped her face with her hand, smearing dust on her cheek.

I looked at her with deep pity.

"Don't worry, I'll think of something. Take it easy for now. I'll go to the engineer, I need to talk to him."

She nodded. Her hair, greasy at the ear level, gave her a miserable look, like a wet dog, her dusty face only had the same eyes as before, but now she had an expression of fear and helplessness. I thought about how I hated Citizen Hakat for what he did to this beautiful, always happy being, but I said nothing more. I kissed Mabel and returned to the office, where Thorvald and Mara were talking quietly.

They fell silent when they saw me.

"And?" Kendra asked, getting up from her chair.

I forgot about her! I didn't know how much I could trust this girl in such a delicate matter. At this point, I chose not to initiate her.

"Could you leave us alone?"

She raised her thin, arched eyebrows, and her eyes hardened. She looked at Thorvald, then at me, then turned and walked away without a word. I turned to the engineer.

"I have a favor to ask you."

"I'm listening."

"This girl is a very important witness in the ongoing investigation against the Mining Company," I began. "She must be hidden until we find her a safe place. Could you take her in for a little bit?"

Sven Thorvald grimaced mockingly.

"Don't take me for an idiot, okay?"

"What do you mean?"

"You know what I mean. I've been alive long enough to know more about police work than I would have liked. This pitiful creature could be anything and anyone, except a witness in a mining investigation. It doesn't matter anyway. Do you want her to stay here?"

"If possible. Your apartment is pretty small..."

He shrugged.

"That's not a problem. This part of the factory was an administrative office. I just need to open one of the other door and I'll be able to arrange it into an extra room. The question is, what do I get from this? I am only allocated food points for one person, and you know as well as I do that you cannot transfer points from an industrial card to a food card."

"I know," I thought about it too. "We can't pay you from the company funds. And I can't visit you just like that without a reason. Someone might get suspicious. We have to think of something else."

He nodded and swung in his chair.

"Do you still have that android?"

"Monty? Of course."

"Well, we have a starting point. We'll prepare an annex to the contract, according to which you will pay me for the maintenance and repair of the robot's servomotors. Yes, I know I am not familiar with this model," he raised his tattooed arm to silence me. "This way, no one will be surprised that you're sending me payments. Each of them should be named Service Subscription. I have a license to repair electronic devices not intended for industrial use, it won't surprise anyone."

He took a piece of computer foil from a drawer and began writing. When he finished, he inserted the foil into a 'cooker', a professional device that solidifies records using a combination of heat and ultrasonic waves. This simple procedure prevents clearing the foil and overwriting it with new text, so it is only used when documenting contracts. He marked the still warm foil with a hand-held hologram generator, and then asked me to sign it. I read the text. It was a simple service contract, with no complicated sub-clauses or small print often pre-pasted on foil sheets designed for this purpose. Sven Thorvald was honest in his own way – he didn't try to cheat his clients.

Constable Maru was waiting for me at the rover, leaning against it. She preferred to stand outside in the filth and cold than stepping inside the vehicle, inside which the android was sitting, without any 'back up'. There was indignation throughout her, and I felt embarrassed.

"I'm sorry, Kendra," I said as warmly as I could as I walked over to her. "It's a nasty matter and I didn't want to involve you in it yet. I need to talk to Scotty before I tell you anything else."

"Yeah, yeah," she snapped. "I have been in this profession for a long time, but I will say one thing: if the police don't trust each other, our effectiveness will be damned. If you haven't yet figured out what solidarity in uniform is, then your training might be a waste of time."

She flung open the hatch and got into the driver's seat. I sat in the back seat next to Monty and activated the mechanism sealing the inside of the rover.

"Don't be mad. I promise I'll tell you everything, I just need to talk it over with Scott first."

She didn't answer.

It was only when the rover turned onto the motorway that she said:

"Your secrets are your secrets, but you should know that in this work, private matters are very easily turned into professional business. The woman you spoke to is clearly hiding from the world since she didn't even come to the office. Do you want to help her? Fine, but be careful not to harm the inspector and the rest of us."

So that's it...

"I swear she... Tanita... didn't commit any crimes," I assured her. "She fell victim to coincidence, nothing more."

She nodded in apparent disbelief. Well, as Sylvanas said, the role of a cop is not to trust anyone, even with a one hundred percent alibi.

"Such coincidences can kill. Be careful."

Oh, Kendra, if you knew how much this particular one could kill... I wanted to confide in the constable, only I would have to tell her too much then. Far too much. Scott was the only one I could talk to about Mabel and ask him for help.

Kendra slowed down so abruptly that I felt sick.

"What happened?"

"Traffic jam," she pointed to the image in the front viewfinder. From the inside, it looked like glass, but in reality it was a screen connected to an array of cameras. "Something must have happened on the road. Possible dome collapse or major collision."

"So what now?" the crowd of cars blocking our path didn't make me feel very optimistic.

Maru pressed a button of the CB radio. They were playing the song of the band Councellor. When it quieted down, we heard the voice of the announcer:

"Attention, drivers. On the B17 motorway, there has been a crack in the ground, causing a sewage discharge. Please be patient. The traffic will be restored as soon as possible."

I looked at my friend.

"Well," she muttered. "Maybe we'll turn back and use the outer tunnel. Better to go around, even if it's far, than to stand in a traffic jam."

I thought so too. Kendra had more experience than me and knew the realities of Lunar life better, this time, however, we were both wrong. This road was also jammed – we forgot that it connects to the main route, so what happened on it affected the underground road to Lunwark.

"We've got no choice. We'll use one of the backup routes," Maru decided. "In truth, I shouldn't be doing that without my supervisor's consent, but in such a crowd of vehicles, too many people may be tapped."

She shrugged.

"What are these 'backup routes'?" I asked.

"Unofficial pursuit routes. Technical tunnels. They were left over from the construction of expressways in lava tunnels, and the city has adapted them as additional infrastructure. Few people know about them. They can be very useful, but you need to know the code key to use them. If I remember correctly, V9 should be the closest."

She stopped the car on the side of the road, turned it around and drove towards Lunwark for a while, passing the overcrowded cars. Then she turned to one of the dead ends, in which there are usually exits for ventilation and treatment facilities, but this one was empty and turned at right angles, quickly hiding us from casual observers. Its end was a wall that opened after the rover emitted a modulated signal, and then closed behind us.

"It's a rarely used traffic route, but I've been here before," Kendra said. "The entrances to the other ones are much further, but that's okay. They all have the same markings, so I definitely won't be mistaken."

She turned on the headlights of the rover. The technical tunnel was not illuminated, only gloomy, 'eternal' emergency blinked inside of it, barely giving any illumination. Their lead casing contained a battery similar to my android's chest that powered an LED light bulb. In their light, only the outlines of the walls were visible. The headlights of the rover literally tore apart the dense darkness, thanks to which visibility improved significantly, at least around us. Through the side view glass, I could see rough walls, fragments of scaffolding, and even abandoned tools here and there. The tunnel curved, probably avoiding depressions, which were not rare on the Moon, and at times other corridors would branch out from it, and I could not figure out how the constable knew which way to turn. I thought that if we got stuck in here it would likely take a long time before someone finds us – and that was an unpleasant thought.

"Are you sure you know what you're doing?" I asked.

"Trust me at least a little bit," Kendra turned again. "I'll bring you home safely like your mommy. I don't even need the navigation. Besides, it doesn't work in here."

"Why?" my voice sounded a little louder than I intended.

"Because of the high content of lead salts in concrete and brass in the reinforcement. They work like a Faraday cage."

"Have mercy..."

Maru laughed.

"Fine, fine, I'll stop being a smart-ass. Constructions like these suppress radio waves and all other waves used in telecommunications. I read about this in the building documentation. This was done specifically by order of the Earth headquarters. I have no idea why this was necessary, because according to the original plan, the auxiliary tunnels were to be dismantled immediately after the completion of construction."

I couldn't guess either, although at that moment technical issues were not the most important. I wanted to leave these dark caves as soon as possible. I felt like I was going to suffocate, and the fact that Monty was next to me didn't help.

Suddenly Kendra stopped the vehicle.

"What happened?"

"Hold on. I want to check something."

"What?"

"I don't like this place," she pointed to the bend in the tunnel visible behind the front visor. It didn't look different from any of the other ones to me, but my companion looked at them, her smooth eyebrows furrowed with displeasure.

"Well, what is it?"

"It's too clean. There is a reason why no one picks up the rubbish left over from the construction site and the remains of tools. They're a hint for us. Here, someone pushed everything aside, as if working in the niche which forms the bend. But working on what?"

I couldn't help her solve the mystery. The only thing I could think of was getting back to Lunnar. Kendra ignored my sour face.

"Stay inside. I'll go take a look," she said.

She opened the entrance hatch, jumped out and closed the rover behind her. Through the front visor, I could see her approaching the bend, trampling concrete and other debris along the way. They cracked with an unpleasant rustle under the pressure of her boots. The instrument system in police off-road vehicles made it possible to perfectly soundproof the interior or, conversely, to eavesdrop on everything that was happening outside. Right now the second option was working.

I watched Kendra study the wall, almost pressing her nose against it, and with all my heart I wished that she would finally finish this absurd exploration. Suddenly I saw as she turns towards the rover and I became worried. She had a strange expression on her face, her eyes were big as saucers. She took a few steps to the car and swayed. She opened her mouth as if she was out of breath, then fell to her knees. I rushed to the control panel of the hatch, but was stopped by the sight of Kendra's hand. She held it out in front of her so that her open palm formed a right angle with her forearm. She was clearly trying to keep me from taking a careless step. I hesitated. The air in the tunnel could have been contaminated, that was the only explanation for her sudden collapse. I couldn't risk it. There were masks somewhere in the rover, but which one should I use? What about the suit? It will take too long to put on.

"Monty, go get Kendra!" I called, with relief remembering that I was not alone in the rover. "Bring her here."

I opened the hatch to let him out and turned on the additional air purification system. The android walked to Maru, picked her up without any difficulty and returned. He put the constable in the back seat and I closed the hatch in relief. I waited a little longer for the purifiers to finally filter out the air, and turned them off so that they did not use unnecessary energy.

"Is Ms. Maru sick?" Monty asked.

I noticed that he put Kendra in a 'safe position', on her side, legs tucked in. Where did he learn this?

"I don't know," I said honestly. "She must have felt bad. Come on, girl, don't joke with me…"

I gave Mara a little nudge, foolishly hoping this was a really crude joke. Of course, I was wrong.

"Everything is blue," Kendra muttered, as if in a trance. "Everything... blue..."

I brought my face closer to her and began to study the pupils, barely visible on the dark brown irises. They were wide and did not react to light.

"This is some kind of a drug," I decided. "We have to get out of here and take her to the doctor."

"Can you drive a rover?"

Good question. I only had a few lessons so far, that's why I took Kendra with me. Even the strict Scott wouldn't allow me to drive one, especially the heavy, serviceable T-4. According to Maru, I won't be able to call the team now, so the only reasonable action is to bring the rover to the surface and then establish communication. Gritting my teeth, I walked resolutely to the front seat.

"Look after Kendra, Monty," I instructed. "Don't let her fall or get hurt."

The rover didn't have a typical control panel like autocars did. Instead, there were two gloves connected to the vehicle's systems using sensors. The driver put on one of them – whichever they preferred – and by moving the fingers could influence the speed, direction and all maneuvers. The brake and soft-release pedal was underfoot. In the description, everything looked simple and with no issues, but I already had the opportunity to confirm that you need a lot of skills to effectively operate the rover.

I put the glove on my right hand, mentally repeating the guide's recommendations:

Thumb, start. Pointing your finger, adding gears. Middle, lowering gears. Whole arm, pivot maneuvers. Instant acceleration, fist clenching. Locking wheels, pressing the hand to the top.

In theory, it all sounded very simple, but theory and practice are different. Gritting my teeth, I put the vehicle in first gear and drove forward. In the inner mirror, I saw Monty holding the restless, half-conscious Mara. There was a tunnel in front of me that I didn't know – so how was I to get the rover out of it? It must have been connected to a main road somewhere, but I had no idea how to get there. The construction tunnels had many branches and turns through which I could wander for a long time. Another solution is to the surface, but... how? On some reflection, I decided there is only one option.

I turned on the 'burrower', a remote measuring device, and turned it to the ground. Observing the indicator, I noticed a slight rise of the ground – I wouldn't have noticed it myself, but the 'burrower' easily caught everything. If I reasoned correctly, the path to the surface should have been uphill.

I didn't dare to switch to second gear. The rover trudged mercilessly slowly, but at least I was sure that I would not slam it against the wall, and with my clumsy maneuvers it could very well happen. It seemed like a long time before I found out I was right.

At the next bend, a massive airlock appeared. I searched desperately through the code database until I found the universal key. The airlock was not as secure as the inner passage. It couldn't be. From the outside, the entrance had to be easy to open so that, if necessary, the tunnel could be used as a bunker. This universal law applies to all underground corridors on the Moon, so I had no reason to assume that the working system would be different.

The key matched. I nervously checked the sensors of the seal. I had to make a maneuver, which I was simply afraid of – lead the relatively small vehicle to the Moon's surface and from there connect to the team. And then? What if I fail? My teeth chattered as I tried to control myself. I've never been so alone in a hostile environment. Admittedly, I was not entirely alone. My comrade was still keeping an eye on Constable Maru, but I knew that I would simply need to call him... but for what purpose? How could he help me now? He was as helpless as I was, especially since he didn't have my knowledge and skills acquired during training.

For a moment, I thought of a crazy idea to send him on foot to Lunnar. He didn't need air, he didn't feel the cold or the all-present dust, and he could make such an attempt. However, given the number of threats on the Moon, the likelihood of a lone android reaching his destination intact was close to zero. It wasn't just about the physical effects of vacuum or temperature. The reduced gravity has caused coordination problems not only for surface researchers, but also for walking machines. The dust, carried upwards by a person's movement, fell back to the ground for hours on end. In the absence of an atmosphere, it became impossible to correctly judge the distance between two points, the height of the cliff, and even the direction of the march. The sun was unbearably bright, and the shadow of the moonlit mountain next to the sun was black and thick as pitch. The perfect place to play hide and seek.

From where I was, I could see high hills and cliffs that I knew were deeper than any bay on earth. They had some kind of strict beauty, but were above all frightening. People used to see them as great destination for rock climbing and extreme sports enthusiasts, but when technological progress allowed people to visit such places, any attempt to reach the lunar summits was prohibited. It was too dangerous. No, I'm not sending Monty on foot to Lunnar.

When I reached the surface, the sun was shining only in the distance. It was about to cross to the other side, and soon a moonlit night would fall on the human colony. The beams were still strong enough that I could see a shiny streak in the distance. Somewhere over the horizon was one of the storage farms – a huge plane covered with panels that convert solar energy into electricity. I did not see the dome of Lunnar, it was hiding behind one of the craters.

The area around the gate was a hard hill, an artificial concrete superstructure, so I managed not to move around the layers of dust. I saw it. It lay around like a gray carpet, and if I went down the hill, it would instantly rise upwards. Only that I wasn't planning on going down. I stopped the rover and turned on my communicator. To my immense relief, after a while I heard a signal from the control panel and was able to switch to the police frequency without any problems. Moss's sleepy voice answered my call. I looked at my watch – it was two in the morning.

"Darren, this is Leeta Ankes," I said. "Is the old man at home?"

"Of course," he replied with obvious displeasure, "he snores so hard that I can hear him here."

"Wake him up."

"Are you crazy?! He'll kill me and then throw me out."

"Darren, are you even listening to me? If I'm telling you to wake him up, then do it. Constable Maru and I are in danger. It's very serious."

"What did you get yourselves into?"

"That's not your problem. Get the old man."

"If you say so, but this is all on you. He just went to bed."

The fact that Scott lived in the bedroom behind his office made his job easier and helped us get in touch with him at any time of the day or night. If he hadn't been such a work fanatic, he probably would have lived in one of the police quarters...

Soon I heard Scott's grumpy voice on the phone:

"What happened? Have you mistaken your left leg for your right?"

"No jokes. I am at the entrance to the reserve tunnel... V9. Not from the side of the motorway, but outside. Officer Maru got sick on the way, she can't help me, and I hardly know how to drive a vehicle. I'm hesitating to, especially on the surface."

"Where did you even go?! To Lunwark?!"

"No. Right on the outskirts of the city, but when we were heading back, something happened and we finally had to make a detour. I won't tell you everything now. It's enough to say that I'm stuck in here and don't know what to do."

Scott was silent for a long time, then I heard him give orders. I looked at Maru again, faintly hoping that she had recovered, but was unconscious. Monty was still holding her arms to keep her from falling off the narrow seat, or turning onto her back. The 'secure position' makes breathing easier and prevents things like a sunken tongue or choking on vomit. My only question was, how did the android even know about that? I didn't teach him first aid, but maybe I should have. I have been neglecting him lately, still busy with work and training. I shouldn't have. He needed a guide to a world he didn't understand, not an owner who put him in the corner when not having the time to play.

He turned his glowing eyes on me.

"Can I do anything else to help?" he asked.

He seemed unaware of the situation, either way he was in less danger than me or Maru.

"Watch over Kendra," I said. "I'll take care of the rest. That's enough for now."

The sound of his voice soothed me, made me feel that I was not alone. I wanted to add something hearty, beautiful, but then Scott spoke up:

"Listen to me carefully, Leeta. Since you are on the surface, you yourself must bring the rover to the second airlock.

"What?!"

"Don't shout, just listen. These vehicles are designed in such a way that no one can get inside without endangering the passengers. They are not designed for ground operations, although they can travel quite far. You have to deal with this. I have turned on the locator and can see where you are on the map. I will guide you."

"What do you mean you'll guide me? You mean the vehicle, remotely?"

"No. I'll just be telling you whether you're doing well."

"But I..."

"Calm down! You are to figure this out, and I'll hear no more of that! It's an order, do I make myself clear?"

There was anger and impatience in his voice. I fell silent.

"Now listen," he continued after a moment. "As soon as you descend from the height, the dust will rise. Turn on the blowers."

I fumbled for the switch and turned it on. The blowers were not actually 'blowing' devices, as the name suggests, but simply retractable pipes with a ventilation system. They dispersed dust sideways, creating centrifugal force – as it was written in the instruction manual. Hope they worked as well as written.

"Now engage first gear and drive down."

I did as I was told, the Rover took off and almost immediately drowned in a cloud of regolith. Despite the blowers, I hardly saw the road ahead. In fact, I could only see it sometimes, and I had no idea how the experienced policemen drove rovers in these conditions without support.

"Now put in second gear," Scott said, "and keep going. Okay... okay... now turn directly right. Hurry up, there's a chasm ahead! That's right. Don't slow down, keep going forward... a little to the left... even more. Good. You will soon run into rubble and the rover will start jumping, don't freak out."

Good thing he warned me. The vehicle started throwing so hard that I could hardly keep my arm in the right position. The armrest didn't help much. I had to rest my other hand on the closed hatch to keep my balance. Scott continued to give me instructions over the loudspeaker, helping to avoid terrain traps and stay on the way to the next airlock. It wasn't easy at all, even with his help, and without it, I wouldn't have been able to do it.

I felt lost and terribly lonely, as if there was no one else in the world but me, Monty, and the unconscious, perhaps dying, Kendra. If it weren't for Scott's calm voice coming from the loudspeaker, I would have gotten hysterical.

The way went on – at least for me – a mercilessly long time, but in the end I found myself just in front of the human building rising above the lunar ground. It was another gate. From the outside, it looked like a huge metal plate framed by a stone. After broadcasting the code sequence, the plate twitched, rising to reveal the entrance. Then it closed behind the rover, and after a while the inner door opened. In the tunnel I saw a second vehicle and Corporal Kunch waiting for me. I almost cried, feeling overwhelming relief.

VIII

Scotty listened to me with an inscrutable expression. He was not angry at my independent action, but he was clearly worried. He didn't interrupt a word, only bit his lower lip and his visual implants twitched slightly. I spoke a little chaotically since my thoughts were still focused on Kendra, who was being taken to the hospital, and besides, the recent terrifying experiences really unnerved me. I wished to take a hot shower made from real water and bury myself under a blanket with the android and my cat, two creatures who loved me just because I was there. But I had to wait.

"This is looking very strange," the inspector finally said. "We'll have to wait for whatever results Constable Maru's research brings, and then figure out what to do next. Now explain to me why the hell did you go to the collection point. You haven't told me that yet."

I sighed desperately.

"Scotty, something strange has happened. Mabel is here."

"What Mabel?"

"Well, Mabel Frost, I told you about her."

"Ah, this floress... Is Citizen Hakat here again?"

"The point is, no. She is here alone. She ran away from Hakat. She is scared to death and refused to tell me why. I suspect your brother-in-law has done something to her or that she witnessed something really terrible."

He nodded slowly, melancholically. I knew what he was thinking about right now. The fact that no matter what Hakat will do, it will not surprise him.

"Then we have a problem," he said.

"Mabel says she covered her tracks well..."

"It's not about the tracks," he interrupted me. "All agents are conditioned. They cannot resist their superiors. Your friend might have escaped while Hakat was away, but all he has is whistle at her and she'll stab you in the back."

"Hold on, but I'm his agent, too..." I objected.

He smiled pitifully.

"Not exactly. Do you remember the training, especially the days when you complained about not absorbing the material you received? Kelley then suggested stimulating your brain with electrical stimuli."

"Well, yes," I admitted.

Initially, I didn't have any trust for the helmet worn over my head, but after two or three times I got the impression that my head was getting clearer.

"The good Samaritan doctor removed the conditioning imperatives from your brain. I wanted to make sure that you don't act like a programmed mechanism when someone says the password."

I shuddered.

"That would have been terrible."

"Unfortunately, conditioning often isn't done only so that the subject doesn't do forbidden things. It's an effective instrument for controlling people. Tell me, Leeta, did Mabel really seem sincere to you? Maybe..."

"Maybe what?"

"She's on a mission given by Hakat?"

I thought. I must admit that at first I had a similar thought, but I dismissed it.

"I don't think so," I said. "She was too terrified. She cut her hair and donned an old jumpsuit to blend in with the miners. She walked through the tunnels to get to the outskirts. When I saw her, she looked like a picture of suffering and despair. A real heap of misfortunes. I don't think she's playing a game.

Scott curled his lips slightly.

"You may be right, but her presence here is very troublesome either way. If Hakat finds her, tragedy could happen. I'm serious. We'll have to think about how to hide her."

"She's staying with Thorvald right now. I discussed it with him."

"That's for now, and what afterwards? She's a floress, she won't last long in a workshop. Trust me, I know this type of woman. Right now she's terrified, but over time the fear will fade and she will want to return to at least a part of her former life."

I had to admit that he was right. Scott knew floresses as 'a type of women', and I knew Mabel. She was not a voluntary prisoner. She has always been freedom-loving, that's why she chose this profession. This made her feel – perhaps in delusion – that she was in complete control of her life.

"We'll think about it later," Cavanaugh said again, "now go home and sleep. Tomorrow we will definitely find out what happened to Maru, and then we will consult about your accident. I really don't like this."

"Me neither."

While talking with my boss, I was still restrained by nervousness and all the stress I experienced, but when it subsided, I was barely able to crawl into the apartment. I didn't have the strength to answer Sue's questions, who helped me undress and wash with Monty. I didn't even want to eat anything. I lay down, hugged Sid, who was purring on the pillow, and fell asleep.

This time nobody woke me up. Scott concluded that I deserved a break after what happened to me and let me sleep for the first time in a long time until I woke up by myself. He must have contacted Sue and Monty about this matter, since neither of them woke me up, saying that it's 6:30 am and that I would be late for work. As a result, I came to the station refreshed and content with my life, despite the difficult experiences.

"Glad you're here," Slavik said when he saw me.

He smiled and slapped my butt as I walked by before I could cover myself with my hands. He had this unpleasant habit, and we – the women of the main police headquarters – couldn't teach him to stop assaulting our physical integrity. We didn't want to complain and give him problems, because we all liked Slavik, but we promised ourselves that one day we would come up with some prank in revenge.

Scott sat at his desk, flipping through the documents on a reader.

"Sit down," he told me. "This is a rather mysterious case. LSD was found in Kendra's blood and on the soles of her shoes. As far as I know, no one transported drugs through this tunnel, and they shouldn't have been there."

"What is the conclusion?" I asked.

"None so far. I'll have to go there myself, and you'll come with me. Kendra will still have to stay in the hospital... I have my suspicions, and if they are confirmed, I don't want to tell anyone, except those who I can trust in one hundred percent."

"I don't understand."

"I'll explain everything, but not here."

I switched on the intercom and demanded an S5 rover with full equipment from the dispatcher. I didn't know what was going on, but I preferred not to ask any more for now. If Scott didn't trust his team, he must have had some really good reasons. I hoped that he really will explain everything to me along the way. At his command, I donned a combat suit made of nanite shielding material and army boots, as well as a belt with additional equipment. I felt like I was going to war and had no idea how to answer Kunch's and Hallie's questions.

Scotty was silent, except for the brief orders he gave me. He was driving fast and no other cars were in our way when the signal lights on the roof came on. He turned them on, although the danger was nowhere to be found. He told me nothing, and I dared not ask why he was abusing police privileges.

He did not speak until we entered the working tunnel.

"Leeta, what I'm about to tell you is not only secret, but also illegal. If you were to turn against me later, I will be lost."

"Oh, boy..."

"Don't interrupt me. As you might have noticed, I don't have much respect for my brother-in-law. I have a reason for that. This isn't a matter of personal prejudice, but something else entirely. Over the years, I've had the opportunity to watch his behavior, and I know that he is capable of anything, of any possible meanness. I saw him grow in power. Now he has opportunities that he never dreamed of, and he is more dangerous than you can imagine. As you may have guessed, people like that have enemies. I have reason to suspect that the owner of the Romain Corporation is one of them. Remember when we searched together for the ownership structure of the moon mines?"

"Yes. It turned out that Citizen Hakat owns a controlling stake in several companies."

He nodded.

"Many of them. My private investigation shows that Romain Corporation is working to block further share buybacks by the people and companies being replaced by Hakat. Someone knows what my son-in-law's goal is and wants to prevent him from achieving it."

"And this someone is here on the moon!"

"That is correct, my dear."

I wiped the sweat from my forehead with my sleeve. This was too much for me. I got the impression that a bit more and my head will start steaming.

"What do you have to do with it?"

For the first time since we got into the rover, he looked at me.

"I support this guy, whoever he is," he said. "Hakat must be destroyed. The owner of Romain Corporation is not acting alone, and it would be impossible for him to. I can guess who is behind this, although I have no proof, so I won't tell you who I think it is. At the moment, something else is more important. Are you with me or against me?"

My throat was dry and I had to clear my throat several times before answering.

"With you, Scotty. Always with you. You know that."

"Yes, I know. I just wanted you to confirm it. I can only trust you and Kelley completely."

I agreed with him. The crew was loyal to him, people liked him, but it's better not to tell anyone about such a serious matter.

"Now you understand why I must consider this floress as a potential mole. I cannot afford to make a mistake."

"I understand," I said after a pause. "Why are you linking Kendra's accident with this matter?"

"You see, Leeta, for a long time now, in every free moment, I have been analyzing unusual electrical signals, radio signals and magnetic vibrations. There are several points in the area of human influence on the Moon that I cannot explain. One of them is located in the delta of the high-speed tunnel and the working tunnel. The ones we are currently traveling through. I suspect that there is an illegal underground structure, something like an apartment in the mine closed by us."

"And the entrance..."

"...could be where Constable Maru stopped the vehicle. As you said, she was alarmed by the sight of a niche in the wall. Since traces of LSD were on the soles of her shoes, it is likely that the drug was in the form of compressed gas in fragile containers. These are the so-called 'gas bombs'. When someone steps on a container and crushes it, gas is released and enters the body through the skin or lungs. Or both."

"How does that help them?"

"It gives them time. Monitoring reports that someone has inspected the wall and residents can move to a safer location."

"So, we're still going for no reason."

"Not necessarily. If we manage to break through the entrance, we can find out who lived there. And where to look for them. We're also acting quickly. It hasn't been a full day yet. Okay, show me where you stopped."

He turned on the headlight harder. I wasn't sure if I would recognize the location of Kendra's accident, but it turned out I remembered it well. It didn't seem to stand out from the other niches formed by the curve of the wall, and yet Maru was right. It was different. It looked newer, had a much less superficial smell.

"Put on your gloves and get your breathing apparatus," Scott told me.

I obediently tossed a can of compressed air onto my back and put the mask on my face. Armed with chemical protective equipment, we got out of the car. Despite wearing a suit and a mask, I involuntarily flinched as concrete crumbs and small objects crackled under the soles of my boots. I didn't know, which were the bombs, and I didn't have time to bend over and check. I preferred to watch what Scott did.

He pulled a flat, wide device out of his bag, turned it on, and began turning the knobs.

"What is that?" I asked.

"An emitter," he replied. "With this, I can tune in to any electrical device and control it as if I had a factory remote control."

"It is legal?"

"Of course not. Will you rat me out?"

I got used to his sarcasm and ignored him. I was more interested in the device that Scott controlled. It looked archaic and awkward, with three rows of old-fashioned pens and five tiny screens on top. I could swear it was put together by some electronics enthusiast and didn't get approval. I had no idea how it works.

"As I thought, behind this wall there is a place literally packed with electronics," Scott finally said. "I suspect... yes, this wall is just a facade. A disguised passage. I'll try to open it."

"What if these people get alarmed?"

He looked at me.

"We'll have to face that then."

He manipulated the knobs at a speed that clearly showed he knew what he was doing. At some point, I heard a click, and something like solid concrete suddenly popped out, opening the entrance. Scott pulled the pistol out of its holster and released the safety. He entered slowly, and I followed behind, trying to keep my footsteps as quiet as possible. We found ourselves in an empty corridor lined with foam, and the passage closed behind us. Scott looked at the miniature screens of his camera and began turning the knobs again.

"I will turn off monitoring and possible weapons," he explained without being asked. "See this screen? This is a biological signal sensor. There are no people around, which means there must be electronic security, it must be good. I can't believe a place like this isn't guarded."

"This device is amazing," I muttered with appreciation.

He smiled, very pleased.

"Yes. Handmade, the only such model in the world. It allows you to enter any place with electronic security. Nobody except you knows that I have it. The underworld, the army, and the politicians would all make a fortune on the design of its construction, which only one person knows about."

"And you probably won't tell me who it is?"

"Someday you'll meet them. Until then, let's get what we came for. We can go now."

The white corridor led us in sharp turns somewhere deeper. It was narrow, probably for security reasons. Two people couldn't walk arm in arm. Finally, we reached a passage closed by a solid metal hatch. Beside it on the surface was a control panel, suggesting a disguised fingerprint sensor.

"Don't touch the door," my boss warned me. "I know this model, it's under voltage."

I backed away, though I had no intention of touching the hatch.

"Good idea. Don't come near. If I miscalculate the code, a current breakdown may occur."

Scott placed a small device against the wall next to the panel, put the headphones over his ears, and began touching various points on the touchpad with the stylus. At some point, a sound resembling a deep sigh could be heard, and the door opened. The inspector left the device, removed the headphones, and grabbed the pistol in one smooth motion, perhaps in a split second. I followed his example. We both burst in, and then froze.

The spacious room was decorated in an oddly familiar way, a bit like a hospital room and a bit like an exclusive living room. An emaciated man in a white shirt with two interfaces on his shaved head was lying on a bed with medical equipment. One was for a speech synthesizer, and the other, it seems to me, he used to control various devices. If I were to guess, he probably used it to lower or raise the back of the bed himself, turn on and off the TV, alarm clock or quadraphonic player. I've seen something like this in films, never before in person.

The man's body was completely inert. Even from the doorway, I saw that only his eyes were alive, and with an effort he turned toward us. It was at this moment that it dawned on me, and I was willing to bet my annual salary on it, that we just found the owner of the Romain Corporation, Leon Beavis Hampton. It had to be him. I wanted to say something, but I couldn't find the words. This was the first time I had seen someone who had been struck so hard by fate, and the thought of arresting him seemed simply absurd.

Near the bunk sat an attractive young brown-haired woman in a dark suit and a snow-white blouse, fastened around her neck with an octagonal brooch. Seeing us, she jumped to her feet.

"How did you get here without alarming the sensors?" she asked in amazement.

Scott sucked in a breath and let it out through his teeth. Then he put the pistol in the holster and, to my surprise, bowed slightly.

"We have our own ways, Your Excellency," he replied.

He looked over his shoulder at me and smiled at my expression. It must have looked very stupid, but I didn't understand anything about this scene. I stared at the lying man, young woman and my boss with wide eyes, unable to utter a word.

"Come over, Leeta," Inspector Cavanaugh said warmly, extending his hand to me. "Meet Number One."

END OF VOLUME TWO